Hidden Part 1

A Michael Sullivan Mystery

LINDA BERRY

First Edition, December 2016
Second Edition, November 2019

ISBN: 978-0-9998538-6-3

Published in the United States of America

www.lindaberry.net

Linda Berry paints a picture with words. A dramatic story filled with complex relationships, emotional growth, and external conflicts that move with perfect pacing, HIDDEN is a gem not to be missed.
—Marie Harte, *New York Times* bestseller

A great novel that makes you want to keep turning the pages! HIDDEN has a cast of richly detailed characters—some we instantly empathize with, others we loath with a feral intensity. Berry combines the beautiful Oregon scenery with a tense and compelling plot. Five stars and highly recommended!
—Dave Edlund, author of award-winning Peter Savage Thrillers

Linda Berry brings the rugged characters and landscapes of Central Oregon to life with detail and emotion. She has an uncanny knack for revealing the soft underbelly of the hardest individuals.
—Paul Bacon, author of *BAD COP: New York's Least Likely Police Officer Tells All*

Five Star Reviews from Amazon Readers

—I was drawn into this book from the beginning. It was beautifully written. The author was so detailed I felt I was right in the story. The characters had a life of their own, and I was invested in their trials. This book can cross many genres, pleasing fans of westerns, drama and thrillers. I highly recommend this book!

—HIDDEN PART 1 is a work of art. Beautifully written and so good that I read it while in hospital and have just reread it a month later. Ms Berry writes with authority about Sully's struggle to adapt to civilian life after two tours in the Marines. One is with him every step of the way as he works to reclaim the family horse farming operation which has been neglected since his father's stroke. A strong focus on relationships is balanced by plenty of action.

To the men and women in uniform
who put themselves in harm's way to preserve
the freedom of our great country,
and to the talented athletes who compete
so fearlessly in rodeo

Books by Linda Berry:

Hidden Part 1

Hidden Part 2

Pretty Corpse

The Killing Woods

The Dead Chill

To learn of new releases and discounts,

add your name to Linda's mailing list:

www.lindaberry.net

ACKNOWLEDGMENTS

I AM DEEPLY GRATEFUL to the many friends who contributed their time and knowledge to the development of Hidden.

A special thanks goes to Joan Steelhammer of Equine Outreach, a horse rescue organization where my volunteer work blossomed into a life-long love of horses. I owe a debt of gratitude to Gracie, my stunning gray-dappled mare, who gave me the joy of unfettered companionship for many years.

For their unwavering friendship, support, and continued belief in my work, I owe a big thank you to JT Gregory, Tim Rubin, LaLoni Kirkland, Sarah Persha, Lindy Jacobs, James Koukis, Mike Lankford, Mark Fasnacht, and Katherine Mattingly

I am deeply grateful for my initial readers, who read my book for pure enjoyment and gave me encouraging feedback: Katherine Mattingly, Bob Kruger, my lovely sister Francine Marsh, and my dearest friend and husband, Mark Fasnacht.

I'm thankful to my toy poodles, Rogie and Jackson, who helped fashion the character of Butch.

CHAPTER ONE

March 2006

A STRONG WIND buffeted the cab as it bumped down the ice-rutted backroads of Wild Horse Creek. Sully slouched in the backseat, his muscles tight with fatigue. The frozen landscape didn't match the memories of home he'd carried through his last tour of duty. Familiar landmarks had been resculpted by ice and snow. There was no delineation between meadow and pasture, just endless white interrupted by pockets of ice-glazed trees. Even the snow-capped peaks of the Cascades jutting into the crimson sky looked different, dwarfed by his memories of the Hindu Kush Mountains of Afghanistan. His pulse raced and he leaned forward in his seat when Dancing Horse Ranch came into view. "This is it on the right."

The cabbie turned onto the gravel driveway and the car shuddered as the tires played over the frozen ridges.

"Could you pull up around back?" Sully asked.

"Sure thing."

The driver carefully negotiated the curve to the rear of the house and eased to a stop. In the paddocks off the barn, several horses lifted their heads and eyed the cab with interest. Despite his weariness, Sully felt a smile tug at his lips. He couldn't wait to get back in the saddle, feel the speed of a powerful animal beneath him.

"Beautiful animals."

"Thanks. We breed champion reining horses."

"Hmmm. I remember a famous rodeo star lived out in these parts. Bare bronc rider. Bred amazing horses. Won a few world titles. Joe …

something."

"Joe Sullivan. My dad."

"No kidding?" The cabbie whistled and caught Sully's eyes in the rearview mirror. "I saw him when I was a kid. Got his autograph. He was a force of nature. Could stay on anything. You follow in his footsteps?"

"Dad started training me the day I popped out of the womb." Sully nodded toward the gable-roofed barn. "My rodeo winnings paid for that, and the last thirty acres we added."

"Sweet." The cabbie looked at Sully over his shoulder, his face half-hidden in shadow. "You must be decent."

Sully shrugged, feeling no connection to his old rodeo triumphs. That glory was all in the past. "I held my own. The armed forces owned me the last four years. Cut my rodeo career short."

"Marine?"

"Just got out." Sully ran a hand over his buzz cut that had grown out a bit during his three-week hospital stay. Though dressed in jeans, western shirt, and a denim jacket, he felt like a Marine. An undercurrent of anxiety buzzed beneath his calm composure. Cut loose from the Corps, out on his own, he felt like a satellite spinning out of orbit. He patted his pockets, searching for his wallet. "What do I owe you?"

The driver tapped the meter.

Sully handed him some folded bills. "Keep the change."

The cabbie smiled his appreciation.

Sully grabbed his duffel and moved carefully as he exited the cab. Still, he grunted from the sharp stabs of pain in his arm and gut. The meds were wearing off.

The cabbie rolled down his window. "Thanks for your service to our country."

Caught off guard, Sully half saluted. Civilian life would take some getting used to.

The cab backed out of the driveway in a cloud of exhaust, the headlights momentarily illuminating the two-story ranch house where Sully was raised. It pained him to see it needed paint. A couple railings sagged on the porch, and a loose shutter clapped in the wind, but the construction was rock solid. Built tough, to last. That's how things were done on the Sullivan ranch.

No lights were on in the house and the windows reflected the last bit of color from the dying sun. An ache of loneliness tore at his gut. If his parents were here, the lights would be blazing, and the two would be out on the porch welcoming him home with open arms. He still couldn't believe they'd separated after thirty years of marriage. His mom moved to town. His dad was rotting in a nursing home. The weight of running the ranch now fell squarely on Sully's shoulders.

He glanced across the yard. No lights on in the bunkhouse, either. Travis Blackwolf, the sole occupant of the ranch, was somewhere off site. Sully had notified no one of his homecoming, but still, the feeling of isolation that enveloped him was unnerving.

He dropped his bag on the porch and crunched through the snow to the trail behind the house, the icy air brittle in his nostrils. Sucking the cold deep into his lungs and panting out white vapor, he hiked to the vista above the hayfields. Ponderosa pines towered at his back and the black tarp of sky rose out of the mountains before him. Oregon, USA. No other place in the world like it. He soaked in the beauty of home with all his senses: the raw, wild land beyond the hay fields, the scent of pine and wood smoke, the wind rustling trees. Peaceful. No distant explosions. No *rat-tat-tat* of automatic fire. Life was simple here. Everything out in the open. A man lived his life by the cycle of seasons—planting, harvesting, raising livestock—not waking up each morning wondering if he'd survive the day. Sully felt naked standing out in the open without his body armor and assault rifle. The undercurrent of anxiety pulsed steadily. He hiked back to the house, his boots stamping holes in the snow, his body now screaming for meds.

He picked up his duffel and switched on the light as he entered the kitchen. On his last leave, he was greeted by friends and family. Big hugs from the women, claps on the back from the men, cold beer, home cooking. Now he was greeted by dirty dishes, pizza boxes stacked around the trash can, and car parts sitting on oil-stained cardboard on the table. The smell of something burnt lingered in the air.

Sully didn't hold the state of the room against Travis. When managing a ranch this size solo, housecleaning fell to the bottom of the priority list. Travis deserved a medal. Sully should give him his Bronze Star. He didn't want it. Didn't deserve it. Squaring his shoulders, he walked through the house to his bedroom, which he found stuck in a time warp. High school and college pennants still hung on the walls, and rodeo trophies lined the overburdened bookshelves. He stood motionless, trying to connect with the person he used to be, the man who needed all these pathetic declarations of self-worth. Anything of true value, he'd come to realize, a man carried within himself. Honor, courage, commitment.

Sully plucked his sweat-stained Stetson from the bedpost and settled it on his head. It felt light compared to his combat helmet with the night vision goggles. He fished his pain meds from his duffel and made a pit stop in the bathroom. He tapped two pills onto his palm, knocked them back with a swallow of water, and studied his reflection in the mirror. Two tours of duty had changed him. At twenty-eight, he felt fifty. A pattern of shrapnel scars marked the right side of his face like pink tattoos. Stress lines were etched on each side of his mouth, and his brow was creased into a permanent frown. Only his blue eyes were unchanged, hiding images of horror behind their blank stare. Here he was back home, safe and sound, while his buddies were still over there, risking their lives every day. Guilt, like crushed glass, rubbed his gut raw.

Sully heard the clopping of hooves outside heading for the barn. *Travis.* He left the house and crossed the clearing, crackling ice underfoot in frozen puddles. He entered the barn and was immediately struck by the serene beauty of the place; the orderly tack room, stacked bales in the loft, horses jutting their heads above the stall doors, soft liquid eyes checking him out. He breathed in the familiar smells of oiled leather, sweet hay, and earthy manure. Incense for the soul. A well-run barn was as close to a temple as a cowboy could get.

Dressed in jeans, a plaid flannel shirt, and scuffed work boots, Travis Blackwolf stood in a stall brushing down Diego, a well-muscled bay quarter horse. After thirty years of working the Sullivan ranch, the old Paiute's body was all knobs, angles, and lean muscle. Sully flashed back to his boyhood when the gray braid that fell down Travis's back was black and shiny.

"Travis."

No response.

Sully entered the stall, touched his shoulder.

Travis turned abruptly, pulling iPod buds from his ears. His face, as craggy as a chunk of volcanic rock, cracked into a wide-toothed grin. "Christ almighty." He pulled Sully into a fierce bear hug.

Sully heard western music pulsing from the iPod tucked in his breast pocket.

Travis held him at arm's length. "You're a sight for sore eyes. Wasn't expecting you till next week. When did you get in?"

"Sixteen hundred hours. Grabbed a cargo flight from Germany. Made a few pitstops stateside. Thirty hours flight time."

"Military express." Travis chuckled. "They spare no frills. You get good medical over there?"

"I'm alive. Can't complain."

"Your gut? Arm?"

"Good as new." In truth, the meds hadn't kicked in. The pain set his teeth on edge. "Clean shots, through and through. Everything stitched neatly back together."

Travis's eyes traced the shrapnel scars.

"I'm okay, Travis. Really."

Travis sighed. "Man, you must be dog-tired. I put clean sheets on your bed."

"Clean sheets. Wahoo. Not used to four-star living." As a Marine, Sully learned to grab shut-eye when and where he could. Trenches, many times. "The place looks good, Travis. Real good." Hard work for one old man.

"I do what I can."

"Well, I'm home now. I'll lighten your load." Like his father, Sully had been blessed with almost supernatural strength and endurance. Under normal conditions, he could do twice as much as Travis. Now he needed to fully recover.

Diego looked over his shoulder and swished his tail, hitting Sully full in the chest. Sully laughed his first real laugh in weeks. "Okay, buddy, I see you."

Diego nudged him with his velvety muzzle, searching for snacks. Travis pulled an oat treat from his pocket. After nimbly accepting, the bay raised and lowered his head, saying thanks, just as Sully had taught him. Agile and fast, the gelding had won dozens of reining competitions, and represented well the Dancing Horse brand.

"You remember me pretty good, eh, buddy?"

"Like his own mother," Travis said.

Sully stroked the animal's damp neck. "He's worked up a pretty good sweat. What've you two been up to?"

"This and that."

Sully watched the old Paiute's bottom jaw saw back and forth, then tighten. He was stressing about something. "What is it you're not telling me, aside from the fact that the ranch needs a helluva lot of work?"

"It can wait," Travis said calmly, but his eyes looked uneasy. "We'll talk in the morning."

Bad news. Sully's gut tightened but he knew better than to press Travis. The old man would give up nothing. The forewarning pushed Sully's stress level up a notch. Picking up a dandy brush, he started brushing Diego's shoulder while Travis worked the horse's other side. It helped to touch a horse, to fall back into a pattern of work he knew and understood.

"Your parents know you're here?" Travis asked.

"No. I need a couple days to get my head straight." Sully heard an edge of guilt creep into his voice, but he couldn't face his parents yet. Not in his current state. He needed time to depressurize. Stepping from the raw violence of war into a world of ease and comfort was like resurfacing from the depth of the ocean too quickly. "I need to check out the ranch thoroughly. Get it ready."

Travis arched his brows, a question in his expression.

"I'm bringing Dad home."

"You might want to give that some thought."

"It's all I've thought about since I heard about his stroke."

"Joe's still in bad shape. Six months ago the doctors told him he'd never walk or speak again. I saw him last week. There was no shutting him up. Probably just to spite them."

Sully chuckled. "Iron will. Nothing ever kept Dad down for long."

"He'll need care, but he won't let you be his nurse."

"Lord, don't I know it. But he belongs here at the ranch, not in some damned nursing home." Sully recalled the sterile hospital room he just left in Germany, haunted by the moans of soldiers suffering from ghastly burns, brain injuries, blown off limbs. An ache swelled in his chest. The edge of grief existed just an eye blink away.

"Bringing Joe home is a good decision, Sully. We'll make do." Travis's brown eyes softened. "We always have."

"There's no way to thank you for holding this place together."

"No thanks needed."

Both men knew the ranch would be in dire straits without him. Travis's name was on the deed. One-third partner. They would all die in their boots working this property.

"You need to drive your pickup," Travis said, raking horse hair from the brush with a curry comb. "Sitting in the garage for four years hasn't done it any good. There's a can of gas in the tool shed."

"It'll be nice to have wheels." Sully recalled the exhausting foot patrols he and his men endured, carting seventy pounds of gear in both frigid cold and sweltering heat, with big fucking targets on their backs. "I've had my fill of foot power."

"I hear ya. In Nam, we waded through miles of swamps and rice paddies. Then more swamps. The whole time, fighting toe rot and leeches. Never stopped raining." Travis raised his eyes to meet Sully's, his expression softening. "Terrible things happen in war. It's not easy coming home. You think nobody here understands. I didn't talk to anyone when I got back. Just stayed drunk for two years. Don't do what I did. You got something to say, come see me. We'll talk."

Grateful, Sully nodded and changed the subject. Combat memories were too fresh, too raw. "How's Mom?"

Travis shrugged. "Haven't seen her since she left."

"In her e-mails, she said you won't talk to her. You blame her for Dad's stroke."

Travis bent down to pick Diego's front hooves. "Your dad was a changed man after she left. Good for absolutely nothing. Had the stroke soon after."

"Smoking, drinking, and working too hard contributed as much as anything," Sully said, tossing the currycomb into the tack box.

"That, too." Travis moved to the rear of the gelding and started picking a hind hoof.

"You know what split them up?"

"Got some ideas."

He waited but Travis offered nothing. Sully knew it was a sore subject. He didn't mention that he hoped to get his parents back together again.

When Travis resurfaced, he cleaned his pick and placed it in the tack box. Then he stretched, arching his back. "You hungry? I've got some leftover pizza."

"How old is it?"

"Few days."

Sully chuckled. "That's a hard offer to turn down, but I'm gonna say no." The meds were finally kicking in, allowing him to focus on hunger and thirst. "Let's go to Beamers. Grab some burgers. I'm thirsty as hell for American beer." Alcohol had been prohibited on military bases in Afghanistan. It'd been a long fifteen months since Sully had tasted a cold one. "I'm buying."

"Well hell then, let's go." Travis wasted no time wrestling into his sheepskin jacket and pulling his wide-brimmed hat low on his forehead. A handful of sleek eagle feathers were tucked around the band.

Out in the brisk cold, breath steaming, they crunched across the tattered ice. Travis fished the remote from his pocket and aimed it at the garage. The groaning door lifted to reveal Sully's white Ford F-350 Super Duty. *A truck with muscle.* Sully ran his hands over the polished surface, grinning ear to ear. "Man, I missed you, baby. Thanks for keeping her clean, Travis. She got enough gas to get to town?"

"We're going in this." Travis circled the truck.

Sully followed. A white pygmy car was parked next to the Ford. It looked like his truck had laid an egg. "A Prius? Who belongs to this?"

"Me," Travis growled. "It gets great mileage. It's good for the planet. I don't want any crap. Get in."

Suppressing his grin, Sully folded his body into the passenger seat. Travis fit in just fine at five-foot-nine, hat and all, but at six-foot, Sully's Stetson rubbed against the ceiling. "Look at this fancy dashboard. GPS?"

"Yeah," Travis said with undisguised pride. "It talks to me in a sexy voice. I have surround sound, too. Wanna hear Garth Brooks?"

"Shit. You spoiled fucking American. I just left a province where folks don't own cars. There aren't any roads. Just goat trails. They live in ancient stone houses without plumbing. The women wear pup tents with peepholes for clothing. It's forbidden for men and women to look each other in the eye."

Travis glanced over and met Sully's eyes. "Ain't this country great?"

"It ain't perfect, but I wouldn't trade it for anything."

***

Miles off the beaten trail, the one-road town of Wild Horse Creek didn't see too many tourist dollars. Sully noticed that a few shops had gone out of business. The empty buildings stood like carcasses with blackened windows and weed-filled lots. The two-pump Arco station, General Store, Mac's Feed and Tack, and Gilly's Pawn and Thrift shop were still in business, some outfitted with hitching posts for folks who rode into town on horseback.

It was after eight p.m. No sign of life except for Beamer's Bar and Grill. The neon sign out front pulsed in the night like a heartbeat, splashing blue and red across the shiny hoods of the trucks in the lot. As he walked into the half-filled restaurant, Sully felt like he was falling forward into the future. Overseas, he'd served himself from steaming metal containers in the brightly lit chow hall, sitting with hundreds of Marines dressed in green and brown cammies, voices raised above the tinny clatter. Here the interior was softly lit and the folks seated at tables looked relaxed, blue-jean casual, voices at a low murmur. The smell of grilled food made his mouth water.

The half dozen men hugging the bar took no notice as he and Travis straddled barstools away from the crowd. It took a minute for the bartender to extricate herself from a rugged-looking cowboy leaning over the counter and saunter over to them. She was a shapely blonde dressed in tight jeans and a low-cut sweater. Her earrings and dainty gold chains shimmered in the soft light.

"Hey, Travis. Haven't seen you for a while." She gave Sully a side glance, eyes brightening with interest. "Who's your friend?"

"This here's Sully. Sully, Britney."

Removing his hat, Sully met Britney's hazel eyes and nodded.

"Hey Sully." She leaned over and wiped off the spotless counter, giving him a ringside view of her ample bustline. *God bless America.* Sully smiled, grateful to see a woman who wasn't dressed in combat gear or imprisoned in a burqa.

"Our tequila drinks are on special tonight," she drawled, looking at him through a fringe of dark lashes. "Can I talk you into a margarita?"

It'd been a long while since a woman had taken notice of him. Unprepared, he looked down for a moment, blinked back up at her. "A Deschutes River Ale, and line up three shots of Cuervo for me."

"Three, hmmm. That happens to be my lucky number."

A snappy comeback eluded him. His talent for flirtatious banter was packed away in cold storage, frozen solid.

"That all?" she asked, tucking a strand of blond hair behind an ear.

"A burger. Extra mayo."

"Fries with that?"

"Yeah. Please. And extra ketchup."

Travis cleared his throat.

Britney tugged her gaze away from Sully.

"I'll have a burger, fries, and a Corona," Travis said.

"Coming right up." She cast a flirty smile at Sully and sashayed through the double doors into the kitchen. Both men followed her with their eyes.

Travis shook his head and grinned. "Man, you sure haven't lost it with the ladies."

"Helluva surprise to me." With his shrapnel scars and pasty face, Sully felt like a dull replica of himself. He didn't have the energy to put into something that had nowhere to go. His personal life was going into cold storage, too. The fear of losing the ranch pushed all self-interests into another hemisphere.

Britney returned, set down two frosty mugs of beer, lined up three shot glasses, and filled them with tequila.

"Thank you kindly," Sully said.

She waited for a moment, but he gave her no encouragement and she ambled back to the cowboy. Without hesitation, Sully threw back two shots and immediately felt the heat spread through his chest and stomach.

Travis raised a brow. "You might want to take it easy. We got time."

"I'm drinking for two," Sully said quietly. He pushed up his left sleeve, revealing a half dozen names tattooed on his forearm in bold, black ink. The first four were buddies he'd lost in the battle of Cusol, 2004. Taliban stronghold. Fierce resistance. House to house combat. The fifth got blown to hell by an IED last year. Close friends. Gone. *And now, Eric.*

"Fucking war." Travis scowled. He touched Sully's forearm near the wrist. "This ink's fresh. Eric Steeler."

"Died three weeks ago."

"Same time you got hit?"

Sully nodded, muscles tightening along his jaw. "He saved my life, and two other Marines. He was my squad's medic."

A glint of understanding flickered in the old Paiute's eyes. No words were needed.

Sully held up his glass and pictured Eric's tanned face grinning under the desert sun. That's how he wanted to remember him. Full of life, a joke always ready to roll off his tongue. "Semper Fi, Doc." He knocked back his last tequila.

"Oohrah," Travis growled.

"Oohrah," Sully growled back, grateful for the company of another vet. It didn't take long for the alcohol in his empty stomach to hit his bloodstream. His mood elevated. The world softened. It felt good. He signaled Britney. "Line up three more for me, sugar."

With a tilt to one corner of her mouth, she refilled the three glasses. "What're you celebrating?"

"Buddies." A little blurry eyed, he turned his forearm upward, revealing the sacred list.

Her smile wavered. "Iraq?"

"Afghanistan."

A shadow of empathy darkened her eyes. "Thanks for your service, soldier. Your first round's on the house."

"Great," Travis said, before Sully refused her generosity.

By the time their food hit the counter, the world had taken on an artificial sheen, everything was slightly off kilter, and Sully felt a lightness of being. He and Travis polished off their burgers and fries and continued drinking, holding tribute to six Marines who lost their lives in a stinking desert on the other side of the world.

Sully couldn't corral his dark thoughts for long. Memories of Eric started shaking loose. His best buddy had grown up in nearby Bend and was planning to go back to med school upon his return. Their deployments were coming to an end, and they had planned to hit Beamer's together their first week back.

Eric should be sitting here right now, getting shit-faced and flirting with the blonde bombshell bartender. Instead, he was dead at twenty-two. Shipped home in a flag-draped coffin.

The alcohol loosened the storm gate that held back combat memories. Bomb blasts echoed in Sully's mind and an image reared up of Eric lying in a filthy ditch bleeding to death. Sully could almost smell the cordite and sulfur clogging the air. As squad leader, he'd been responsible for the safety of his men, but he failed to bring Eric back alive. Shame seared his brain like a hot branding iron. Blinking hard, he forced the sickening image into some dark hidden chamber of his soul.

Longing for just a few hours of oblivion, Sully threw back his last drink, but he was unable to rein in his untamed mind. Tomorrow, he'd wake up to a slew of ranch problems, including the bad news Travis was holding back. He rested his forehead on his folded arms over the bar and heard Britney slap the check on the bar top.

"Your friend dead?" she asked Travis.

Sully opened one eye.

"Just dog-tired."

"Too bad. Tell him next time, maybe ease up on the shots."

"Yeah, poor kid," Travis chuckled. "Can't hold his liquor."

"I can hear you," Sully said, slurring his words. He pulled his wallet from his pocket and placed a few bills on the counter, then started sliding off the barstool.

Travis propped him up against the counter. "You ready?"

Sully nodded, his head in a fog, the room spinning around him.

"Hang tough," Travis said.

The blonde beat them to the door and held it open. "Welcome back to the states, Sully."

CHAPTER TWO

THE LAB PANTED over her shoulder from the backseat as Maggie Steeler pulled into the driveway and parked her Prius next to Brennen's Mercedes. She turned off the engine and watched the snow feather the windshield. The office was tucked away in a grove of juniper trees, their branches drooping under a heavy burden of snow. It made her think of the shoulders of weary soldiers stationed in cold places far from the comforts of home. She thought of her son. Dead. Killed in some shithole in Afghanistan.

The world looked cocooned and soft under the billowy mounds of white, but the peaceful landscape was at complete odds with the storm raging inside her. The pain of grief washed through her in waves, sometimes so intense she could barely breathe. Crying jags erupted without warning, triggered by any small memory of Eric, and the house was booby-trapped with memories. Maggie slogged through the endless hours of the day and took pills at night to sleep, but there was no escape. Her dreams were invaded by nightmares. The challenge started all over again as soon as sunlight spilled across the windowsill.

Today she'd had enough of her self-imposed exile. It was time to get back to her life. Shivering as the heat dissipated in the car, Maggie did a quick check in the mirror. Her eyes were red-rimmed and puffy. Mascara wasn't an option.

Behind her, the Lab whined, his tail thumping against the window. She opened the door and the dog was out in one bound, ecstatic, paws imprinting the flawless snow, powder flying. Maggie watched in wonder, wishing she could absorb even a modicum of his joy.

Breath steaming, she followed Homer up the stairs to the craftsman-style house she co-leased with Brennen. The Lab shook off his dusting of snow and they entered the warmth of the small waiting room. Six comfortable chairs, a table covered with glossy magazines, and framed photos of flowered meadows awaited their patients.

The aroma of coffee and sounds from the kitchen told her Brennen was conducting his morning ritual, bonding with his expensive espresso machine. She crossed the room quietly, hoping she could make it to her office without alerting him.

"Maggie, what are you doing here?"

"Morning, Brennen."

Middle-aged and stiffly collegiate, Brennen stood in the doorway of the kitchen holding a mug crowned with foam. Gray-haired and distinguished, his carefully put-together style of casual elegance reminded her of Ralph Lauren. A transplant from the Upper East Side of New York, he never quite adjusted to the small town lifestyle of Bend, where most people dressed down in jeans and athletic wear. Brennen still imported coffee beans from Ethiopia, loafers from Milan, and cobbled lamb's wool sweaters from Scotland.

"You're supposed to be off for another week," he said in a slightly accusatory tone.

"Nope. My exile has run its course. I e-mailed my clients to let them know I'm back."

He lifted his cup above his head as Homer jumped up against his thighs.

"Down, Homer. Sorry." She gently grabbed the dog's collar. "He's excited to be back."

Frowning his distaste, Brennen brushed snow from his gabardine slacks. "Espresso? Cappuccino?"

"No, thanks. I've already had three cups at home."

He approached her noiselessly on his cushioned loafers and peered at her over his reading glasses. "You look worn out."

"Thanks, I needed to hear that."

"What I mean is, you look like you should still be recuperating."

"I get it." She unlocked the door to her treatment room and switched on the light. Immediately, the peacefulness of the room soothed her. It was a place of quiet healing, where she had comforted countless suffering people over the years.

"Sure you're ready to get back to work?" he asked gently, following her.

"Yes." Sitting home alone was a torment. Eric's ghost haunted every corner.

Brennen sipped his coffee, brown eyes studying her, which put her in a defensive mode. She unwound a red wool scarf from her neck, removed her down jacket, and hung them on the coat rack. She smoothed the wrinkles from her cream-colored turtleneck and olive green stretch pants. "My patients need me," she said firmly. "And I need them."

He randomly picked up objects from her bookshelves that her teenage patients found amusing—a Rubik's cube, a beetle entombed in a chunk of amber, a conch shell that held the sound of the ocean. He looked at her over a trilobite fossil. "Do you think you can be present with your patients right now, Maggie?"

He was a psychiatrist. She was a therapist. The differences in their degrees, and their incomes, were never an issue, though he found subtle ways of pulling rank. Normally, it amused her, and they engaged in playful banter, but today, he was just plain annoying.

"Homer, off the couch," she said, ignoring Brennen.

"Patients aren't here to take care of your needs, Maggie." A flicker of disapproval passed over his face. "They aren't a distraction."

Maggie caught herself before she snapped out a reply. She answered in a calm voice. "My patients are in good hands, Brennen. I'm fine." She gestured toward the door, and smiled. "I have a busy schedule."

"I'm here all day, Maggie." To make some obtuse point, he studied a photo of her son dressed in full combat gear, e-mailed from Afghanistan two months ago, and put it down on the wrong shelf. "Come talk to me."

The door shut softly behind him.

Maggie picked up Eric's photo and sank onto the couch. Her son looked so young. Just a boy. His sensitive face looked out of place beneath his combat helmet. As a medic in a combat zone, he had been asked to do an extremely dangerous job, but he served his unit fearlessly and saved countless lives. Her heart swelled with pride for her son's accomplishments.

He would have made a fine doctor.

The ever-ready tears spilled down her cheeks. Grief was such an abstract injury. Invisible. Each of her clients was dealing with the anguish of loss in some respect—divorce, death, estrangement, betrayal. Now she, too, was lost in a vast, barren, unmapped territory. Stumbling blindly.

But doing something purposeful was the first step to healing. Here in her work setting, Maggie could put her own desolation aside and focus on her patients—and settle into her other self—the confident, empathetic counselor and skilled navigator.

Homer laid his head on her lap and watched her with sad brown eyes.

"I'm okay," she murmured, stroking him tenderly. He'd been a good therapy dog, bringing comfort to many troubled souls.

Maggie replaced Eric's photo, turned on the gas fireplace, and took stock of her room. Everything was neat and orderly. Outside, the snow fell softly past the window and she felt insulated and safe. Yes. This was good. It was right that she should be here.

She heard the front door open. That would be her new patient, fourteen-year-old Sean Decker, with his mother, Rebecca, whom Maggie had spoken to by phone. Rebecca had compiled a list of grievances about her son. Maggie specialized in working with families in crisis. She hoped to manage the session in such a way that the list would never surface. This mother was going to be her son's toughest obstacle. Parents usually were.

Maggie opened the door and smiled warmly. Rebecca and Sean shook out of their snow-flecked coats and hung them on the coat rack, faces flushed with cold. "Sean and Rebecca?"

"Yes," Rebecca said, her expression tense.

"It's so nice to meet you. Please come in."

Rebecca nudged her son. He shot his mother a hostile look and shuffled toward Maggie with the enthusiasm of a prisoner on a chain gang.

"Hello, Ms. Steeler." Tall and lanky, Sean provided a limp handshake and avoided eye contact, his long dark hair covering one side of his face.

Rebecca breezed in behind him, all business, neat and professional in a gray pants suit, hair and makeup perfect. A manila folder was tucked under one arm.

"Make yourselves at home," Maggie said.

Rebecca and Sean seated themselves on opposite ends of the sofa.

"Is it okay if Homer says hello?" Maggie nodded toward the Lab, who waited obediently on his bed.

"Yes. Absolutely." Rebecca spoke for both of them.

The Lab took his cue and came to the couch, momentarily sniffing

Rebecca but paying more attention to Sean. Sean half smiled, stroking Homer as though he were a long-lost friend.

"Homer, pillow," Maggie said. Homer settled back on his bed.

"He's well trained," Rebecca said curtly. "He listens to you. Dogs are easy. Kids are hard."

Maggie saw Sean's smile vanish. He stared at his feet, hair falling across his face like a curtain.

"Look at him. This is what he does," Rebecca said. "Goes someplace else. He ignores me most of the time."

"Rebecca," Maggie said in a soothing tone, "I wonder if you'd mind if I just talked to Sean for a minute?"

Rebecca nodded and leaned back in her seat, gripping the folder on her lap.

"Sean," Maggie asked, "have you ever talked to a therapist before?"

He lifted his head and Maggie saw a glint of suspicion in his eyes. "No."

"I don't bite. I promise," she said gently. "I'm wondering if you'd mind sharing some of your interests."

He looked up and blinked.

"Something you're good at, that makes you happy."

He looked at his hands, then back at Maggie. "I don't know."

"Answer her," his mother said sharply.

His shoulders slouched and he hung his head.

Rebecca jumped in. "This is what I deal with every day. Sean doesn't talk. Doesn't do his chores, or schoolwork. He shuts himself in his room and plays video games." Frustration tightened her features. "He has a Teflon shield where I'm concerned."

Sean's face flushed red with anger. The tension between the two was as taut as barbed wire.

"I'm seriously thinking about putting him in a private school back east," she continued. "Maybe military."

"I won't go," Sean said, clenching his fists in his lap.

Rebecca ignored him, talked directly to Maggie. "He needs to get away from the influence of his low-life friends."

"They're not lowlifes," Sean said.

"They smoke pot," she said coldly.

"Not all of them. It doesn't mean I do."

"Not yet."

The animosity between the two, Maggie guessed, had been running at full throttle for some time. Unfortunately, Rebecca was now ready to wash her hands of her son. Bringing Sean in to see a therapist, Maggie imagined, was her last-ditch attempt to mend their shattered relationship. At this stage of the game, it would take time, a lot of hard work, and cooperation.

"Sean, you were about to tell me a little about your interests. How do you like to spend your free time?"

Sean studied his hands, said nothing.

"Skateboarding," Rebecca said grimly.

"I can talk for myself," Sean mumbled.

"What do you like about skateboarding?" Maggie coaxed.

"When I'm skating, I'm not thinking about anything else." He kept his eyes on his tightly clasped hands and talked in a monotone. "It's just me and my friends having fun."

"Do you practice a lot?"

"Every day after school." He peeked at her through strands of hair. "I do lots of tricks."

"For two or three hours," Rebecca interjected. "I wish he'd put as much time into his schoolwork."

Maggie focused on Sean. "Are the tricks you do pretty tough?"

"Yeah."

"Can you get hurt?"

"They're dangerous," Rebecca said. "But he doesn't listen to me. He comes home bruised and scraped all the time. His clothes torn."

"Sean, please continue," Maggie said.

"I guess I do a lot of things that are pretty crazy. But the guys that are really good take a lot of risks."

"Are you really good?"

He nodded, his voice a little more energized, a hint of a smile touching his lips. "I'd like to compete ... but ...." He looked at his mother and his smile disappeared.

Rebecca opened her mouth to make some remark, thought better of it, and remained quiet. Maggie felt empathy for her. It couldn't be easy living her life shuttered off from her son, but that was her survival response, something Maggie would address later in the session. "What's your relationship like with your friends, Sean?"

"They come to me and talk about shit." He looked at his mother to see her response.

Her expression was closed off and long-suffering.

"Most of them are older," Sean continued. "But they talk to me and tell me their problems."

For the next thirty minutes, Maggie encouraged Sean to talk about himself. He went on to explain his high-ranking position in his hierarchy of friends, how the boys shared confidences about their problems at home, their romantic relationships, and how he spent a lot of time teaching others the mechanics of his tricks so they would avoid injury.

"What I hear, Sean," Maggie said, "is that when you're skating, you're facing a challenge. And you have an opportunity to be brave, because you're facing the possibility of injury."

Sean pulled his hair back, revealing a thin, intelligent face.

"You like being part of a group," Maggie continued. "Your friends look up to you like you're a leader. They listen to you. That's interesting to me because you have to be a fair-minded guy for people to talk to you about their problems."

"I guess so." Sean glanced at his mother, who sat listening with a keen expression.

"Rebecca, I know you have your own concerns here, and that's important, but I'm wondering if you would take a moment to think of a time when your son was happy."

She reflected for several long moments. "When we were all together as a family. It's just been hard the last couple years … since the divorce …."

"Can you think of a time when he did something that really mattered to you?"

Rebecca slowly smiled. "Yes. A few weeks ago I was out of town on business. The day I came back was my birthday. When I got home, the house was clean, and Sean had made dinner. I didn't even know he could cook." She looked at her son with affection. "It was probably the best dinner I ever had. Because you made it for me."

Sean's face brightened.

"But what's the point of reflecting on one good evening?" Tears welled in Rebecca's eyes and her voice trembled. "Sean needs an attitude change, and I don't know how to make that happen."

Maggie handed her the tissue box. Rebecca wiped her eyes and blew her nose. The three sat in silence while she regained her composure.

"Before you make a major decision about Sean, Rebecca, I wonder if you'd be willing to make a two-month commitment to these sessions. I believe we can work through some of these issues where you and Sean seem to be at odds. We can look at ways you can talk to one another that may be more productive and respectful."

Rebecca's face tightened again. Maggie knew she wanted to believe that Sean was solely responsible for the fault lines in their relationship. Maggie would have to be gentle with her. Therapy wasn't easy. Untangling the knots of deeply held beliefs could be very painful.

Rebecca pursed her lips, eyes focused on the file in her hand.

"Say yes, Mom," Sean said. "Don't send me away."

Rebecca heaved out a sigh. "Let's give it two weeks, Sean. Then we'll reevaluate."

Maggie spent the rest of the session playing peacekeeper. Communication had opened up a little and mother and son were being cordial to one another, choosing words carefully. Maggie gave them both home assignments. As he walked out the door, Sean's eyes sent out a plea of help, which tugged at Maggie's heart. Two weeks of therapy wouldn't win him any battles, but it might put a few cracks in Rebecca's unyielding attitude.

After the Deckers left, Maggie was haunted by the similarities between Sean's predicament and that of her own son. Her husband, David, had been as critical of Eric as Rebecca was of Sean. She remembered David's compulsive, restless nature, and how it drove him to work sixty-hour weeks, striving for perfection. His idea of recreation was competing in triathlons, pushing himself to exhaustion. She could barely recall moments when her husband just sat still. She was convinced stress led to his fatal heart attack ten years ago. She was reminded of his enormous talent every time she drove through her upscale neighborhood and saw the stunning luxury homes his architectural firm had designed.

Maggie loved David, but when his critical eye turned on Eric, trouble erupted. In sports and academics, her son's achievements were above average, but that was never good enough. David belittled Eric for lack of effort. "Don't push him so hard," she often chided. "Let him be a child."

"Children need to learn discipline to become successful adults" was one of David's battle-worn responses. After years of exhaustive arguments on child rearing, David just tuned her out, preferring to take advice from the carpenter or the plumber, or some witless neighbor down the street. Anyone who agreed with him. Maggie countered David's criticism by over-praising Eric. Their parenting model, she knew, was dysfunctional and polarized. *Poor Eric.* Stranded in the middle, trying to find a sense of balance in his life.

No one survived parenthood without collecting a trunk load of regrets. Self-forgiveness was what most parents needed to work on, what she still worked on, whenever she reflected on some dispute with Eric that she could have handled better. The pressure of tears warned her that she needed to get out of her head and focus on her work. She picked up the file for her next patient and began reviewing notes from their last session.

CHAPTER THREE

THE MERCURY was soaring, topping out at a scorching hundred and five degrees. Beyond the rodeo stadium, the monotonous desert landscape stretched for miles, wavering on the horizon as though underwater. The air was so dry Justin could barely rustle up enough spit to swallow. A fine layer of dust coated his chaps, boots, protective vest, and every inch of exposed flesh. Even his eyeballs felt grainy. The smell of livestock and manure hung in the air, shifting when the smoke drifted over from the fast food stands, carrying the smell of grilled meat.

His gaze swept the inside of the arena. Bleachers half-full. A few hundred spectators. A surprising turnout for a tiny hick town hidden in the Sonoran Desert. By national standards, this rodeo wasn't even on the radar, but bull riding attracted folks willing to drive in from Tucson and Phoenix.

Fighting a bad case of nerves, Justin wiped the sweat from his forehead with his shirtsleeve and pulled on his helmet. This was his first Professional Bull Riders rodeo. Until now, he'd only competed at high school and college level. Back-road rodeos nobody ever heard of. But some top riders were here today, and the bulls looked bigger and badder than anything he'd ever ridden. Watching seasoned cowboys getting tossed in the dirt within two or three seconds wasn't boosting his confidence any. He felt a jolt of panic when his alias came crackling over the loudspeaker.

"Next up folks, our last bull rider, Alex Hamilton from Beaverhead, Oregon. Riding Cyclone. A bull with a whole lotta mean. This cowboy's gonna need some serious talent to last more'n a second on this animal."

As Justin climbed up on the bucking chute, a hush fell over the crowd and he picked up on their edgy excitement. They'd been waiting on this bull. Compact and powerful, Cyclone had thirty wins, no outs. No rider had ever lasted more than three seconds on his back. No one here thought Justin could ride him, and no one would hold it against him if he dismounted early to save his tail.

He lowered himself into the chute and straddled Cyclone, and the hot sweat from the bull's hide soaked into his jeans. The bull shuddered and thrust back his massive head. Justin jerked away from the horns. The bull thrashed to the right, crashing into the side of the chute. Justin kept his feet up on the rails. Shit. He wasn't even out of the chute yet. Fighting down a wave of fear, he shoved his gloved hand farther into the rope handle and curled his resin-sticky fingers around it tightly.

The cowboy handler shot him a sympathetic look before yanking the rope tight around Cyclone's chest. The world closed in. Nothing existed but Justin and this bull. He sucked in a breath and nodded. "Let 'er rip!"

The gate opened and the bull exploded into the arena. The world blurred. The ground jerked skyward and crashed back down. Cyclone's hindquarters rose like a tidal wave, spine almost vertical, then hit the ground like a ten-ton truck. Justin moved with the propulsion, his free arm thrusting skyward, his spurred heels digging into hide for all he was worth. The bull lurched to the left, then to the right, and bent into a spin. Justin posted himself over the center, every muscle screaming as he strained to hold on. Spine-ramming bucks came one after the other.

Justin held on.

The buzzer sounded.

He freed his rope hand, flew off the bull and landed in the dirt on all fours. Fifteen feet away Cyclone pawed the ground, horns thrust forward, ready to charge. A bullfighter clown darted between them. Cyclone turned momentarily. With loud snorting right behind him, Justin sprinted to the railing and flew over it to safety.

Holy fucking smoke! His heart hammered his chest. He could barely catch his breath. That was close. He'd been a hair away from dead. But he did it. Stayed aboard bad-assed Cyclone for eight seconds. Adrenaline electrified his system. His focus sharpened. Colors brightened. The applause from the crowd was deafening.

The emcee's excited voice blasted his win. "That bull ain't never been rode for eight seconds before! Out of thirty tries. We seen a first here in

Red Rock today. You gotta get it done on the dirt. This cowboy got it done."

As he waited for the verdict from the judges, Justin evaluated his performance. His style points weren't the greatest, but still, it was his best ride ever.

"Alex Hamilton moves into number two position," the emcee said. "Good ride, cowboy."

Second place. Thank God. He made some cash.

Cowboys grouped around him, high-fiving, slapping him on the back. "Way to go, cowboy."

"Good ride."

"How'd you stay aboard that freaking thrashing machine?"

When the attention died down, Justin took off his vest, chaps, and spurs and squatted in the dirt to pack his gear bag. He crowned his damp, sandy-colored hair with his brown Stetson. Nerves had stymied his appetite all day, and now he was starving. He needed something wet and cold to flush the dust out of his parched mouth. He hiked over to a food stand being dismantled by a couple of teenage boys, paid for the last three lukewarm hotdogs, a bag of barbeque chips, and a king-size soda, then sat in the shade of the stands wolfing down his food. The crowds were dispersing into a mowed-down field of weeds, and dust clouds were billowing as cars headed out.

By the time he picked up his prize money the arena had emptied and the hall behind the chutes was deserted. The sudden echo of boots moving swiftly behind him made him glance over his shoulder. His heart skipped a few beats. *What the hell?* The three roughneck cowboys he'd bet against in a bar last night were headed his way. This had bad written all over it. His prize money was in his pocket. Three thousand dollars in one-hundred-dollar bills. He aimed to keep it there.

Pulling his hat low over his forehead, he sprinted out to the contestants' parking lot and slipped behind a row of horse trailers, aiming to get to his truck. The sound of boots running behind him grew louder. A Dodge Ram towing a trailer pulled out of a slot in front of him and blocked his path.

Silently cursing, Justin turned to face the men braking to a halt behind him. A hard-looking lot. Hats marbled with sweat. Faces as sun-cured as old saddles. Men who scraped by doing shit rodeo jobs and gambling.

Justin had seen them at dozens of rodeos in the Pacific Northwest and had taken pains to avoid them, until last night. "Whaddya want?" he asked, taking an offensive posture.

Porky, the ringleader, resembled a starving coyote. Bone-thin, long-pointed nose, hollow cheeks, hand-rolled smoke tucked between chapped lips. "Jus' wanna talk," he said.

"I'm kinda in a hurry here," Justin said. "Make it fast."

Porky shared an amused expression with his sidekicks. "We'll try not to take up too much of yer precious time. You owe us money."

"The hell I do," Justin said.

The three men closed him in against the side of a trailer.

Justin's heart started pounding.

"Yer ride don't square up with the bullshit you fed us last night," Porky said.

"Ya said ya hardly ever bull rode before." This from Waters, a shorter version of Porky, only bowlegged, with a wandering eye that twitched like a needle on a seismograph.

"That ain't what I said."

"That what he said?" Waters asked his partners.

"That's what he said," Porky answered, smoke curling up from his cigarette.

Their dusty companion grunted in agreement.

Justin spoke slowly. "What I said was, I'm an amateur. That don't mean I hardly ever bull rode."

"You knew we was putting money on Chet," Porky said. "But yer ride pushed him into third place. He got a damned belt buckle. We lost our paychecks."

Justin assessed the situation. It appeared the men didn't have the IQ of an earthworm between the three of them. Something wild and violent stirred behind Porky's amber-colored eyes. "And what, you 'spected me to warn you off? Sorry to hear you took a loss, boys, but I ain't no gambling adviser. I'm in the game for myself, just like you."

"Ya rode that bull like a pro," Porky sneered. "You ain't no greenhorn. In gambling circles, we call that cheatin'. We's getting our money outta you one way or another." He punctuated his words with a sharp jab to Justin's chest.

Justin jerked the man's hand away. "Ain't my fault Chet messed up."

He had watched the high-ranked cowboy stagger out of the bar stinking drunk last night, just minutes before Porky and his pals blew in. That kind of drinking would throw any rider off his game. All the more reason why Justin bet on himself. "I ain't giving you nothin'."

Porky's fist caught Justin hard in the gut. He buckled over, barely able to breathe. His good rodeo hat fell to the ground and Porky crushed it with his boot, then he whipped Justin back up by his hair.

"Screw you," Justin said hoarsely.

"Cocky bastard." Waters shoved him violently and Justin's head slammed against the trailer. White pain exploded in his brain, then blackness started rushing in. The pounding of blood in his ears turned into the clopping of hooves and he saw a blurry figure approach the group mounted on a horse. His vision cleared enough to recognize Pastor Bob. The pastor had conducted the church service from horseback in the arena that morning, wearing the same clothes—an orange-and-green-plaid blazer, bolo tie, and purple dress shirt. Justin had attended, praying with every ounce of conviction he could muster for God to give him a break today.

"What's going on here?" the pastor asked sternly.

Porky scowled, said nothing.

Beneath the brim of his hat, the pastor's face was flushed from heat. Beads of sweat collected along his jaw line and dripped onto his collar. He inched his Appaloosa forward. "You all right, son?"

Justin shrugged, probing his throbbing head with his fingers. He was relieved to find his scull still in one piece.

The pastor leveled a steel-edged gaze at Porky. "Three against one?"

Porky flicked his cigarette into the dirt. "This ain't church business, Preacher."

"But it is the sheriff's business." All eyes followed the pastor's gaze down the narrow dirt road that ran between the trailers. A police car cruised toward them. Justin sensed sudden nervous tension rolling off the three cowpokes. They assumed relaxed expressions as the car slowed down and the sheriff looked them over. Pastor Bob waved him on. The sheriff nodded, and drove on, covering them all in an extra layer of talc-like dust.

"You all know the sheriff's my brother." An unveiled threat crept into the pastor's tone.

Porky's gaze followed the sheriff's Yukon until it disappeared, then he turned back to Pastor Bob. "This piece of shit asked for it. He's trying to cheat us."

"Cheat you?" The pastor's eyes narrowed. "You boys been gambling again?"

No response.

"Gambling's a vice, Porky. No better than fornicating with whores." The pastor slipped into his sermon tone. "There's already plenty of volunteers running 'round doing Satan's work. He don't need no more help from you three. You better take care to protect your souls. Got any idea how to do that?"

The men exchanged looks.

"Clean living?" Waters offered.

"Clean living. That's right." The pastor nodded at Justin. "This young man came to service this morning. Asked me to pray special for him."

Porky spat in the dirt near Justin's boot.

"He promised if he won anything he'd donate half to our church."

What the hell? Justin never had private words with the pastor, and he certainly wouldn't have offered half his prize money. He kept his mouth shut. It was an expensive payoff, but at least he wasn't getting the crap beat out of him.

"Plenty of folks in our congregation have been pressed with hard times." Pastor Bob locked eyes with Justin. "Now our prayers have been answered."

Amen to that. Justin figured most of the money would go into the pastor's pocket. He quickly did the math. After half his money went to the preacher, he'd be left with fifteen hundred. After collecting his winnings that night from the bookie, he'd be ahead another couple grand. Thirty-five hundred. He could live on that for a while. Eat better, stay in a motel from time to time.

"Here comes Maria. Watch your mouths." The pastor pulled a handkerchief from his pocket and mopped his dripping face.

Justin's jaw dropped a little as he took in the striking Mexican woman sauntering toward them. She wore a short sundress and western boots, her caramel-colored skin glistening in the sunlight. She looked around his age, twenty. Justin tried to focus on her face, but his eyes scanned the lines of her body of their own accord.

Pastor Bob dismounted and wrapped a protective arm around her waist. Justin saw the gold wedding band sparkle on her finger. How'd the big sweaty ox get a woman like her? The pastor could easily pass for her father.

Maria relaxed against Pastor Bob's sturdy frame and her dark eyes flashed with recognition when they fell on Justin. "You cowboy ride Cyclone, yes?"

"Yes, ma'am." Justin had no talent for talking to women, especially one as pretty as Maria.

"That bull, he loco." Maria smiled, flashing even white teeth. "He throw every cowboy. Not you. You get beeg monies, no?"

Justin felt his face warm. "I did okay." Avoiding Porky's eyes, he retrieved his hat, smacked off the dust and reshaped it, then pulled it down over his throbbing head.

"He's giving the church a big donation," Pastor Bob said.

"Good man." She flashed a grin that lit up Justin's insides like a firecracker.

"You boys better clear outta town," the pastor said sternly to Porky, then his tone lightened when he turned to Justin. "Let's go, son. Where's your vehicle?"

Hoisting his gear bag over his shoulder, Justin followed the pastor's Appaloosa past the trio of cowhands who made no attempt to clear a path. Porky shoved him hard and Justin picked up the scent of sour sweat and tobacco. Once a safe distance away, he glanced back. Porky's eyes bored into his with what Justin interpreted to be murderous intent. He knew their paths would cross again at future rodeos. He'd made a dangerous enemy.

Justin noticed that a handsome, silver-haired man was standing off the road, watching intently from the shadow of his oversized motorhome. A rig like that, Justin knew, cost top dollar, probably a quarter million or more. The air-conditioned livestock trailer hitched to the back wasn't shabby, either. An air of confidence and success swirled around the man, and Justin felt a sharp jolt of envy for his secure place in life. He also felt humiliated that his ass-whipping had been witnessed.

His feeling of shame faded as Maria linked her arm through his and matched his stride. Despite the brutal heat, she looked incandescent, shoulders and legs glowing in the sun. Her lips were painted the color of a cactus flower and her black hair was held in place by scarlet combs. Silver earrings dangled from her lobes like tiny wind chimes. It'd been a while since he'd had a kind touch from a woman. The fragrant scent of her hair stirred inside him an intense longing for an easier life, a stable life, and a woman like Maria he could call his own.

As they approached his camper truck, Justin toyed with the idea of jumping into the cab and screeching out of the lot. Keeping his money.

As though reading his thoughts, Pastor Bob got a sudden hard glint in his eyes. He opened his jacket and placed his hand on his hip, displaying a holstered .38 Smith & Wesson.

Justin's stomach twisted as he counted fifteen of his hard-earned greenbacks into the pastor's hand. The pastor tucked the wad of bills into a pocket and turned to help his wife into the saddle. He mounted behind her, tipped his hat, and rode off across the emptying lot.

Tight-lipped, Justin climbed into the cab. Spewing curses, he hit the dashboard repeatedly with the heel of his hand. He'd just been played by a conniving swindler. A thug walking around in the guise of a good Christian. But who could he turn to? The sheriff, who was the pastor's crony brother? The two were power players, committing crimes with impunity in a town so small it didn't exist on most maps. Justin revved the engine and fishtailed out of the lot, raising a storm of dust that followed him out to the paved county road.

After several miles, he pulled onto a dirt road and parked under an outcropping of smooth gray boulders that provided shade from the relentless sun. Trying to calm the angry beast inside him screaming for justice, he sprawled on his sleeping bag on the sand, his hat covering his face. There was nothing to do but wait. As soon as the cash from the bookie hit his wallet this evening, he'd break the sound barrier getting out of this dried up, degenerate town.

CHAPTER FOUR

AS HE LAY dying on a rutted goat trail in Kunar Province, Sully imagined Canadian geese flying across the war-tattered sky. The geese broke V formation and reconfigured, forming letters that spelled *HELP*. Sully weaved in and out of consciousness, his thoughts jumbled, the ground tilting at an angle. He wanted to grab hold of something to keep from sliding off the earth, but his arms wouldn't move. His legs felt heavy and far away. At the edge of consciousness, a mortar round whistled, grew louder, and exploded with an ear-piercing blast. The ground rumbled beneath him. Dust and rubble sprayed his face. Whop whop whop whop. Apache gunships! Seconds away. Thank God. They'd blow the Taliban to hell.

The din of choppers receded. The nightmare abruptly shattered. When he opened his eyes, sunlight stabbed his retinas like needle pricks. His body was tangled in the covers. The doorbell was buzzing, an insistent pulse as irritating as a dentist's drill. Sully got up too quickly and braced an arm against the wall until a wave of dizziness passed. He didn't remember getting into bed last night, or putting on the pajama bottoms he'd worn in high school. The buzzing stopped. He heard the back door open, then the sound of boots scuffing the kitchen floor.

"Sully?" a baritone voice boomed. "You home?"

Head ringing, stomach lurching, Sully shuffled down the hall past the living room and entered the kitchen. Pain radiated from his wound sites. Even his hair hurt.

Dressed in his olive-green uniform, western boots, and wide-brimmed Stetson, Sheriff Carl Matterson stood holding a Styrofoam cup in one hand and a foil-wrapped pan in the other. The sheriff was a big man with strong features, nose bent slightly to the right from college football, his paunch more rounded than Sully remembered. The kitchen looked smaller with him standing in it.

"Hang on, Carl." Sully picked up the prescription bottle from the counter, shook a couple pills onto his palm, and gulped them down with water from a mug sitting in the pile of dirty dishes in the sink.

"Too much partying last night?" Matterson asked in a jovial tone.

"Something like that." Fighting a wave of nausea, Sully turned to greet him.

Matterson's grin faded as his eyes traveled over the red scars on Sully's abdomen, arm, and face. "Man, you got banged up over there."

Sully ran a hand over his throbbing bicep. "No worries. Still got all my vital parts."

"Thank God for that." Matterson pushed his hat back from his broad forehead. "You got bigger. More muscle. The military will do that to you." His gaze fell to the names etched on Sully's forearm. "New tats?"

Sully extended his arm and Matterson scanned the names. Something like empathy glinted in his eyes. "That's rough."

Sully shrugged. Matterson missed nothing. Training from years on the job. He'd been sheriff for as long as Sully could remember. Tough on crime. People slept better at night. "That pie you're carting around, Carl?"

"Oh, yeah. The wife made it yesterday. Gotcha coffee, too. Strong, black."

"Hell, Carl, I like this delivery service. Have a seat."

Matterson made no comment about the mess in the kitchen. The smell of the motor oil on the car parts made Sully's stomach churn. He transferred them from the table to a countertop, making room for plates and the only two clean forks left in the drawer.

With a squeak of leather from his gun holster, Matterson settled into a chair, hung his hat on a bended knee, and stripped the foil from the pie pan.

Sully sliced into the crust. "Strawberry-rhubarb? Sweet."

"None for me, Sully." Matterson patted his belly. "Watching the gut."

"You sure?"

"Well, maybe a thin slice."

Sully sliced a sizable piece for each of them and the two chewed silently for a moment.

"That's tasty. Give Susie my thanks. My first home-cooked food in months." Sully served them both another piece. He gulped coffee in between bites and his brain began to sharpen.

Matterson leaned back in his chair and his jacket fell open, revealing his holstered Glock 9mm and the badge clipped to his belt. "Travis called this morning. Told me you were back. Said to let you sleep. Guess I woke you anyway."

Sully glanced at the clock above the sink and said with a touch of panic, "Hell, it's after ten. I've wasted half a day."

"Relax, Sully. You're not on military time anymore. You work for yourself now."

"You notice the state of this ranch, Carl?"

Matterson glanced around the kitchen. "Needs some work, sure. But hold steady, son. Me and my guys at the station are coming out this weekend to lend a hand. Hardware store donated paint. The pastor's organizing something with the women, too. All hush-hush. You don't know anything about it, of course. We'll get this place looking like Graceland in no time." He grinned. "Might even be more pie."

Sully looked down at his plate. The idea of charity made him uncomfortable. If his father were here, he'd have none of it. "I appreciate that, Carl. I really do. But we don't need help. I'm able-bodied, and so is Travis."

"You and Joe never said no to anybody needing help in this town. You're a war hero. Can't keep people from respecting what you did over there."

Sully didn't feel like a hero, but arguing with Carl was a waste of time.

"Travis said you wanna bring Joe home. To get him here, you're gonna need help."

Sully's voice softened. "Point taken."

"There's another reason I'm here." Matterson's brow creased into multiple folds. "Unpleasant business. Travis thought it'd be better coming from me."

Sully recalled Travis being troubled about something in the barn last night. His breathing slowed. Here it comes.

"There's been some horse thievery going on around the county the last few months."

Sully was genuinely surprised. Wild Horse Creek was a close-knit horse community. Most of the ranching families went back generations. Folks trusted one another. Horses were routinely left unattended out in pasture. Stealing another man's horse was unthinkable. These days, horses were microchipped, papered, had photos on the Internet. "Whose horses?"

"Patterson, Cannon …."

Sully whistled. Those two highbrow neighbors owned million-dollar horse farms. One bred hunter jumpers, the other dressage champions. "How many?"

"Seven, between the two."

"Jesus," he said, alarmed. "You're talking serious money."

The sheriff looked down at his hat, then back at Sully. "Gunner's gone."

"What?" Sully didn't think he heard right.

"Sorry, Sully. They got him two nights ago."

Sully sat stunned. He pictured his high-spirited chestnut stallion with the white blaze, black mane and tail. A reining champion. "Two nights ago? I was getting on a plane in Germany." Sully shot off his chair and paced, anger building in his chest.

Matterson shook his head, said gruffly, "It's a mean business. Horses are damned personal."

"Christ, it feels like I just had a kidney ripped out." He'd rather lose a kidney than Gunner, his most valuable horse.

"He's insured, isn't he?" Matterson asked.

"God, I hope so." Sully had no idea who was looking out for their finances these days. "No amount of money can replace Gunner. His reining instincts are inbred. He brought in top dollar in stud fees. How're we gonna replace that income?"

The sheriff looked down with a sullen expression, turning the brim of his hat in his hands.

"It was too much putting all this on Travis," Sully said in a morose tone. "Dad gone. Mom gone. Valuable horses just sitting in the barn. Guess I'm lucky they only took Gunner."

"He's a prize, all right. It's a changing economy, Sully. Hard times. Pushing people into crimes we haven't seen here. A horse like Gunner can be sold on the black market overseas, or South America, for a small fortune."

Sully struggled to pull himself together, embarrassed to show emotion in front of Matterson. He heard Canadian geese honking as they flew over the roof preparing to land in the creek. "What do you know about the thieves?"

"Not much," Matterson said. "They operate at night. No one's ever seen them. They get in and out without raising a stir. They've been at it awhile, we found out. Horses have gone missing in other counties, too."

"How do they know the layout of the ranches? Which horses to take?"

"Evidently, Sully, they're working with someone local. Someone who knows ranches around here." Matterson's expression tightened. "Could be a trainer, farrier, veterinarian. Who knows? So many of these people come and go every year."

Sully stacked the plates and placed them on the counter, his mind racing.

"It's got all our neighbors riled up," Matterson said. "Wondering if it's someone we know and trust."

"He's gonna end up pretty damned dead if anyone finds him before you do."

"Let's hope that doesn't happen." Matterson shifted his weight. "Travis was out tracking with my deputies yesterday. They picked up two sets of boot prints leading Gunner out of the barn across the north end of your property. They lost the tracks out on the fire road where they crossed the creek. Spent hours trying to pick them up, but …." The sheriff shook his head. "Nothing. Had to pull my men off the chase. Travis went back out this morning."

"I gotta help him," Sully said with a sense of urgency.

"Travis doesn't need your help. Nobody can track better than him, and he's got a three-hour jump on you." Matterson wiped pie crumbs from his shirt, scraped his chair back from the table, and unfolded his large frame. "The best thing you can do right now is get the ranch ready. Joe's gonna get word you're back and he'll be chomping at the bit to get home." With a sympathetic look, Matterson settled his hat over his thinning hair and crossed the floor. He paused with his hand on the door handle. "Glad to have you home, son." He walked out pulling the door shut behind him.

From the window, Sully watched the morning sun glint off the sheriff's windshield as he backed up his patrol truck, then it disappeared around the house. Feeling like he needed to smash something, Sully strode out to the porch barefoot and shirtless, barely noticing the cold.

He was greeted by honks echoing across the yard from the nearest pasture. Heads thrust skyward, the two donkeys, Gus and Whiskey, were braying like drunken sailors cut off from liquor. This was a cue for the horses to buck, squeal, and gallop at breakneck speed through the pasture, kicking up snow. Chickens came fluttering out of the coop, cackling and scurrying around the yard, flapping wings, feathers flying. Pistol, the mule, rattled the locks on his paddock and thumped his body against the gate, his lips pulled back in a yellow-toothed grin.

Sully felt the urgent need to mount up and join Travis to track the rustlers, but the animals were letting him know they were hungry. They should've been fed hours ago. His anxiety rose. Pressure built in his chest and his heart started racing. He had a sudden strange sensation of being detached from his body. He sank back against the steps, barely able to catch his breath. Long minutes of anguish crawled by and he tried to calm himself by training his eyes on the cumulus clouds drifting in the blue sky. After a long while, the hammering of his heart started to ease. He drew in a thin, ragged breath, and released a tendril of frozen air.

What the hell? He was losing it. Must be the stress of coming home. The doctor at the hospital told him it would take time to adjust. *Take it slow.*

The world he left behind was centered around order and protocol. Sully understood the rigors of military life and his place in the chain of command. He did his duty and followed orders. In return, everything he needed—clothes, food, housing, a paycheck—had been military issue, handed down from the powers above. Solid. Unbreakable. Reliable.

He returned home to chaos.

He was now responsible for the care of these animals. He needed to pull this ranch back together, with limited labor and dwindling capital. And here he was, spiraling out of control, paranoia gnawing at the edges of his confidence. He had to push through this wall of anxiety, like he did every time he sat on a wild bronc before it cut loose in the arena, and like he did when he went out on patrol in hostile territory—and get the job done. His breathing was almost back to normal. He was freezing.

He peeled himself off the icy planks and hurried to his room. Dressed in his old work clothes, Sully went back outdoors and started his chores. After piling hay bales onto the flatbed truck, he dropped off feed to the equines, heifers, and bulls, and filled the water troughs. He threw feed to the chickens and watched their beaks peck the earth like pistons.

With the most pressing tasks taken care of, Sully headed out to the stable behind the barn to inspect Gunner's stall. In high school, he had saved a portion of his rodeo earnings to buy a quarter horse from a champion bloodline. At sixteen, he brought Gunner home; a four-year-old stallion with perfect conformation, agility, and a willingness to learn. Full of pride of ownership, Sully spent hundreds of hours training him. The stallion came to respond to his commands instinctively, and he was electrifying to watch in the arena. The dozens of reining competitions Gunner won sealed the reputation of Dancing Horse Ranch as a top-notch breeder.

Stealing a man's horse was stealing his livelihood. Fuming, Sully grabbed a pitchfork and sifted through the pine shavings in Gunner's stall looking for any small clue left by the thieves. *Nothing.* He opened the stall door and went out into the paddock. The snow had been packed down by the boots of the lawmen who conducted a search yesterday. A maze of tracks led out of the paddock across the fields to the north end of the property. The sheriff said the tracks continued for several miles and ended at Smoke River. Hopefully, Travis would find something today that they had missed.

He fished out his cell phone, called Travis, and got his voicemail. No cell coverage.

Sully got back to work. He pulled down the brim of his hat and put on his shades to protect his eyes from the glare. It was a crisp March morning. The sun reflected brilliantly off the white hillocks and snowdrifts rippling across the fields. To the west, fingers of timber reached down from the Cascade Range into the desert sage. To the south and north, the ranch was bordered by ponderosa forest. It was good land. Beautiful country. Now his family was in danger of losing it.

The sun warmed his back as he examined the livestock and found them in good condition. He applied antibiotic ointment to minor cuts on an Appaloosa and the mule and took note of horses needing farrier work. Like oversize dogs, the horses followed him through the pastures and nudged him for attention. He had sorely missed being in the company of intelligent animals who gave their affection freely and never judged you. As he mucked out stalls, took inventory of the farm equipment, and worked on repairs, Sully felt his blood pressure drop.

***

The sun melted into a sea of red and gold that stretched across the range of snowcapped mountains—a stunning show nature put on for free. Despite his exhaustion, Sully moved indoors and scrubbed down the kitchen, including the floors and the dusty pots and pans hanging over the island. His glance kept darting out the window, hoping to spot Travis riding home. The old man was mentally tough, but he was getting older, and Sully felt uneasy that he was alone in the frigid cold after dark.

By the time he polished off two cans of chili for dinner, Sully's whole body ached and his right arm was throbbing. He swallowed his pain pills, peeled off his work clothes, and took a hot shower, relishing the hot water pelting his tight muscles. The flannel bathrobe that had been loose on him in college was now too snug. As a bronc rider, he had stayed lean. Every extra pound of weight on a horse's back was a detriment. But as a Marine, Sully worked out hard to build up muscle. In hand-to-hand combat, strength could make the difference between life and death.

Next, he turned his attention to the office, where everything was coated in dust. Looked like no one had turned on the computer since his mother left. A financial whiz, she skillfully ran the ranch on a tight budget, making every dollar work like two, and justifying every expense. In the warm months, they grew their own food. In the fall, they canned the surplus. His mom did all the cooking and ran the household like clockwork, while the men labored outdoors from dawn until dusk. It was a good life. They worked hard and religiously deposited money every month into savings.

As he sorted through six months' worth of unopened bills in the inbox, his back stiffened and the muscles grew tight across his scalp. With trepidation, he got on the computer and started going through the books. *Not good.* Anger at his mother's neglect started simmering in his gut. How could she coldly walk away from her responsibilities at the ranch, from the family that depended on her, from the animals? No food had been canned last year. The pantry was empty. Travis was living on pizza. Bills were unpaid. It would take a lot of hard work to get the ranch right side up again.

The pain pills, combined with exhaustion, made his brain fuzzy. He shuffled into his bedroom, sorely tempted to get under the covers and pass out, but his duffel still sat on the floor where he left it last night. The prospect of confronting its contents made his gut tighten, but he'd made a promise to Eric. It had to be done.

Opening the bag released the dusty smell of canvas and desert sand. He was transported back to his Marine compound as he unpacked. On top were plastic bags containing toiletries. The middle was filled with clothing, rolled up to take less room. Socks and underwear were tucked into the sides, filling up the cracks.

He stacked everything neatly on the floor, then pulled out his medical kit, air and water tight, small enough to fit in a pocket. It contained antiseptic, a needle and thread to sew wounds, and a maxi pad to soak up blood. It had come in handy on many missions. Grains of desert sand spilled onto the carpet as he lifted out the sturdy cardboard box sealed with packing tape. The address and phone number of Eric's mother were scrawled across the top. *Maggie Steeler.* Sully would have to call her tomorrow.

He checked his cell. No message from Travis. He planted the phone on the nightstand and burrowed under the covers of his bed, sleep pulling at him like a rope on a calf.

CHAPTER FIVE

JUSTIN SAT HUNCHED over the scarred bar at Chester's Bar 'n Grill working on his second cold beer, struggling to keep his patience in check. His gaze darted from the yellowed rodeo posters curling on the walls to the marbled mirror behind the counter. He saw himself reflected with the empty room behind him, except for a pair of drunks leaning into their drinks by the window. Outside, the neon sign splashed garish color across the sidewalk and headlights from an occasional car flooded the bar with light. Useless, the buzzing metallic fan moved hot air from one side of the room to the other. His shirt was damp under the armpits and stuck to his back.

The rotten turn of the day had his nerves on edge. As a consolation, he had treated himself to a steak dinner with all the trimmings. The best meal he'd had in weeks. He glanced at the clock and cursed under his breath. Smiley, Red Rock's version of a bookie, was an hour late.

The door opened, but it wasn't Smiley. Justin recognized the silver-haired man he'd seen standing in the shadow of his fancy motorhome. The man who had witnessed his ass-kicking by Porky and his misfit amigos. The man's style looked more Jackson, Wyoming than this hick town lost in the Sonoran Desert. His boots were hand-tooled, and his well-shaped Stetson was free of stains. His straight posture and confident expression gave him an air of authority. The stranger looked right at him, crossed the room, and straddled the stool next to his. He removed his hat, met Justin's eyes in the mirror, and nodded.

"Howdy," Justin said, barely polite. He didn't want company.

The stranger ordered a Corona and sat in silence until the bottle and a frosted mug were placed in front of him. A slice of lime was hooked to the lip of the mug. He poured the beer, squeezed the lime, and took a long pull, then wiped the foam from his mouth. "Man, that's good. Cold. Hell of a rodeo today."

"I seen better. Seen worse," Justin said.

"Going to Boise next?"

"Don't know nothin' 'bout Boise. Just staying local."

The man looked at him long and hard. "You can cut the act, cowboy."

Justin glanced at him, sizing him up. "Whatchu gettin' at, mister?"

"Lose the cowpoke vernacular. You're way too smart to use English that poorly." He swiveled in his seat, half facing Justin. "Those cowhands who roughed you up today may have fallen for your bumpkin act, but it doesn't fly with me."

"What's it to you?" Justin finished his draft beer and signaled the bartender for a refill.

"Let's say I'm an interested party. I've seen you on the circuit."

Justin said nothing, waited. The bartender placed a fresh mug in front of him.

"You're good," the man said. "But you could be better."

"I'm learning."

"You'd learn faster with a trainer."

"Trainers cost money."

"You travel alone?"

"Yep."

"Most cowboys travel in groups. Support each other. Share the costs."

"I like my own company."

"That may be. But you're playing a dangerous game getting mixed up with Porky and Waters."

"Bad losers." Justin met the man's piercing gray eyes. "They took it out on me."

The man took a swig of beer. "Men like that don't take kindly to losing money. Leading them to believe you're a rookie was a con."

"I *am* a rookie."

The stranger's eyes locked on his, unflinching.

"This was my first PBA rodeo," Justin said, suddenly feeling defensive.

"How many amateur shows you do this year?"

"Too many to count."

"You earn money?"

"Half the time."

"You're a pro."

The man's intense stare unsettled Justin and he looked into his beer.

"You think you got it all figured out, Alex? No accountability? The last guy who messed with Porky ate through a straw for six months." A ghost of a smile. "I'd hate to see anything happen to your pearly whites."

"I can take care of myself."

"Yeah? What if Pastor Bob hadn't saved your ass?"

"That crook?" Justin scowled, shifted in his seat. After a moment of reflection, he added, "Guess I'd be drinking this beer through a straw right about now."

"Damned straight." The man finished his beer and pushed away his empty bottle. The bartender set down another Corona. "You paid a high price for the pastor's salvation. Half your earnings."

"Don't I know it."

"Got a name besides Alex Hamilton?"

"That name's working just fine." Justin tightened his jaw. He was using the name and accent for a semblance of protection from his hidden past, but that was no one's business but his own.

"As in Alexander Hamilton, founding father?"

Justin was feeling his alcohol. "He may be someone I admire."

The man laughed, loud and confident. "Funny that you'd pick the name of some old coot from the dawn of American history."

"Hamilton was a great man," Justin said with a touch of indignation. "Possibly the most misunderstood and under-appreciated of all the founding fathers. He was a heroic leader in the American Revolution, he was George Washington's chief of staff, and our first secretary of the treasury. He helped form a strong central government, which united the colonies when they were floundering. Just a few of his many, many accomplishments."

The stranger looked impressed. "You like history?"

"Yeah." Justin could win a quiz show he'd read so much history.

The man's face sobered. "It's ironic you chose that particular handle, considering Hamilton was preoccupied with matters of honor and decency."

Justin felt his face warm. The stranger had no right to judge him.

Justin used the name because he and Hamilton had eerily similar childhoods. Both were born bastards, were abandoned by their fathers, lost their mothers early in life, were raised in foster care, and faced lives of hardship and struggle. Hamilton developed his mind, worked hard, and pulled himself out of an anonymous, impoverished existence. Justin intended to do the same.

"This the life you want, Alex? One step ahead of men who want to beat your brains in?"

"Hell no," Justin said, frowning. Presenting himself as a rookie to Porky had been an act of desperation. It just happened. It wasn't planned. "What do you care? You got a guardian angel complex or something?"

The man laughed. "You could use one. You're a smart kid, Alex, but you need to be smarter. You won some money today, which should've put you halfway to Phoenix by now." The man shook his head. "But here you are."

Justin was more curious than annoyed by the stranger's interest. Roaming solo, eating fast food and doing second-rate rodeos was taking its toll. It'd been a long while since he'd had a real conversation with anything but a horse.

"You sticking around means only one thing. You're waiting for Smiley."

"I intend to get my money," he said fiercely.

The stranger's eyes narrowed momentarily. He rubbed his jaw. "It's a damn shame you're too young to see your potential. I own that bull you rode today. You're the first cowboy that wasn't thrown off him. I don't know where you learned how to stay on a bull, but you're a natural. Good instincts." He met Justin's gaze. "You're also a hothead. That's going to get you into trouble."

Justin stared into his beer, troubled by the man's prediction.

"If you decide to stop throwing your talent down the toilet, I could offer you some honest employment."

Justin shrugged.

"Self-worth is about finding out what you do best and working hard at it."

"Some great philosopher say that?" Justin asked.

"Hell if I know. It's just a little something I learned myself by doing things the hard way." The stranger placed a card on the bar with a few bills, covering Justin's tab. "If your attitude changes, call me." He settled his Stetson on his head, placed a hand on Justin's shoulder, and walked out.

Justin stared at the card for a long time before picking it up.

Hank Sterling, Sterling O Ranch, Beaverhead, Oregon.

Justin blinked hard. The man was a legend.

***

It was after eight when Smiley slithered into Chester's. A little glassy-eyed and smoldering after two hours of sipping beer, Justin watched him from his perch at the bar. The man was oily, from his small eyes, pockmarked skin, and greasy hair to the insincere way he conducted business. Justin figured he'd repel water if he bothered to shower. The bar was now clouded by cigarette smoke and full of tough-looking cowboys who drank hard and played hard at the card tables in back.

Smiley slouched on the barstool next to Justin and motioned for the bartender. A shot glass appeared and was filled with cheap whiskey. The bartender left the bottle. Obviously, Smiley was a regular. The bookie gulped back two shots before gracing Justin with his full attention. "Sorry I'm late. Got your goods." He patted his shirt pocket.

The obvious bulge made Justin's heart pick up a beat. "Hand it over."

Smiley scowled. "In here? You crazy? Let's go out back." He motioned to the bartender. "Watch my bottle for me, Murry."

Built like a sumo wrestler, the bartender eyed Justin with an unreadable expression and went about his business.

Justin's balance was off when he got to his feet. He'd drunk too much. He followed Smiley through a dark passageway past the restrooms, looking over his shoulder twice. He didn't like the setup, but his truck was on the other side of that exit door. He'd grab his money and run. They stepped into the dimly lit alley and the heavy door clanged shut behind them. Quiet. No movement.

Smiley unbuttoned his breast pocket, made a show of taking out a thick roll of bills, and began thumbing them into Justin's hand, slow and precise. Mostly twenties and fifties.

"Hurry it up, will ya?"

Smiley glared up at him. "You made me lose my place. Where was I?"

"Give it to me." Heart racing, Justin grabbed the bundle of bills, shoved it into his back pocket, and strode toward his truck.

Two men rounded the back of his camper before he reached the driver's side. Silhouetted against the dim light, one was tall and skinny, the other was stocky with bowed legs. Justin turned in time to see Smiley slip back through the exit door.

The men came at him fast. Justin turned to run, but a third figure sprang out from the shadows and tackled him. The concrete flew up hard and fast. Someone's boot heel came down like a sledgehammer on his skull. White pain exploded in his brain. He curled up, covered his head, braced himself. Rapid-fire kicks from two pairs of boots thrust him into instant, agonizing hell.

"Enough!"

The assault stopped.

"Mind yer own business, Murry," Porky grunted.

"Beatings behind my bar are my business. Keeps tourists away."

Silence.

"You did the kid enough damage. Get your money and go."

More cursing. Justin felt hands pat down his body, find his wad of bills, then he heard his wallet slap the ground.

"Let's go. Count it in the truck. Take out Smiley's cut."

The footsteps moved away down the alley.

Justin heard the door clang shut behind Murry.

Light-headed, drifting on a sea of pain, Justin heard a set of boot steps return. A vicious kick found his hamstring. Someone moaned like a dying animal. Was it Justin? Vaguely, faraway, he felt his boots being yanked off. Then he was floating off the ground. The last thing he remembered was sinking into oozing, stinking, rotting food.

As he emerged from darkness, Justin became aware of three things: his labored breathing, hellish pain, and the claws of squeaking rats scurrying over his body. With a yelp, he batted a large rodent off his head. The creatures scattered as he tried to rise, his hands grabbing blindly for the rim of the dumpster. His fingers slipped off the greasy edge and he teetered backwards onto his ass.

It took another couple of tries before he tumbled over the side to the asphalt below. Coated in grease and rotting food, Justin leaned against a brick wall with both arms and retched his steak dinner, then he dry-heaved, feeling like pieces of his gut were spewing out. Bile burned his throat, his body pulsed with pain, and he could hardly breathe, which probably meant fractured ribs. He was hatless and bootless.

Momentarily, white-hot rage blocked out the pain. Then it came back again, full force. Tears squeezed out of his eyes.

Sucking in ragged breaths, he picked up his wallet and staggered like a drunkard to his truck. He wiped dust off the window with his sleeve and peered into the camper shell. *Thank God.* All his meager possessions—sleeping bag, carton of books, laptop, beat-up guitar, rodeo gear bag—were untouched. He unlocked the cab door, threw an old tattered blanket over the seat, climbed in, and peeled out of the alley.

As he raced away at high speed from his nightmare in Red Rock, Justin was tormented by his own stupidity. Why had he followed Smiley into the alley? Why didn't he see it was a setup? Porky, Smiley, and even the bartender had played him. This, after the preacher got a sizable piece. He'd ricocheted like a pinball from one con man to the next after cruising into town with *sucker* pulsing in neon on his forehead.

Hank Sterling, the only decent man he'd met today, had warned him not to stay but he'd been too pigheaded to listen. Now he was paying a heavy price. Beaten up, no money, and no way to make a living until his body healed up.

He drove for hours with the windows rolled down to dilute the nauseous smell, the barren desert flashing by on both sides of his truck. Around three a.m. the lights of Phoenix appeared on the horizon and familiar landmarks swept into view. The neon signs of cheap motels and gas stations pulsed in the night.

Justin pulled off the highway, bounced over a pitted road, and parked at a rest stop. The restroom reeked of urine and bleach. Graffiti covered the walls. As he relieved himself in the urinal, his eyes scanned vulgar poetry and primitive drawings of body parts. Fighting back an urge to heave, he stripped off his fouled clothes, shoved them into a trash bin, and did his best to wipe grease off his skin with powdered hand soap and paper towels. After doing a piss-poor job, he slathered on a layer of soap just to stifle the odor. Pain shot through his body as he pulled on his last pair of clean jeans and t-shirt. He wormed his feet into a pair of worn-out running shoes and limped out into the warm desert air.

He drove a short distance into a gritty suburb, parked outside a Motel Heaven, and entered the dimly lit office. The closet-size room smelled of stale coffee and cigarettes, and the pimply-faced clerk behind the counter swiped his card without looking him in the eye. Justin figured his odor must be offensive, even frightening. He paid in advance for three nights and located his room.

At thirty bucks a night, Justin knew what to expect and wasn't surprised. Musty, dismal, poorly cleaned. Stains in the toilet and sink that would never wash off. He parked his old leather bag on a chair and searched for some oxycodone left over from an old injury. After popping two in his mouth and washing them down with water from a plastic cup in the bathroom, he undressed and stood in front of the mirror to gauge the damage

He looked like he'd been trampled by a herd of bulls; his body a patchwork of welts and bruises. Covering his face with his arms during the assault left it untouched, but the back of his head throbbed like it was being used as a conga drum. Something like rancid bacon grease dripped down his face from his hair.

Justin showered in tepid water. He shampooed his hair twice and scrubbed his flesh with two cakes of tiny soap, sucking in his breath against the pain. He withstood a cold spray of water for several minutes, hoping to reduce some swelling. Shivering, teeth chattering, he toweled dry, got into bed, and pulled the covers over his shoulders. Bad mattress. Starchy sheets. Made no difference. He was in agony, waiting for the meds to kick in. Now that he was safely holed up, he surrendered fully to the depression his anger had kept at bay.

With the splurge for the motel room, he had maxed out his credit card. Tomorrow he hoped to rustle up enough change from his pockets and glove compartment to order a large pizza, which would have to provide his calorie intake for the next three days. In his entire life, Justin had never felt so low, so desperate. Only yesterday, he thought he had bottomed out on bad luck and was on his way up. He recalled the feeling of triumph after riding Cyclone. Ecstatic high, cowboys slapping him on the back, a big wad of cash waiting for him. Because of his stupidity, his luck had changed with the speed of an ax chopping through kindling.

As he contemplated a survival strategy for the next few weeks, one far-fetched idea kept resurfacing—finding a sympathetic woman to shack up with. Around the circuit, women were always hitting on him. They liked his athletic build and neon-blue eyes. A good number had invited themselves into the back of his camper truck for some gratification. Quick. Easy. Stripped down to raw emotion. No attachment. No expectations. Like riding a bull, the second he started thinking was the second he made a mistake. Best to just stay in the moment and enjoy the ride. He didn't remember faces or names, never kept a phone number. After sex, he just wanted them gone. "Catcha next time around" was his usual parting remark.

Living the way he did with no house, no savings, and an insufficient education, didn't foster a desire to hook up with a dependent female, though one or two had expressed an interest in hitting the road with him.

Now things had changed. He was desperate. He'd have to piece himself together, venture out to some singles bar and try to find a gal with a tender heart. Despising himself, he drifted into a pain-filled, fitful sleep.

CHAPTER SIX

"*INCOMING! INCOMING!*" A panicked voice barked over the loudspeaker. Sully heard the whistle of Taliban mortars and then the ground concussed, shaking his cot. In an instant, he was on his feet with his M16 in his hands. A round burst right outside the concrete-and-sandbag bunker, spraying his men with rubble. Dust and smoke stung his eyes. The air reeked of explosives. He couldn't hear his own voice screaming, "Take cover!"

Another detonation. Shrapnel blasted through the embrasures. Two men got slammed to the floor. A rocket-propelled grenade hissed through the doorway and skidded across the floor.

"*Get out! Get out!*" Sully frantically searched the floor until his fingers touched hot metal. Snatching the grenade beneath his gut, he waited for oblivion.

The bunker and his men vaporized. The sudden silence was deafening. He opened his eyes to find a sliver of light peeking through the bedroom door from the hallway at the ranch. He was home in Oregon. USA. Drenched in sweat, heart racing, Sully lay motionless, waiting for his emotions to cool. He kept his eyes open, not willing to witness more of the horror stored behind his eyelids.

The clock on his nightstand read six thirty. Gray light seeped in along the edges of the window shade. He pulled himself into a sitting position, his feet found his worn sheepskin slippers, then he shuffled through the house to the kitchen clad in pajama bottoms. The smell of last night's chili reached his nostrils before he turned on the light. It felt good to see the kitchen scrubbed and orderly, all the pots shiny. He put water on for coffee and set two mugs on the counter.

Coffee dripped into the pot and the aroma filled the room. A knock at the door alerted him before Travis walked in, accompanied by a cold blast of air.

"Morning, Travis." Sully smiled, happy to see his friend in one piece. "You smell coffee a mile away, don't you?"

"Heard the water hitting the pot from the bunk house." Travis rubbed his reddened hands over a gas burner.

It bothered Sully that his friend looked stiff with cold. The old bunkhouse was drafty, but Travis insisted he liked his privacy. "I don't know why you don't stay in the house. There's a perfectly good room sitting empty while you're freezing your ass out there."

Travis ignored him and grabbed a box of powdered doughnuts from the cupboard. "Want one?"

"How old are they?"

He shrugged. "Two weeks. Maybe three."

"I'll pass." Sully poured two mugs of coffee and set one on the table in front of Travis.

Travis hung his jacket on the back of the chair and placed his hat in the middle of the table. Sully thought it made a nice centerpiece, with the sleek feathers jutting out like a rooster's tail. The old Paiute's skin was sun-cured from his collar to the middle of his brow where his hat normally sat. After stirring sugar into his coffee and adding cream, Travis wolfed down a doughnut and started on a second, powdered sugar dusting his collar.

"I got a visit from Carl yesterday," Sully said, leaning against the counter with his hands wrapped around his mug. "He gave me the good news."

Travis grunted and gulped down a half cup of coffee. He wasn't much of a talker until he had about half a pot.

"Thanks for going out tracking."

Travis looked around the room. "Thanks for cleaning the kitchen. Where'd you put my auto parts? I need to work on the truck."

"In the garage. You find anything?" Sully asked.

"Yeah."

Sully waited until Travis took another gulp.

"When I was out with the sheriff's men, we lost the tracks on a forest road a few miles up the creek. Yesterday, I picked them up again where the creek runs into Smoke River. The tracks disappeared from time to time, but I'd find them again. They just kept crossing those horses back and forth across the river where the water was shallow." He paused to drain his mug.

Sully refilled it and waited while Travis stirred in sugar and cream.

"In an old campsite, I found tire impressions made by two trucks hauling big horse trailers. There were four pairs of boot prints and the tracks of about a dozen horses. The horses were loaded into the trucks. Gunner was one of them."

Sully cursed. There could be no mistake. Gunner's tracks were easily recognized, embossed with the initials DH for Dancing Horse. "The other horses?"

"Don't know where they came from."

Sully mulled this over. "Big trucks. Careful planning. Sounds like a well-organized operation. Sheriff said they've been at this for a while. Horses have gone missing in other counties." He spoke in a quiet tone, but anger stewed in his gut. "The bastards could be anywhere in the country by now."

Travis pulled a plastic baggie from his jacket pocket and handed it to Sully. "Found those scattered around the campsite."

Inside were three cigarette butts. Hand-rolled, pinched on one end, stained with nicotine. "Sloppy, leaving those around."

Travis shrugged. "Probably some stooge they hired to wait with the trucks."

"We'll drop this off at the sheriff's office. Maybe they can trace some DNA." He looked at Travis. "You're better than a hound dog at tracking."

"Takes time and patience, is all." Anger flashed in his dark eyes. "I want Gunner back as much as you do. Yesterday was my last chance to track. Snowstorm's coming in."

Sully arched a brow. "Snow gods tell you that?"

"That, and I saw it on the Weather Channel last night." Travis stood and crossed the floor, refilled his coffee mug. "You planning on cooking breakfast, or letting an old man starve?"

"Last time I lived here you knew what a frying pan looked like."

"You remember my cooking?" Travis asked.

"Point taken." Sully recalled the stack of pizza boxes he threw out last night. "Time to wean you off pizza and doughnuts. I'll cook. Think you can make toast without burning them?"

Travis grunted.

Sully pulled eggs, butter, and bacon from the fridge, and placed two cast-iron skillets over the burners. He lined one with strips of bacon and cracked eight eggs into the melted butter in the other. The bacon sizzled and popped. After a while, he poked the strips with a fork and turned them over. He divided the food onto two plates and they sat down to eat. Travis doused his eggs with hot sauce. He smothered everything in hot sauce, probably even pizza.

"I looked over the books last night," Sully said, swiping egg yolk off his plate with buttered toast. "We have enough savings to cover the next two months. That's the good news." He paused for a moment and then dove in. "Now the bad news. Dad's medical bills have pushed us close to bankruptcy. We owe the General Store for feed. Long and short of it, we're about thirty grand short to meet overhead and property taxes by the end of the year."

A trace of anger tightened Travis's face.

Sully knew the old Paiute was blaming his mother. Sully, too, felt a burn in his gut. "With Gunner gone, we're losing stud fees. It appears Gunner wasn't insured. No payment was made this last quarter."

Frown lines deepened on Travis's brow.

Sully was sorry to dump the whole load on him at once, but he needed to know. "I figure we'll have to sell a horse or two, one of the bulls, and think about boarding other folks' horses. Maybe do some training clinics."

Travis pushed his empty plate aside. "What about hay money?"

"That'll help," Sully said. "Who are the folks Dad leased the hay fields to?"

"Shankles. Last year they agreed to lease for two years. Fifty-fifty split on hay."

"Who delivers the hay?" Sully asked.

"Todd Shankle. Until he broke his hip."

"That explains why we're behind on payments. You and I need to make deliveries today and collect what's due."

"I'm not much good at asking for money," Travis said, leaning back in his chair and crossing his arms.

"How long's it been since you've seen a paycheck?"

"Can't remember."

"Six months," Sully said.

"Don't need anything. I got room and board and my veteran's check. Doing fine."

"You want to keep that roof over your head?"

Travis grunted.

"Come on, tough guy," Sully smiled. "You can be my muscle. Wear your shades."

Travis grunted.

"That a yes?"

"What're you waiting for? Get your duds on. I'll start piling hay on the truck. And grab my shades."

Sully went to his bedroom to get dressed and spotted Eric's box sitting on the carpet. A nagging sense of duty welled up. He picked up his cell and dialed Maggie Steeler.

CHAPTER SEVEN

MAGGIE HEARD the distant jingle of her cell as she stepped out of the shower into the steaming bathroom. Wrapped in an oversize towel, she rushed into the bedroom and tried to pinpoint the phone's location. The jingle came from the rumpled covers of the bed. She threw back the comforter and grabbed it on the fifth ring. "Hello?"

"Mrs. Steeler?" A man's voice.

"Yes," she said, impatient. A telemarketer? Water dripped down her back from her hair and she shivered from the chill in the room. She started to head back into the warm bathroom, but the voice stopped her.

"This is Michael Sullivan. I was stationed with Eric in Afghanistan."

Maggie stood motionless, speechless for a moment. She found her voice. "Yes, of course. Eric's squad leader."

"Yes, ma'am." A pause. "I'm home in Wild Horse Creek. I sent you an e-mail from Germany a week ago?"

"Yes, Michael. I remember." Her voice softened. "You have some things that belonged to Eric."

"Yes. I'd like to get them to you."

Tears welled in her eyes. She didn't trust her voice to speak. She didn't know if she was ready to meet the last man to see her son alive.

"Mrs. Steeler?"

"I'm sorry. I was thinking about my schedule." She stared at the frigid world outside the window. Everything sheathed in frosted white. "I'm free this evening after work. Around six?"

"That works."

"Let me give you directions."

"No need. Google Maps."

She heard him expel a breath. This meeting would be difficult for him, too. "Welcome home, Michael."

"My condolences, Mrs. Steeler."

"Thank you." Maggie ended the call. No noise inside the house. Outside, the snow muffled everything. The silence deepened her sense of isolation. Every day she was assaulted by acts of kindness. A well-meaning neighbor in the grocery store. Her patients. And now this young man who was Eric's closest friend and wanted to do the right thing. She understood people just wanted to hear she was okay, as though she could fast-forward through grief like a bad movie.

Death was a difficult concept. A sucking black chasm that outsiders didn't want to get close enough to peer into.

Over time, the stranglehold of grief would loosen its grip, but for now the pain had nowhere to go. It filled her entire being. She knew she would carry it with her for the rest of her life. Damp and shivering, she willed herself into motion. She had to blow her hair dry, put on makeup, dress for work. One minute at a time. She would endure.

CHAPTER EIGHT

SULLY AND TRAVIS spent the day delivering hay and collecting payment. Driveways were slick with ice, making it challenging to negotiate the big flatbed truck weighed down with hay bales. Horse theft was the topic of conversation at every stop. The wealthier ranchers had installed security systems, while the poorer ones were doing double duty, working during the day and patrolling at night. Spending extra money and missing sleep made folks short-tempered. There was plenty of anger going around.

Old Monty Blanchert was last on Sully's list. Records showed that he had picked up hay from Shankle for six months straight without making a payment. Sully fondly remembered doing odd jobs for Monty when he was a kid. He paid well, and his wife, Betty, still alive at the time, had always sent him home with fresh eggs or a basket of muffins.

Monty used to tell him stories about the history of the county. The Blanchert family once owned thousands of acres and ran cattle. Over the years, they sold most of their property in parcels, forming the smaller ranches that now made up the county, including Dancing Horse Ranch. Blanchert switched to breeding some of the finest quarter horses in the country. Unlike many breeders who hit upon hard times, Monty was well bankrolled and ranched as a hobby. His three hundred acre property was prime Oregon real estate, with rolling pastures and commanding views of the Cascades.

Snow started feathering the windshield as Sully pulled off the highway. With all the hay delivered, the flatbed truck was easier to navigate. He drove a half-mile up Monty's private driveway and parked in front of the sprawling lodge-style house.

Sully sat for a long moment before turning to Travis, whose tense expression matched his own. Something was wrong. Normally three or four barking dogs would have loped across the yard to greet them and a few horses would be standing at attention in the corral. It was mid-afternoon, yet the porch and yard lights were on, and he noticed numerous sets of boot tracks in the snow between the front door and the barn. That much activity was out of character with Monty's quiet lifestyle. Sully lifted his pants leg and pulled his .38 from its ankle holster.

Travis arched a brow, not totally surprised.

Sully had been a civilian for two days. He wasn't ready to walk around unarmed. Maybe he never would be.

They left the truck with Sully in the lead. Using hand signals, they inched along the wall of the house to the front door. Sully dipped his head in front of the paned window and saw a body sprawled on the floor. Adrenalin shot through him like a bolt of electricity. He prayed it wasn't Monty. He tried the door handle. Unlocked. He threw the door open and pressed himself back against the wall. No noise. Just a smell he'd grown too familiar with in Afghanistan.

Travis caught it at the same time and raised his bandana over his nose. Holding his gun at eye level with both hands, Sully entered the warm living room. Travis followed. Their eyes darted around the great room, noting the overturned furniture, opened drawers, and books scattered across the carpet. Monty Blanchert lay face up in a wide pool of dried blood in the middle of the floor.

Sully made a slow orbit around the room, scanning it in slices, missing nothing, then he squatted next to the body. From the state of the corpse and the temperature in the room, he guessed the death had taken place within the last three days. The dead man's eyes were covered by a milky film and stared sightlessly at the ceiling. Bruise marks covered his face and his bottom lip was swollen and split. Two bullets had pierced his chest. Sully's throat tightened and he was momentarily speechless.

"Someone beat him up good," Travis said sadly, crouching next to him.

Sully studied Monty's right hand. "Looks like gun powder residue on his hand and shirt cuff. He shot a handgun several times." No gun lay nearby. "Maybe he wounded someone."

"Hope to hell he did."

Both men were silent.

"Let's get away from this smell," Sully said.

They strode out of the house into the gripping cold. Vapor steamed from their mouths as they gulped in clean air. No matter how many times he'd seen a lifeless body, Sully would never get used to violent death. "Call the sheriff, Travis," he said, voice neutral, gut tight with fury. "I'm gonna check on the horses."

Gun lowered, he followed the multiple footprints to the barn. The door was wide open. With his back to the wall, he peered quickly into the interior. Quiet. No movement. He entered and searched every stall. All twelve were empty.

Something moved behind him. Sully spun around, finger on the trigger. A feral cat shot out from behind a grain bucket and knocked it over with a sharp clatter. Sully's finger froze. He lowered his .38 and took a moment to steady his nerves. Through the back door, beyond a soft veil of falling snow, he saw bare trees in the pasture pocked with ravens. Something else was dead. Several ravens flew out of the stiff grass as Travis joined him. Together they took in the carnage; the carcasses of four dogs frosted with snow, blood pooled beneath their bodies.

"Four good ranch dogs," Travis said bitterly, squatting over them. "Shot dead."

Feeling a tremor of sorrow, Sully turned away and holstered his weapon. He studied the maze of boot and hoof prints crisscrossing the ground. "A shitload of tracks have passed through here, Travis."

"At least a dozen horses," Travis agreed. He crouched and brushed new snow from a few frozen tracks. "These are the same horses that were hauled away with Gunner."

Sully squatted next to him.

"Monty's farrier stamped his shoes with this symbol that looks like an arrow," Travis said, pointing it out. "It was on all the prints at the campsite."

Sully blew out a breath. "Stolen the same night as Gunner. Gives us the time of Monty's murder."

They followed the tracks the full length of the pasture to the edge of Monty's property. Wild Horse Creek ran beyond the fence, stretching fifty feet across at that point. The streambed was strewn with boulders and the water cascaded noisily into rapids for a quarter of a mile. "The tracks go through the fence and into the creek." Sully fingered the fence wire. "It's been cut and loosely rewired."

"If a neighbor glanced over, he wouldn't notice anything out of place."

In both directions, the banks of the creek were hidden by evergreens, now coated in white. "No use looking for their exit point," Travis said. "The tracks will be covered by now."

Anger rose in Sully's chest and spilled into his words. "These rustlers are smart. They targeted ranches along the creek. The water covers any noise and the creek gives them an escape route no one can see."

"They're smart all right." Travis scratched his head. "What the hell are they doing with all these horses?"

"Black-market buyers, the sheriff said. Sold offshore where they can't be traced back to American owners."

Travis's hat and shoulders were layered with snow and he was rubbing his chafed hands.

"Where're your gloves?"

Travis shrugged. "Left 'em at one of the ranches."

Sully slapped him fondly on the back. "Let's head back."

Through the gauzy curtain of snow, they watched a patrol truck bounce into the yard and ease to a stop. Sheriff Matterson got out wearing a thick jacket, collar turned up, hands gloved in leather. The muffs of his hat were pulled down over his ears. Sully and Travis met him in front of the house and quickly relayed what they knew.

"Christ. Can't believe Monty's dead." Matterson shook his head, breathing out puffs of white. "The thieves cleaned him out?"

"Ain't a horse left," Travis said, stamping his feet, hands shoved into his pockets.

Matterson flipped the bill of his hat up from his face. "Jackson's place is just across the creek. Last month, when four of his jumpers were taken, Monty didn't hear a thing."

"The roar of the creek covers the sound," Sully said. "They could've entered from anywhere, exited anywhere."

"Now we got this damned snow," Matterson said. "Hides everything. Well, let me take a look inside." He entered the house and came out five minutes later, his ruddy complexion darkened with anger. "Every room's been tossed. Safe's open. Gun cabinet's cleaned out."

The three men stood silently for a long moment, expressions tight. Big, light flakes floated to the ground like goose down.

"This the first time they entered a house?" Sully asked, feeling his ears going numb.

"Yeah. My guess from these boot tracks, Monty came out and surprised them in the act, shot at them. They got the best of him, brought him back to the house. Then who knows what happened."

"He may have recognized them," Sully said. "If so, he figured he was a dead man, so he fought back."

"Forensics will scour the place. They'll find the attacker's blood, if there is any." Matterson shook his head. "Poor old Monty. Senseless."

"I found a few things out tracking yesterday," Travis said.

The sheriff looked hopeful. "Whatcha got?"

"Follow me."

The three men headed to the truck, now covered in snow. Travis retrieved the baggie and handed it to the sheriff. "I found those butts at an abandoned campsite out on the McKenzie."

"Hand-rolled," Matterson said, studying them. "Forensics might be able to trace the paper and tobacco. Maybe pick up some DNA if it hasn't been compromised by weather."

"There were tire tracks made by a couple hauling trucks. They were used to move Gunner and Monty's horses out."

"How do you know they were Monty's horses?"

"Monty's farrier stamped his shoes with an arrow symbol. Didn't know they were his horses until I saw the same prints here."

"This happened the same night they took Gunner?"

"My best guess. I took pictures of the tracks left by the trucks. They're on my cell phone. I'll e-mail 'em to you."

"Good work," the sheriff said with warm appreciation. "Having a timeline helps."

They all turned toward an approaching white county car, tires grinding over the icy drive. "Forensics," Matterson said. "Coroner's on his way, too. Looks like it's gonna be a late night."

"Let us know if there's anything we can do to help," Sully said.

"I'll keep that in mind."

Sully scraped snow off the windows of the truck and joined Travis in the cab, his hands and face numb with cold. He started the ignition, got the heat blasting, and pulled out of the driveway. Two men dressed in coveralls toting forensic kits were crunching through the snow toward the house. Matterson went to meet them, baggy in hand.

"Don't envy their job," Sully said.

"Nasty," Travis agreed.

They drove home in silence. The smell of death seemed to linger on their clothes, in Sully's nostrils. He pulled over at the mailbox, climbed back into the cab sorting through bills and junk mail, and found an envelope with their address hand-scrawled across it. "From Monty," he said sadly. "Postmarked the day he died." Sully tore it open and pulled out a business check. "He paid for all six months."

Travis nodded at the note attached to the check. "What's it say?"

"Hi, Joe. Sorry this is late coming. Never got a bill. I heard Sully's coming home. Tell him to stop by for a beer. Monty."

The two men sat in silence, listening to the wipers squeak across the windshield. Sully heard Travis blow out a long breath.

"One day, Travis, we'll find who did this."

"You can count on it. Then they're gonna pay."

"Damn straight."

Back at the house, Sully took a long, hot shower. No matter how much he scrubbed, he couldn't erase the memories of Monty and his slaughtered dogs and the smell of death. He didn't have time to eat before heading out to see Eric's mother. Just as well. He had no appetite.

CHAPTER NINE

MAGGIE'S HEAD and eyes hurt. Weeping made her face feel like a washcloth that had been wrung out too tightly. Here at home she could cry without restraint, but she'd have to put on a brave face for Eric's squad leader.

She stripped off her work clothes and tunneled through her walk-in closet, grabbing stonewashed jeans and the cashmere sweater Eric gave her for Christmas. "This teal matches your eyes, Mom." Eric said the color reminded him of the Caribbean Sea and the cruise they took after his high school graduation.

As she slipped the soft fabric over her head, memories surfaced of sunbaked days, salty air, burns on noses and shoulders. She recalled the gentle sway of the dock and the shimmering heat on her body as she basked in her lounge chair. Occasionally, she glanced away from her novel to watch Eric. He glided under water as clear and smooth as glass, his snorkeling tube carving a V on the surface. He came up with a splash from time to time to show off some treasure he'd found: polished glass from an old bottle, an orange starfish dislodged from a coral reef. "Throw it back in. Don't disturb nature," she'd told him. On their many hikes through national parks, they tried to leave nothing behind but footprints.

Then he left for OSU, pre-med. Still recovering from the shock of being an empty nester, Eric stunned her with his decision to drop out of school after his second semester. He wanted to enlist in the Marine Corps. Christ almighty! What a trying period. She'd tried to reason with him to stay in school, but discussions turned into fiery debates, often punctuated by Eric's bedroom door slamming shut against her voice. In the end, Maggie accepted his decision. She and David raised him to be a man of principle, to follow the noble calling of his heart. The country was at war. Terrorists had attacked American soil three years earlier. Many of his friends had enlisted. "The only way evil can triumph is for good men to stand by and do nothing," Eric said, quoting Edmund Burke. His idealism both impressed and saddened her. His motives were so pure, so naive.

Homer circled the bathroom rug twice, and finally settled into a resting spot while Maggie took inventory in front of the mirror. Her shoulder-length auburn hair looked dull. Easy fix. She pulled it back into a ponytail. Her face was another story. She looked haggard from sleepless nights, and older than her forty-two years. A little concealer covered the violet shadows beneath her eyes. Lipstick added a touch of color. *Voila.* Back to the realm of the living, barely.

Michael Sullivan was her son's closest friend from that alter-world, Afghanistan, where men and women died sudden, violent deaths. This young man understood her son in a way she never could. He understood Eric's warrior mentality. He understood the controlled insanity of protecting an alien land where the enemy looked just like the people they were protecting. Michael had witnessed her son's bravery firsthand. Eric had tended to Marines with horrific wounds while his squad was under fire. Expedient medical treatment saved lives. But in the end, the odds were against her son. Eric became a casualty no one could save.

Maggie went through the motions of making dinner, throwing a salad together and placing frozen lasagna in the oven. If Michael's visit dragged on too long she'd use dinner as an excuse to hustle him out the door.

At six o'clock the doorbell chimed. Homer shot down the tiled entryway and skidded to a stop, barking, until Maggie grabbed his collar and opened the door. It was a frigid night, yet the young man standing on her porch with a cardboard box under one arm was coatless, dressed in a long-sleeved t-shirt, jeans, and work boots. Around six feet tall, startling blue eyes, straight posture, muscular build. A Marine. The right side of his face was pocked with fading scars. Inflicted the night her son died?

"Hello, Mrs. Steeler."

"Hi, Michael." She smiled and took his outstretched hand. Strong grip. Calluses. "Come in." Maggie led him into the great room, seated herself on the couch, and gestured toward the brown recliner. Eric's chair. Homer sniffed Michael enthusiastically until he patted his big blond head, then he settled at Maggie's feet.

With his tanned face and casual dress, she thought Michael could pass for one of the local snow boarders. Someone with a carefree life. Then she imagined him as Eric must have seen him, dressed in combat gear with an M16 strapped across his shoulder—tough, seasoned, protective of his men, and even more so of Eric. Medics didn't carry weapons. The image seemed at complete odds with the culture of this small resort town, where the war in some remote corner of the world didn't touch most lives.

Michael sat on the edge of the chair with the box balanced on one knee. She sensed he didn't want to get too comfortable or stay too long. Just do his duty and go. Sunlight from the window highlighted the grave, angular contours of his face. Something raw behind his eyes. Wounded. She understood.

"I'm sorry for being here under these circumstances, Mrs. Steeler," he said.

"I'm sorry, too."

"Eric and I were pretty tight. We served together for two years."

"Eric wrote about you in his letters. He called you Sully."

"Yes, ma'am. Everyone calls me Sully."

"May I?"

"Please." He took in a long careful breath, released it. "I know most of Eric's possessions were already sent to you, but he wanted a few personal things hand-delivered if anything happened to him." Sully crossed the space between them and handed her the small sturdy box, then reseated himself.

A keen longing to reach across time and touch a part of her son welled up inside as she pulled back the cardboard flaps. Inside, wrapped in newspaper, she found treasures. Eric's cell phone, holding priceless photos and video clips, a few dog-eared paperbacks, and a worn packet of letters tied together with a shoelace. Maggie lifted the letters to her nose, inhaled the ghostly presence of Eric, and felt quick tears spill down her cheeks. Wiping her eyes with her fingertips, she noticed something small and shiny lodged in a corner of the box, as though thrown in as an afterthought. She pulled out a St. Christopher medal on a silver chain, lifted it to her lips, and smiled. "I gave this to Eric when he was fourteen."

"Eric wore it twenty-four-seven," Sully said with a ghost of a smile. "He said you had it blessed by the pope, a shaman, a leprechaun, and the Dixie Chicks. He believed it had mystical powers that protected him. He had us believing it, too." Sully paused a few beats, then continued. "No matter what artillery was flying around, Eric had the ability to push everything aside and just focus on his job. That concentration saved lives. He was a hero many times over."

She listened attentively to this glimpse into her son's private world. "This shouldn't be in the box. Eric gave it to you."

His eyes widened with surprise. "You knew that?"

She nodded, adding softly, "A week before he died, he wrote me that you saved his life in a firefight. He wanted you to have it."

Sully looked away, clenched his jaw, turned back to her. "I wish he'd never given it to me."

"Why?"

A haunted look crossed his face. "I was wearing it when he got hit."

"You believe this medal would have saved him?"

His blue eyes darkened. "For two tours of duty, bullets never touched him. He seemed to have an invisible shield. Then he gave me his lucky medal. A week later he died. I lived."

She said nothing, reflecting on his words.

"The night it happened we were ambushed out in the open. We were taking a lot of fire. Me and three other Marines were shot up pretty bad. Eric ran from one of us to the other, giving emergency care. He saved our lives. Then he got hit. We couldn't save him." Sully's voice choked. He looked down at his hands. She saw a tremor pass through his shoulders. "Sorry, Mrs. Steeler. I better go." Not meeting her eyes, he stood abruptly and started for the door.

"Sully …."

He paused without turning. "Ma'am?"

"Please, stay."

She watched him straighten his shoulders and then he turned almost in military fashion and reseated himself. He cleared his throat, all trace of emotion wiped from his face.

Maggie sat forward and spoke in a soothing tone. "Eric saved your life, Sully, because that's what he was trained to do. He died doing his job, and doing it well. There's no greater honor for a Marine than that." She held the St. Christopher medal on her opened palm. "This medallion doesn't have supernatural powers. Only God has the power to take a life. He chose to take my son."

Sully didn't meet her eyes, and when he spoke, it was almost to himself. "I can't shake the feeling that I could've saved him, if only I was paying more attention."

Maggie thought for a long moment, choosing her words carefully. "It's common to feel guilty about surviving when others didn't. Feelings of guilt can be intensified if someone died while rescuing you. There's a name for what you're feeling. Survivor's guilt."

He sat listening, his expression troubled.

"A part of you wants to trade places with Eric, but punishing yourself can't reverse the natural order of things."

"On some level, I know you're right, but ...." His voice trailed off.

"The message hasn't made the leap from your brain to your heart, but it will in time. One day you'll accept that there was nothing you could've done to save Eric."

They sat without speaking, listening to the silence of the house. Wind passed across the windows with a low moan.

"I knew my son," Maggie said. "He wouldn't want you to suffer."

Sully looked at her with warm appreciation. "Eric told me you were a therapist. He said you always knew the right thing to say."

Maggie smiled. Helping Sully also helped her. She held the medal out to him, the chain dangling from her fingertips. "Please take this. Eric wanted you to have it, and so do I."

He took the medallion and she saw something soften in his face. Maybe it did have magical powers.

"This means a lot to me, Mrs. Steeler. I didn't have anything of Eric's."

Maggie was moved. She felt concern for this war-weary young man who was trying to assimilate back into civilian life straight from the heat of combat, alone, while his buddies were still in a war zone trying to survive. Civilians didn't understand the challenges facing vets coming home. There should be more counseling, but unfortunately there wasn't.

It saddened her that these men and women were asked to sacrifice everything, were put through the meat grinder of war, and then were shipped home and discarded. It was immoral. She knew Sully was struggling to control emotions that weren't controllable. Many vets, deprived of healthy outlets for grief, spiraled into self-destructive behaviors; drug and alcohol abuse, even suicide. She wanted to help steer

Sully away from a tragic outcome. "Honor Eric, Sully, by living life fully. Find your own personal peace. Make your life count for something. That's what he would want."

"That's my intention, ma'am." He pulled the chain over his head, held the medallion in his fingertips, and surprised her by bowing his head and silently moving his lips.

Maggie felt humbled by his unembarrassed show of faith. Her own faith had evaporated. A cold, merciless God governed the universe. He had taken her son.

The gray light coming through the windows suddenly shifted and the room was infused with a luminous golden glow. It seemed otherworldly somehow. A message perhaps. A sliver of hope. The room turned gray again.

Sully opened his eyes and gazed around the room, seemingly taking it in for the first time. "This is a beautiful home. Eric said your husband was an architect."

Maggie took in the fluid beauty of David's design: wood-beam ceilings, walnut floors, river rock fireplace, and oversized windows that offered stunning views of the Cascades. The furnishings had been picked with comfort in mind; overstuffed chairs, colorful pillows, and art pieces from their travels. Photographs chronicled Eric's childhood from baby to adult. "David poured his soul into this house," she said. "He died soon after it was finished."

"He died young."

"Forty." She sighed, recalling the shock of suddenly being a single parent. Life had been a whirlwind, a challenge balancing her career and motherhood, and the years sped by too quickly.

"I'm so sorry for your losses," Sully said gently.

"Thank you." Coming from a man who had also suffered enormous loss, his empathy felt genuine, and soothing. A moment of poignant understanding passed between them.

"Eric talked a lot about his home life," Sully said. "He appreciated the way you raised him. He said the values you taught him made him a better medic."

"He told you that?" She smiled, gratified.

"He did." He smiled, too, his eyes brightening. "He used his hands a lot when he talked, just like you do."

Maggie's smile deepened.

"I'm sorry I missed his funeral. I was laid up in Germany."

"Are you fully recovered?"

"Pretty much."

Maggie thought back to the colorless day her son's coffin was lowered into the earth. The American flag, folded into a precise triangle by white-gloved hands, had been placed in her hands. The memory made her shudder. "Funerals are supposed to bring closure, but for some, it reinforces the sense of loss."

"I don't like funerals. I've been to too many." He pushed up his left sleeve and revealed a list of names tattooed on his forearm in bold black letters. "Here's my tribute to Eric and five other buddies I lost to war. I look at their names every day, so I never forget what they sacrificed."

Maggie's breath caught. "May I see that up close?"

In answer, he came and sat next her.

Oh dear God. Five other families suffering a loss so big it swallowed your entire life. She read down the list, reciting each name like a prayer. Her son's name was etched at the bottom near Sully's wrist. "This is the most beautiful memorial I've ever seen."

Sully's eyes were glassy. He pulled down his sleeve and clenched his jaw.

"I told myself I wouldn't ask you this, but I feel I have to." She swallowed. "Did Eric die alone?"

"No," he said softly. "I was there with him, holding his hand."

"Did he suffer?"

"No. It was fast. He died peacefully."

Thank God. Maggie didn't want any more details. Not yet. She felt a sense of relief emerging from a deep black void. Eric wasn't alone. He didn't suffer. This remarkable young man was at his side.

"Would you like to see Eric's room?" she asked, knowing it would be healing for Sully, and Eric would want it.

"Yes, I would."

Maggie led him down the hall and opened a door. Homer, who had slept with Eric since he was a puppy, leapt up on the bed and curled near the pillow.

Sully moved through the room slowly, lightly touching Eric's belongings, the way she did when she wanted to conjure her son's spirit.

Her son dwelled here in an archive of memories. The shelves overflowed with books, electronic gadgets crowded the desk, sports trophies lined the windowsill, and his skateboard and gulf clubs leaned against the wall. The bed was neatly made, and Eric's clothes hung in the closet, just the way he left it on his last visit. "No one else has been in here since Eric died. Everything is …."

"Sacred," he filled in for her.

Maggie nodded, impressed by Sully's sensitivity. Young men, it seemed, came back from war morphed into older men, seasoned by unnatural experiences taking place in an unnatural compression of time. Eric, too, had changed. When he came home on leave he was more guarded, more private, and he never spoke of the war.

"Joseph Campbell, Lao Tzu," Sully read from the titles of books lining the shelves. "Eric always had his nose in a book. Always quoting one philosopher or other. One in particular. Blaze something …."

"Blaise Pascal," she answered.

"Here he is." Sully pulled out a book, leafed through it to a bookmarked page, and read, "Between us and heaven or hell there is only life, which is the frailest thing in the world." He looked at her. "Your husband gave him this."

She nodded. Sully's familiarity with intimate details of her family was both surprising and comforting.

"Eric and I spent hundreds of hours together," he said. "There wasn't much to do but talk about our lives, our families, our girlfriends. How much we missed everything American. He was always showing me photos of home."

"He sent me hundreds of photos from the Middle East," she said, sitting at Eric's desk and revving up his laptop. "Want to take a look?"

"Sure." He leaned over her shoulder as she started scrolling through pictures of Afghanistan.

"That's our squad," he said, pointing to a group of Marines in combat gear posing in front of a dusty Humvee. The silver skin of the Pech River snaked through the background, framed by the steep blue mountains of Korengal Valley. Sully squatted in the foreground. Eric stood behind him. Two Marines were watching the high ground on either side of the Humvee. To Maggie, it had seemed like a casual shot, but now she recognized there was a tension in the way they held their M16s, gloved fingers near the triggers.

Sully breathed deeply and she knew he was reliving memories.

"This is my favorite." Maggie scrolled quickly to the next photo. Sully and Eric stood with their arms thrown casually across each other's shoulder, relaxed, faces tanned, grinning. Eric's hand was out of the frame holding the camera. They could have been two California surfers instead of Marines caught in the crucible of war.

"I remember the day this was taken," he said quietly. "We'd just returned to base after completing a three-day mission with almost no sleep. Being back was like being in a resort. My squad slept twenty hours straight. We ate real food in the cafeteria, hot, on a plate. Played video games. Watched movies in air conditioning. It was good down time."

"He told me about that mission," she said. "Your squad took fire, yet everyone made it back safely. Eric said you had uncanny instincts for survival that the Marines couldn't teach."

Sully reddened and stood up straight. She saw he didn't take praise well.

"What kept us alive was everyone working as a unit. You're only as good as the guy watching your back. I didn't know Eric wrote about missions. We try to spare folks at home."

"Don't worry. He didn't give details. Mostly he talked about his buddies. He referred to you as Big Bro."

"I called him Lil' Bro."

"I think he adopted you as the brother he always wanted."

A ghost of a smile. "Goes both ways."

"Let me make you copies."

"I'd like that."

She waited for the photos to print and then handed them to Sully.

Sorting through them, his face relaxed. "Brings back fond memories. Eric was always snapping pictures. Everything interested him. Everything. Mostly, I took pictures of kids. They crowded around us in droves. They loved Marines. Reminded me of why we were there."

Maggie was touched.

They heard the timer go off in the kitchen.

"Oh, my lasagna. Are you hungry, Sully?"

He thought for a moment. "I don't wanna put you out."

"No trouble." She smiled, realizing she didn't want the visit to be over yet. "Follow me."

"Yes, ma'am."

"Do me a favor, Sully."

"Sure. Anything."

"Stop calling me ma'am. Eric's friends call me Maggie."

He smiled. "Okay, Maggie."

CHAPTER TEN

WITH ITS FROSTED GLASS, burnished wood, and cushioned booths, Saguaro Cactus was a classier bar than the ones Justin normally frequented. He'd only been here once before, with a buddy after a win, and they had a little money to burn. The men, mostly weekend cowboys, were dressed in expensive western wear. The ladies, rodeo groupies from the suburbs, dressed in short skirts and cowboy boots. He figured very few of them had ever straddled a saddle, or even wanted to.

Unable to afford a drink, Justin slipped into the shadows against the back wall. The prettiest girls were all up front, hugging the bar, or making sultry moves on the dance floor. Justin didn't know much about the workings of the female mind, but he knew enough to stay clear of pretty, take-charge women. They'd have expectations he couldn't begin to meet. Instead, he scouted out the darkened area in the back, occupied by couples or clusters of giggling girls. His eyes returned repeatedly to a plump redhead sitting solo in a corner booth, a diamond ring on her right hand. She had a timid way about her, which made him think she might be a recent divorcée out testing the waters as a single. Justin watched her for twenty minutes, trying to build up his courage.

As she sipped her second drink, the redhead's posture thawed a little, she started bobbing her head to the music and casting shy glances around the room. Justin waited until the DJ played a slow song, then he made his move. Forcing a natural-looking gait, he cut a path around tables to the redhead's booth, enduring some god-awful pain from his throbbing hamstring. As he closed in, her eyes caught his and darted away. "Howdy, miss." He tipped his hat and smiled. "Care to dance?"

She stared, her mouth opened a little, not answering.

He leaned in. "You're not gonna make me walk back across this room alone, are you?"

"No. No." She stood up too quickly, knocking over her glass of water and she started dabbing the table with a napkin.

"Don't worry 'bout that." He took her hand, led her to the dance floor, and pulled her into his arms. Not too close. Polite. They both slipped into the rhythm of the music which had an easy two-step beat. Up close, she looked about thirty, and had a plain, round face. She had some extra meat on her, but he didn't mind. He liked the feel of a woman in his arms. "What's your name?"

"Avery."

"I'm Justin."

"You live here in Phoenix?"

"Nah, just passing through."

"You in rodeo?"

"That I am. Just took second place in Red Rock. Bull riding."

"Oh my gosh. You ride bulls? Wow."

"You like rodeo?"

"I like cowboys."

He smiled. "When I asked you to dance, you looked like a scared filly, ready to bolt. Am I that bad?"

"No, no. Not at all. I guess I just … don't trust men who look like you."

"How do I look?"

"Like Kenny Chesney. Maybe cuter. Bluer eyes."

"That a bad thing?"

"Not if I was a supermodel." She smiled, and the sprinkle of freckles across her cheeks made him think of poppies in a mountain meadow.

"Why'd you pick me?" she asked. "All the hot girls are up front."

"They're too skinny," he murmured in her ear. "I like a real woman. Hmmm, you smell good, like roses."

Her smile widened and he realized he'd misjudged her. When she smiled and her eyes lit up, she was pretty as hell. He spun her around, and they two-stepped side by side, then he pulled her into his arms again. Her eyes glistened in the soft light and she pressed in closer. Justin winced. His chest was tightly wrapped in an Ace bandage, and the pressure on his ribs made his eyes tear up. Likewise, his leg was on fire. He was thankful when the tune ended, and he could limp behind her to her booth.

"Want to join me?" she asked.

"Sure." He slid in beside her. She caught the server's attention and they ordered drinks. When the drinks arrived, he patted his pockets and pretended to have forgotten his wallet. She paid, happily. Tucked away in their dark cove splintered off from the rest of the nightclub, he and Avery spent the next couple hours drinking, laughing, and flirting. He refilled his mug from a pitcher of beer, she ordered sweet drinks: a Cosmo, a white Russian, a banana daiquiri. The music washed over him like a warm river on a summer evening, sometimes gentle, sometimes rocky, steadily heightening his emotions. The alcohol, the music, and Avery's easy laughter were doing a good job of easing the pain he'd walked in with.

Over time, she allowed his touch to linger on her hand, her shoulder, her waist, her damp neck, until his senses were filled with the smell of her rose-scented perfume. He wanted to kiss her and taste the sugary drinks in the well of her mouth. A nice heat coming from his groin spread through his torso, and he started spinning pictures of Avery lying in bed, arms open and inviting.

When the blinking lights signaled closing time, Justin and Avery strolled out into the parking lot knitted as tightly together as Siamese twins. He kissed her under the dim yellow light of a lamppost, pressing her back against her shiny Ford Expedition.

She pulled away, murmured, "Wanna drive me home? I'm a little bombed."

"Hell yeah, I wanna drive you home."

She smiled sweetly. "We'll pick up your truck in the morning."

She wants me to spend the night. Justin was immersed in feelings of gratitude. He hungered for a woman's gentle touch and some down-home genuine kindness. He lifted the keys from her fingertips, helped her into the passenger's seat, and climbed in on the driver's side.

CHAPTER ELEVEN

MAGGIE HEARD Sully whistle his appreciation as he followed her into her spacious kitchen. He took in the granite counters, professional chef stove, oversized cooking island, custom cabinets, and built-in appliances.

"My mom would love this kitchen. You must be an amazing cook."

"Actually, that was my husband. I've never used half of these appliances." Maggie donned mittens, pulled the pan of lasagna from the oven and placed it on the counter. "Voila," she said triumphantly. "A frozen entrée heated to perfection. This is more my style."

"Mine, too," he laughed. "Can I help with anything?"

"You can grab the salad out of the fridge."

"Sure, give me the hard job."

Maggie smiled. She poured kibble into Homer's bowl and heard the Lab crunching as she got out plates and flatware and set them on one side of the island. Sully seated himself and she joined him. "Help yourself."

"Suddenly I'm starving," he said, crowding his plate with cheesy lasagna and salad.

She held out a basket of crusty French bread.

"Thanks." He took two slices and slathered them with butter.

"While Eric was growing up the house was always full of kids," she said, serving herself. "Seems like I spent every weekend grilling hot dogs, flipping pancakes, and bussing kids to sports events. It's nice to have someone to feed again."

"Happy to oblige," he said, eating heartily.

"Would you like some wine?"

He paused, fork midair. "I'm more of a beer man, but I'll try some wine."

"This Cabernet goes great with Italian." She uncorked a bottle sitting on the counter and poured the wine into two long-stemmed glasses.

He took a swallow. "Hmmm. Tastes better than the boxed stuff I drank in college."

"I hope so. My husband was a collector. This wine has aged in the cellar for years. I figure it's time somebody started drinking it."

"Again, I'm happy to oblige." They toasted. Sully drained his glass.

"This isn't tequila, Sully," she laughed, refilling his glass. "You're supposed to sip. Enjoy."

"Right. I've forgotten my manners. I should sniff first, say something about the fruity bouquet, roll it around on my tongue, and then finally, swallow."

"You're watching too many bad comedies."

"Sorry, I've been camped out in the dust for too long with foul-mouthed Marines." His voice held a touch of pride.

She knew he missed his buddies. Leaving a tightly knit brotherhood behind was one of the hardest adjustments for a returning vet. "I bet you're a quick study."

"Watch me." He took a dainty sip and delicately patted his lips with a napkin, his little finger straight out.

They both burst out laughing.

"Where'd you go to school?"

"I'm minimally educated. Got an AA here in Bend, at COCC," he said. "I couldn't go away to school. My dad needed me on the ranch. I'd competed in rodeo my whole life, so I turned pro. Dad and I took off most weekends, working the circuit."

"What did you do at the rodeo?"

"Rode broncs. Bareback." His blue eyes flashed passionately. "No high in the world comes close to staying on a bucking bronc for eight seconds. Pays well, too, if you're good."

"You were good?"

"I held my own. I'd probably still be doing it if it weren't for 9/11. Me and a bunch of cowboys got plastered after rodeo, got a good patriotic head of steam going, and we all enlisted in the Marines. Next day when I sobered up, I was stunned. But I decided to stick to my commitment."

"How'd your parents feel?"

He paused for a moment, chewing. "Mom was relieved. To her, it looked safer than rodeo. I'd had my share of broken bones, sprains, and stitches. Goes with the territory. Mom figured it was just a matter of time before I showed up at the kitchen door with no teeth and a steel plate in my head. She hoped the military would set me on a new course. We all thought the war would be over in a few months."

"And your dad?"

"That's a different story." Sully's brows knitted together and his tone turned serious. "He'd been training me for rodeo my whole life. At twenty-four, I had just ranked second in the world. We were planning on going for the title." Sully paused and Maggie thought she saw a look of sadness cross his face. "It was tough on Dad." He shrugged. "Now I'm back, and I can do what I really love."

"What's that?"

"Work with reining horses, and compete." Sully drained his glass. Maggie refilled it.

"Horses are amazing animals. Powerful. Fast. So sensitive they seem to know what you want before you ask." He scraped the last bite off his plate. "You like to ride?"

"I've never been on a horse," she confessed.

"How's that even possible?" He squinted at her, accentuating lines around his eyes that added maturity to his face. "I see, you're more the Mercedes type."

"Prius, actually. There's something to be said for parking your transportation in the garage and forgetting about it."

"Amen to that."

"I'd like to try riding. I love animals. I volunteer at the Humane Society."

"One day I'll have you out to the ranch. We'll put you on Sam, a gentle ol' gelding with no ambition. He can't do more than walk fast. Let you feel a little wind in your hair."

"I'd like that." Maggie meant it. She picked up the empty plates and rinsed them off at the sink. "There's chocolate ganache cake in the fridge, Sully. Dessert plates are in the cabinet next to the stove."

"Chocolate? You're talking my language."

Sully kept Maggie company until the wine bottle sat empty on the counter and he had polished off two servings of chocolate cake. Maggie was enjoying herself. The first tinge of happiness she'd felt in weeks. It pleased her that Sully, too, had managed to push sadness aside for an evening. She found him to be a grounded young man. Smart, with solid values. So much like Eric.

"I hope I haven't kept you up too late," he said, glancing at his watch. His face was flushed from the wine and his eyes stood out like polished turquoise.

"No worries. I'd just be sitting around drinking warm milk and knitting doilies."

"Sorry, I didn't mean to say you're over the hill. Far from it." His eyes gently appraised her, and he smiled. "You're more like Eric's sister than his mother."

Maggie felt her face warm. "A compliment of the highest order."

"Well, I best be gittin' on home," he said in a hayseed accent, pushing himself up from his chair. "I take my weekly bath on Friday night."

Maggie laughed. She wrapped the remaining lasagna and cake in foil, placed them in a brown paper bag, and handed it to Sully. "Lunch tomorrow."

"Thank you kindly." He smiled his slow, easy smile that she found totally charming.

Maggie and Homer accompanied Sully out to the driveway as they always had with Eric. There was a piercing chill in the air and sleet slanted under the lamplight like slivers of glass. She crossed her arms against the sharp needle pricks of cold.

Sully got into his shiny white truck, revved up the engine, and rolled down his window. "Thanks for the nice evening, Maggie. It's the most relaxed I've felt in weeks."

"Hey, don't talk like it's your last visit."

His face brightened.

"Please, come over again for dinner."

"I'd like that."

"Next Sunday?"

"Good deal. I'll bring dessert."

Coughing out a few clouds of exhaust, the truck backed out of the driveway and she stood watching until the taillights disappeared around a curve in the road. Scurrying back inside, Maggie found herself smiling. A fragile bubble of pleasure had bobbed up from the depths of her gloom, reminding her of happier times.

After drying Homer's back with a towel, Maggie busied herself in the kitchen, grateful that Sully had appeared during this bleak period in their lives. On a level that words could not describe, they understood each other. Sharing hurt with another wounded person eased the feeling of isolation. She recognized how tempting it was to fill the void left by Eric by mothering his best friend. Sully already had a mother. He didn't need two. Maggie cautioned herself to keep a healthy perspective on their growing friendship.

***

The icy roads were slippery and the wipers were working double-time scraping sleet off the windshield. Inside the warm cab, Sully's thoughts drifted back over the deeply emotional evening. Seeing Eric's childhood home in his absence had been a painful pill to swallow. If Eric were alive, Sully would have met Maggie at his friend's invitation, and the evening would have been one of celebration and laughter. Eric had been one of the funniest guys Sully ever met, and his spontaneous humor had defused a lot of stressful situations when their squad was on patrol in dangerous territory.

Sitting in Maggie's living room holding Eric's most personal possessions in a box had been one of the toughest moments of his life. Looking into his mother's eyes had been like looking into an open wound. He had lost it for a moment and would have walked out the door and probably never seen her again if she hadn't called him back. Pushing her own grief aside, Maggie had reached out to him, and her words loosened a knot of guilt that had been twisting his gut since Eric's death. She didn't hold him responsible. Now he just had to forgive himself.

Maggie had controlled the entire evening, serving him dinner, pouring the wine, guiding the conversation, gently probing into his history. But it hadn't felt intrusive. He came away feeling like he'd been cared for.

From the many stories Eric had told him about his family, Sully knew his friend had been raised on a pampered leash; ski passes to Mt. Bachelor, a car at sixteen, expensive vacations. Sully now understood that the refinement he admired so much in his friend had come from the cultured atmosphere created by his mother.

Sully on the other hand, had never been given a free ride. Growing up in the Sullivan family had been a life-long lesson in self-reliance. A man earned his own way. Reward came from the accomplishment reaped from hard work, and more hard work. His clothes, boots, rodeo gear, and even the right to sit at the table had been earned by his contribution to the ecosystem of the ranch. Each person relied on the other, and cooperation was the fuel that kept the machine running smoothly. Joe's word was law. His mother enforced that law, but with a softer hand. Responsibility and resourcefulness had been ingrained into Sully's character like the rings in a tree. There was no waste, no excess, and no luxuries when times were lean.

Unlike Eric, Sully considered his own manner to be rough, his intellect more grounded, not layered with lofty visions and beautiful ideals. But he didn't resent his upbringing. It had prepared him for surviving in a war zone and moving quickly into a leadership position, where he was able to protect his men—until the assault that killed Eric.

As he pulled into the driveway behind the house, thoughts of Monty's murder crowded into his mind, and the smell of death crept back into his nostrils.

A blue TV light flickered from the bunkhouse window. Travis was still awake, probably watching Leno. The ranch house was dark. Sully parked in the garage and made a detour through the hard-driving sleet to the barn to check on the horses. Everything was quiet, the animals calm, dozing. He crossed the yard to the house, pulled his .38 from his ankle holster and stood just inside the kitchen door, listening while his eyes adjusted to the dark. The clock above the sink ticked out fifteen seconds before he cautiously made his way to his room and stripped off his wet clothes.

He cleaned up in the bathroom, donned a pair of pajama bottoms, and plopped back against the bed pillows leafing through the photos Maggie gave him. All but one had been taken in Afghanistan—a photo of Eric and Maggie standing on the caldera of Crater Lake, overlooking the clear blue water. Eric had the untroubled look of a kid who'd never faced real hardship. When he transferred into Sully's unit two years ago at twenty, Eric was starting his second tour and had already experienced his share of combat. He'd packed on more muscle and had a steady, mature look in his eyes that came with the weight of a medic's responsibility. IEDs, the chief cause of injuries to troops, could blow multiple limbs off a man in an instant. As a medic, Eric was the last hope for a Marine who could bleed out in minutes without medical intervention. Life or death lay in his hands.

In the photo, Maggie looked fit and athletic. She had an unfussy kind of beauty that might be considered plain if not for her expressive sea-green eyes. More than her physical appeal, he was attracted to her gentleness and keen intelligence. She was easy to talk to. She listened. He didn't have to carefully edit everything he said like he did in his e-mails to civilian friends and his parents. For a few hours tonight, he had escaped the hardships of his life. Tomorrow he'd bring his father home from the nursing home and try to talk his mother into moving back to the ranch. Try to get life back to normal. The way it used to be.

Sully studied a framed photo on the nightstand of himself riding a spirited bronc named Rowdy. That was the ride that won him second-place standing in the world. Decked out in custom chaps and a protective vest that bore the logos of his sponsors, Sully looked every bit the rodeo star. Rowdy had all four hooves three feet off the ground, back rounded, tail and mane flying. Sully was balanced on the horse in perfect form, seemingly floating on air.

With a feeling of remoteness, he removed the photo and stuck it in the drawer next to his .38 and 9mm Berretta, then he slipped the photo of Maggie and Eric into the frame. He didn't feel guilty about lying to Maggie tonight. Eric's death had not been quick, or easy. Moaning like a wounded animal, Eric clung to Sully's hand for long tortured minutes in stinking, fetid ditch water that swirled red with his blood. His moans still echoed in Sully's head.

Sully positioned the photo facing his pillow. It was the last thing he looked at before turning off his light.

CHAPTER TWELVE

AVERY, JUSTIN discovered, was separated from her husband and owned a nice little house in a quiet, middle-class suburb. After living in his camper for six months, a space he couldn't even stand in, a real home with nice furnishings seemed beyond luxurious. Avery's homey touches—throw rugs, pillows, plants, framed pictures on the walls—intensified his yearning for a home of his own. Property with acreage, a good barn, quality livestock, grassy pastures. Avery had swept the place clean of a man's presence, and her sorrowful tone when she alluded to her ex told him she was going through a nasty divorce.

He waited patiently while she played hostess, offering a drink, which he declined, and finally, inviting him into her bedroom. She turned down the light, disappeared into the bathroom and reemerged wearing a wispy nightgown, her hair freshly brushed, face scrubbed free of makeup. Nice. He loved the smell of clean on a woman. Clean wasn't easy to do when living in a truck. The grind of driving solo hundreds of miles between rodeos and the continuous exposure to hard men and wild livestock had worn him down. Now the company of a soft woman wearing nothing but a silky concoction brought out his tender side. He wanted to be touched gently. He wanted to touch her gently. But first, it was time to get real. See if his gamble was going to pay off.

Stammering a little, he told her about being jumped, beaten, and robbed of his prize money in Red Rock—leaving out the gambling and bookie part. Avery sat on the edge of the bed listening attentively. When he removed his shirt, unwound the ace bandage and revealed his extensive bruising, Avery gasped, brown eyes wide with shock. To his relief, she transformed into Nurse Nightingale, jumping to her feet, anxious to get him ice packs and pain relievers.

"I'll pass," he said, sinking onto her bed. "The best pain reliever I can think of is for you to come over here right now."

Eyes still showing concern, she sat next to him.

Breathing in the smell of her skin, he kissed the cove of her neck, his fingers sliding the silky straps off her shoulders. Her breasts were pale and smooth, her nipples as delicate as rose petals. Avery blushed deeply, covered herself with one arm, and turned off the light. He quickly removed his jeans and boots and slipped between the cool sheets beside her.

"You're beautiful," he whispered. He was accustomed to quick, hot sex in his cramped camper. Most of the time he didn't even bother to shed his clothes, or his lover's. He just focused on the driving force of lust. But with Avery he took his time, kissing and touching her gently, as though she was the one who was wounded. Holding her close was the most lush, sensual pleasure he'd ever known. He did his best to give her pleasure, his senses filling with her womanly scent. She in turn was sweet and soft and mindful of his injuries.

Afterward, lying in the dark flushed with contentment, Justin understood for the first time the difference between carnal lust and making love, and the pleasure a man derived from taking care of a woman's needs before his own. Riding a bull until the buzzer sounded now seemed like a cruel metaphor.

Finding Avery had been a miracle; an experienced woman who wanted more than a cowboy conquest to gossip about with her girlfriends. Exhausted, grateful for a comfortable mattress, he spooned Avery from behind, holding her damp body close to his, caressing the soft, round bowl of her belly until her breathing turned into quiet snores. He slept deeper than he had in months.

CHAPTER THIRTEEN

SULLY TRIED to get his bearings as he merged into the fast-moving traffic on the parkway. He had to get used to this concept of being his own boss, hopping into his truck and driving anywhere, anytime, on paved roads as smooth as silk. He glanced at his fellow Americans speeding by in their nice cars with only an occasional patrol car keeping the peace. In Afghanistan, he traveled on rutted trails in armored Humvees beneath tiers of ancient houses carved into stone cliffs, passing women dressed in burqas and goat herders dressed in baggy kurtas who barely concealed their looks of contempt. No one could be trusted. Villagers who acted as friends by day could be harboring Taliban by night. Most villagers wanted the Marines gone, dead or alive.

Recalling his tension when riding in a vehicle vulnerable to an IED, his stomach tightened. His heart raced and his hands started going numb. Yanking his thoughts away from the past he gazed at the lead-bottom clouds hanging low in the steel-wool sky. Another snowstorm was barreling in. A good one. Probably ready to dump a few inches.

Focus.

Breathe.

His heartbeat crept back down to normal.

Sully pulled off the parkway and wove through side streets until he found his mother's small rental house, barely visible behind a stand of juniper trees. Mist rose through the boughs and smoke curled from the chimney. A peaceful scene. Still, his eyes scanned the yard looking for any small disturbance on the ground that might be a concealed explosive. He knew it was irrational, but he couldn't shake the feeling he might get a leg blown off walking up to a strange house.

The world was a dangerous place. Sully didn't like his mother living on her own, away from the safety of the ranch. And he didn't like the expense of supporting an extra household.

Hopefully, her separation from his father would be short-lived now that Sully was home. He didn't relish the conversation they needed to have about her neglect of the bills. What had gotten into her? He'd called her from the hospital in Germany last week. She didn't expect him home until next week, but an opportunity came up to catch a ride on a cargo flight, and he grabbed it.

The last two days he'd spent at the ranch had been productive and necessary. He'd had time to process horse theft and murder and understand fully the financial state of the ranch. Though still working on getting his emotions under control, he could now sit down with his parents and have an honest conversation about their finances.

He left the truck and spotted Ronnie vigorously sweeping pine needles off the front porch. She was bundled in a red parka and fuzzy wool hat, her breath steaming in the frozen air. A beautiful sight. For a long moment, Sully just watched her, overcome with emotion. It had been a year since he laid eyes on his mother, and something keen and piercing and tender stabbed his heart. "Mom!"

Ronnie froze for a moment and turned slowly, as though not trusting what she heard, and then her eyes opened wide. She dropped the broom and her hands flew to her mouth. "Oh my dear God! Michael!"

Sully sprinted up the stairs and pulled her into his arms. Her head found the curve of his shoulder and his chin rested on the crown of her head, just like old times. He held her close for a small eternity.

When she pulled away, tears were streaming down her cheeks. "My dear, dear boy!" She sniffed and wiped her eyes with her fingertips. "You're home early. My heart's about to burst."

"A chance came up to get home fast and I took it. I barely had time to pack a bag." He fondly refreshed his memories of his mother's worn, beautiful face; the strong cheekbones, wide mouth, high forehead. Worry lines around her eyes and mouth had deepened, and instinctively, he wanted to protect her.

"Thank God you're all in one piece," she said. "You're safe. I was so worried. Look what they did to your face." She tenderly touched the scars on his cheek. "You were too handsome for your own good, Michael. This adds character. I don't like how close they came to your eye. Can you see okay?"

"Yeah, Mom. Perfect."

"The rest of you?"

"Good as new," he said, ignoring the pain in his arm.

"If I'd known you were coming, I would've cooked all your favorite foods. At least cinnamon buns."

"I'm home for good, Mom. There's plenty of time for cinnamon buns." He pulled a small, gift-wrapped box from his pocket. "I got this for you in Kandahar."

She beamed. "You've always been so thoughtful. I'll open it inside. Come in. Let's get out of the cold." She opened the door and something small darted at his heels and clamped onto the cuff of his jeans. He shook his leg, but the creature held on tight. "What the hell is that?"

"Butch, no," Ronnie scolded, and scooped up the squirming animal. Big brown eyes gazed at Sully through a tangle of curly blond hair. "Say hi to Butch."

"Is it a dog?" he teased.

"Of course it's a dog. A toy poodle. He just needs a haircut. Badly."

After giving the dog's head a mandatory pat, Sully stepped past his mother into the warmth of the house. He silently groaned. His mom was back to her old, destructive habit. The place looked like a storage locker. Columns of file boxes and plastic storage containers took up most of the floor space around the perimeter of the room. One of the two chairs was fairly hidden beneath stacks of magazines and books.

He felt especially concerned when he noticed the fire burning brightly in the fireplace had no protective screen. "Mom, if a spark flies from the fireplace and hits some of this tinder, the house would be a deathtrap in seconds."

Cheeks flushed with cold, Ronnie glanced around the room as though seeing it for the first time. Still holding Butch, she pulled her mittens off with her teeth. "You're right, Michael. I won't put on another log."

"Where's the screen?"

"Behind those boxes."

Sully found the screen and placed it securely in front of the fireplace.

"Thank you. I've been absent-minded lately. Busy with work." She made no excuse for the state of the room.

His mother always had an obsession with collecting printed material. "Information gathering," she called it. "Research." Sully and Joe had managed her "necessary hobby" by restricting it to a small storage room and routinely recycling when it got out of control, with Ronnie pecking right behind them like an angry hen. His dad sometimes negotiated a trade deal. They got rid of "stuff" and she got the acquisition of a new goat or hen. It worked. Sully was now seeing what happened without intervention.

The anger he felt about her neglect of the finances shifted into concern for his mother's mental health. Granted, she was a talented writer; producing copy for local publications, and lifestyle articles to a host of web publishers, but it didn't warrant turning her house into a data bank. "How'd you collect all this material since you left the ranch?"

"Library drops it off, and folks from churches," she said cheerily.

"What's in all these boxes?"

"File folders packed with news articles. I clip them from magazines and the paper."

"Mom, I understand you need to do research, but everything can be found online these days."

She shook her head. "Not true, Michael. Not in great depth. I need facts, not abbreviations. I know it looks a mess, but I know exactly where everything is filed."

Upon closer inspection, he noticed that all the neatly stacked boxes had colored labels fitted precisely in the left corners and the contents were listed in alphabetical order. She'd put hundreds of hours into this. Everything tidy and organized. To Sully it looked a little crazy. Compulsive.

"Come into the kitchen, dear. I'll make coffee."

"Sounds good, Mom." Sully followed her down a hallway, also stacked with boxes, into a brightly sunlit kitchen. The smell of home cooking seasoned the air, igniting childhood memories.

The kitchen had always been his mother's nerve center, and cooking was her most passionate past time. A meal always started with her studied journey through the garden, carting wicker baskets. Ingredients were carefully selected from an array of herbs and vegetables—sun-ripened tomatoes, squash, eggplants, kale, spinach. Carrots, potatoes, and onions might be shaken loose from the soil. Then she swept into the kitchen like a tornado, peeling and chopping and stirring and tasting, turning her bounty into sweet and savory dishes. No one, even the chefs on TV, could turn out a better meal than Ronnie.

His mother abruptly shoved Butch into Sully's arms, removed her jacket and hat and looped them over a chair at the table. The static momentarily stood her short red hair on end. He noticed she had dropped some weight and her jeans and sweater looked a size too big. Sully's concern deepened.

"Sit, dear. Take off your hat. You know I don't like hats in the house."

The surface of the table was laid out with stacks of paper that seemed to be aligned on a perfect grid pattern. He dropped the poodle to the floor, but the animal attacked the hem of his jeans again, growling in a little pipsqueak voice. Sully dragged him a few feet to the table and lifted a pile of papers to clear a spot.

"Michael, no!" Ronnie's voice held a touch of panic.

He froze. His mother's eyes looked wide and anxious.

"Please put those down exactly as they were. Those are my research papers. Let me clear away the laptop."

"No problem." *What the heck?*

The papers were replaced, the computer whisked away, and his mother took a breath.

When did she become this anxious? She'd always been calm and reasonable, a steadying hand when his father was stirring up his usual shit. Sully hung his hat and jacket on the back of a chair and sank into it. It wobbled a little and squeaked beneath his weight. He'd have to tighten it before he left.

While busying herself with the coffee, Ronnie glanced at him as though he were an apparition. "I can't believe you're here." She measured the ground French roast into the coffee pot. "Coffee will be up in a minute. Have you seen Lilah?"

"No." His jaw muscles tightened at the mention of his girlfriend's name.

"Bring her over to dinner soon."

He said nothing. After the letter he received in Germany before he left, there was nothing left to salvage from their relationship.

"She's come to visit, you know. She's too pretty to be running around on the loose. You should think about marrying her."

Jaw clenched, Sully didn't reply.

Ronnie set down a plate of homemade chocolate chip cookies with walnuts. His favorite. "You're not getting any younger," she said. "Lilah has waited a long time."

He wolfed down a few cookies, the thought of Lilah dampening his pleasure.

"My goodness. You're starving. Let me pack up these cookies to take back to the ranch."

"Great, Mom." He dropped Butch to the floor. The dog bit into his cuff again and pulled, growling for all he was worth. "I just came by to pick you up. I'm going to get Dad. I knew you'd want to come."

Her eyebrows shot up. "You're taking him home?"

"That's the plan."

"So soon?"

"Well, yeah. You said in your e-mails he's improving. Travis said he's walking and talking up a storm."

She crossed her arms, hands gripping her elbows, and frowned. "Yes, he's talking. But walking? Not really. A few steps with a walker, but …." Her eyes darted to the floor.

"But what?" Butch growled. Sully shook his leg. Butch held on.

Ronnie turned away, opened a cabinet, and took her time pulling out two mugs and placing them on the counter.

"Mom, you're making me nervous."

She faced him with a solemn expression. "Your father's never going to get well, Michael."

Her words caught him off guard, a hard jab to his chest. "Who says?"

"His doctor."

Sully pondered this, emotions lurching. "The same doctor who said he'd never walk or speak again?"

"Yes, but—"

"I don't believe it for a second. Dad's as strong as a bull. Nothing's ever kept him down for long."

In the silence that followed they listened to water drip into the pot. The aroma of coffee filled the room.

"He's receiving good care around the clock," she finally said. "You should leave him where he is."

Sully's gut twisted.

"He'll be a burden to you." Ronnie dry-washed her hands, a gesture she made when she was nervous or stressed. "You don't have time to be his nursemaid."

"Does Dad know you feel this way?"

She didn't answer.

"When did you see him last?" he asked.

"It's been a while …."

"How long, Mom?"

Her eyes flashed. "I've never been out there, okay?"

Sully sat stunned. "You never visited Dad? In six months?"

With a guilty look, Ronnie turned and busied herself locating the cream in the fridge.

"Mom, don't ignore me."

She placed the cream on the table and leaned back against the counter. Her face was drained of color, accentuating her freckles. "I talk to your father every day, Michael, and to his nurses. I'm managing his care just fine."

"By telephone?" Sully breathed deeply. "How can you turn your back on Dad when he needs you the most?" He knew he was glaring but he couldn't help himself. "Jesus, Mom. What's going on with you? Do you hate him?"

"Of course I don't hate your father." Her Irish came up, green eyes sparking with fire.

"Then why did you leave him?"

"For good reason."

They stared at each other, faces tight.

"I know you think I'm the villain, here, Michael. But I'm not. Do you think I wanted to leave my home? My garden? The animals? The life we built together?" Her chin quivered. Quick tears streaked down her cheeks and dripped off her chin.

Alarmed, Sully rose from the table and put his arms around her. He felt her trembling.

Ronnie pulled away, dabbing her eyes with a tissue.

"Mom, what's going on?"

"I can't talk about it," she sniffed. "It's between Joe and me."

Damn it. The set of her jaw told him she wasn't going to confide in him. He knew better than to drill her. Ronnie was stubborn as hell. So was

Joe. Sully remembered the tension in the house when his parents were at odds with each other, barely speaking for days, and both using Sully as a referee. His father especially was short-tempered, letting off steam by bullying Sully, accusing him of taking his mother's side. Then miraculously, the two would be back to normal, his mother smiling at the breakfast table, his father whistling while he did his ranch work, and Sully relieved to be out of his father's crosshairs.

Now here they were, living separate lives while the ranch and animals suffered. His mother's slumped shoulders and sad expression told him something disastrous had split them up. He felt a cold chill creep along his spine. Maybe what was broken couldn't be fixed.

"Can I make you lunch?" she asked, struggling to compose herself. Trying to sound normal.

"Have I ever said no to food?"

"Never. Not even in your sleep." She smiled thinly. "I made pot roast last night. I'll make sandwiches."

"Sounds good," he said, hiding his frustration.

Ronnie pulled the roast and condiments out of the fridge. "Everything on it? Onions, cheese?"

"Sure, Mom. No hot peppers." He took his seat, chair squeaking. Butch sprang onto his lap, pressed his forepaws against Sully's chest, and licked his chin. "Christ." Sully scratched around the dog's ears. "Friggin' mutt."

"He likes you. Butch is a man's dog. He never kisses me." Ronnie pulled a jar from the fridge. "I have your favorite pickles. When you were a little boy, you used to say Hickles Pickles was your favorite vegetable."

"I remember. Fried chicken, pickles, and a side of Skittles. My dream meal."

Ronnie poured coffee, added cream to both, and handed him the larger mug. He took a sip. Even in his disgruntled mood, he could appreciate a good cup of coffee. She served the sandwiches and he noticed the crusts had been trimmed off with surgical precision. He started wolfing down the sandwich and gulping the coffee. "How's work, Mom?"

"Busy. I'm up against five deadlines." She picked at her food.

"Don't get yourself too stressed."

"It's under control."

Yeah, right.

"How's the ranch?" she asked, guilt raw on her face.

"Needs work." This was no time to bring up Gunner and their finances, he decided. He wasn't going to further aggravate a bad situation. "Travis did a good job looking after the place."

"How are the horses?" She topped off his mug.

"Well cared for. Fat. I need to start working them. Mom, why don't you come home for a few days? Work with your mare. Help me with Dad."

Ronnie's mouth tightened.

He backed off and quickly finished his sandwich. "That was good, Mom. Well, I'm heading out." He dropped Butch to the floor and took his time getting into his jacket, pulling his hat low on his forehead, hoping she'd volunteer to come. She didn't.

"Take Butch to your father. It's his dog. He'll want to see him."

The poodle stood poised to go, brown eyes eagerly watching him. "This fashion accessory is Dad's?"

"Surprised me, too. After Jaspers died, he went to the pound to get a ranch dog, but he came home with Butch."

Jaspers, he thought with affection. Now there was a good ranch dog.

"And Michael …." She was quiet for a long moment.

"Yeah?"

"Bring Joe back here."

"Mom, you just said he can barely walk. How's he gonna maneuver around your mountain of—" he almost said *shit*. "Boxes."

"Do you think he'll do better at the ranch? You don't have time to take care of a disabled man. Cooking, cleaning up after him, managing his meds."

"You should both be at the ranch," he persisted. "Dad would be more comfortable there."

"Michael, don't try to fix this. You can't." She released a long, controlled breath. "If you insist on getting him out of there today, it's best he stays here. It'll give you time to prepare the house. You'll need to build a ramp up to the porch, and put hand bars in the bathroom."

Of course, she was right. It never occurred to him to make changes to the house.

"I'll move some of this stuff out of the way," she said.

"No. I'll do it. What goes first?"

"Everything in the living room. Put it in the garage. And clear out the guest room for your father."

Outside, the snow was falling gently to the earth. Slipping a little, Sully made quick work of emptying the rooms with the hand truck and organizing the boxes in the garage so his mother could easily access them.

"I'll be back soon," he told her when he finished. He tucked Butch under one arm, hugged Ronnie goodbye, and walked out into the falling snow. His truck was camouflaged in white. He dropped Butch onto the passenger seat and wiped off all the windows. He got into the cab and revved up the engine.

Shaking from cold or fear, Butch peered up at him through gaps in his tangled hair. "Man, you need a haircut. Marine style. Oh, hell." Sully cranked up the heat, pulled Butch onto his lap, and stroked the little tangled head. Butch licked the top of his hand. Oddly, the pipsqueak dog had a calming effect on him.

Butch lowered his eyes in a Zen-like state of meditation.

"Give me some life direction, Yoda. I could use it."

Butch tilted his head to one side, lifted his ears, and released a chorus of little yelps.

"Yeah, I know. You're receiving instructions from the mother ship. Too bad I don't understand dog speak."

Sully glanced back toward the house and shook his head, puzzled by his mom's behavior. Feeling as though he was swimming upstream, he pulled away from the curb and headed for St. Mary's Convalescent Haven, his tires forging tracks in the pristine snow.

CHAPTER FOURTEEN

"GET THAT PIG SLOP outta my face!"

Though the words were slurred, Sully immediately recognized the gravelly tone of his father's voice. He quickened his steps on the polished linoleum in the sterile hallway.

"I'll force this down your throat, if I have to," came a gruff voice with a Mexican accent.

Sully stood motionless in the doorway, taking in the scene. A muscular nurse's aide stood over the bed holding a spoon in front of his father's face. His other hand held Joe's wrists down on the tray table in a vise-like grip. Joe's lips were compressed into a hard line, his blue eyes shooting sparks.

"Get the hell away from my dad," Sully growled, resisting the urge to grab the man by the neck and throw him into the hallway.

The aide shot Sully a startled look, stepped back from the bed, and crossed his beefy arms over his chest. Sully recognized old gang tattoos on his hands and neck.

Joe's eyes blinked hard. His mouth formed words, but no sound came out. "Sully ...." A raspy croak.

Sully crossed the room, swept aside the tray table, and folded Joe in his arms. He had waited long months for this moment, to see his dad in person and make sure he was okay. He felt his father's bony ribcage through the pajama top. The smell of medicated soap wafted off him.

Pulling away, Sully hid his astonishment. Joe was no longer the strapping, rugged man Sully had seen on leave fifteen months ago. He had shed a good thirty pounds. His dark hair had silvered, and his once iron-hard muscles felt like putty. Joe's perpetually tanned face was gaunt and pale and he looked a decade older than his sixty years. Only his intense blue eyes were unchanged, now staring at Sully in wonder.

Sully noticed bruises on his father's wrists. Other forced feedings? "You're shrinking, Dad." Sully scowled at the nurse's aide.

The man glared back. "You saw for yourself. He refuses to eat."

"Get me outta this hellhole," Joe said fiercely. The right side of his mouth drooped and saliva foamed in the corner. He nodded toward a wheelchair against the wall. "That's mine."

"Help me get his things together," Sully said sharply.

"You can't just take him out of here," the aide said.

Sully stood close to the man, and hissed, "Try stopping me."

The aide's expression withered. He lurched into motion, helping Joe peel off his pajamas.

"My suitcase is under the bed," Joe said, wiping drool from his mouth, his excitement palpable.

With a couple sweeps of his arm, Sully emptied his father's drawers and closet.

While the aide helped Joe worm into a pair of baggy gray sweats, Sully collected toiletries from the bathroom. He packed everything easily into the weathered suitcase that still bore faded rodeo decals. His father's presence had been stripped from a room designed for interchangeable people who came to rehabilitate or die. "Where're his meds?"

"Front desk." Glowering, the aide finished tying Joe's shoes, then stormed out.

His father's left arm and leg were spindly and weak, and he looked shrunken in his sweats. Sully supported his weight until he sagged into the wheelchair. With the suitcase balanced across Joe's bony knees, Sully wheeled him down the hallway. Joe's big-knuckled hands clutched the sides of the suitcase, and his head bobbed with the motion of the chair. The back of his thick, shaggy hair was matted down from months of lying on a pillow. Recalling Joe's almost supernatural strength and endurance, Sully felt a piercing sorrow. What happened to the ruggedly handsome Joe Sullivan, former world champion bareback rider and rodeo legend?

At the front desk, a nurse with a sour expression was placing a dozen prescription bottles into a plastic bag. Sully fought down a feeling of dread. The hard reality of what he was doing struck him with sudden force. "You got my dad on all that stuff?"

"Yes. Doctor's orders." She pursed her lips, shot him a scornful glance. "You understand we can't be responsible for what happens to him once he leaves the premises."

Sully nodded.

"Please sign these papers." She shoved forms across the counter.

Sully hesitated.

"Sign the damn things," Joe barked, spit flying.

Sully scrawled his signature on each page, folded his copies into a square, and shoved them into his breast pocket. He gripped the chair's rubber handles and pushed it out of the lobby into the brisk March air. Falling snow had softened the edges of the world with a thick layer of white. Sully removed his hat and settled it on his father's head.

Joe flashed him a crooked grin and inhaled deeply. "Damn, it feels good to get that hospital stink out of my nose."

Sully felt the same way. Both men filled their lungs, breathing out smoky vapor. As the wheels of the chair squeaked through the snow in the parking lot, Sully felt sharp pinpricks of remorse. His mom was right. Joe was unable to care for himself. Sully would have to be his nurse, housemaid, and cook. His newfound freedom faded into dark shadows.

Working out the logistics of getting Joe into the cab gave him a taste of what lay ahead. White-hot pain shot up his arm as he half lifted, half pushed Joe into the passenger seat. Clearly, a pickup wasn't a good vehicle for transporting a disabled man. Breathing hard, Sully folded the wheelchair into the back seat and joined his father up front. Butch was licking Joe's face like a bear on a honeycomb, his stump of a tail wagging a mile a minute.

"You missed your ol' man didn't you, lil' fella?" Joe grinned ear to ear. "You need a haircut, scout. You look like a haystack after a windstorm. You should see 'im when he's groomed. Looks like a show dog."

They didn't need a high-maintenance dog at the ranch, but Sully was grateful to see his father smiling. That alone earned Butch his keep. As they pulled out of the lot Joe rolled down the window, stuck out his head, and whooped a high-pitched rodeo yell, showing fiery sparks of his former self.

Sully grinned. "It's liberation day, Dad! Yee haw!"

"I'll shoot myself before I ever step into another nursing home. Or you shoot me, if I can't," Joe said, rolling up the window, his hair wind tousled.

"Come on, Dad. Aren't you gonna miss the sponge baths?"

He gave Sully a steely look. "They were given by Frank, the asshole you just met." Joe seemed to see Sully fully for the first time. "You look good, boy. Real good. The best damn thing I've seen since I first laid eyes on your mother." Joe shook his head, looking a bit dazed by the swiftness of events. "Thought you weren't coming till next week. How long you been here?"

"Couple days."

"How's the ranch?"

"Travis did a good job looking out for the place. You, on the other hand, look like crap. We need to fatten you up. Get you back in the saddle."

"Amen to that. We can start right now. Pull into that driveway right there, son. Let's get us some real food."

Sully braked, pulled into the lot of McGillys Barbeque, and got in line at the drive-through. The snow suddenly turned into a legitimate hailstorm and white balls pinged off the hood like marbles. Oregon hail could appear out of nowhere and sweep in and out of the area in minutes, even on a hot summer day. It had ruined many a flower garden, to Ronnie's despair.

"After we get our food, I want you to take me to see your mom."

"She said the same thing."

"She wants to see me?" Joe's voice faltered.

Sully gave him a sharp look and glanced away, alarmed.

The old man's eyes were watering. In his entire life, he'd rarely seen Joe shed a tear. Sully used to tell his friends that his dad was made of barbed wire and dried rattlesnake gut, and was just as tough. Over the course of his childhood, when he and his dad were in the arena training, Joe had been all fire and brimstone. Rodeo was his religion and he made it Sully's religion, too. He had no patience for whining or any show of weakness. Sully's many injuries, sustained from flying off a bronc and hitting the dirt, had been met with cold contempt.

To this day, Joe's stern voice echoed in Sully's head. "Get your behind back in that saddle, boy. No quitting. When you hammer steel, it only gets harder." Like the tip of a spear pressing against his back, Joe's unrelenting toughness pushed Sully steadily up the ranks until he reached number two bareback rider in the world: a feat Joe always expected, and

Sully faithfully delivered. Failure was unacceptable. It showed weakness of character. Now Joe was showing weakness. The stroke had somehow changed him. Sully didn't know what to make of it.

Outside the hail let up as quickly as it started and was replaced by snow, heavier now. The two men sat motionless in the sudden silence, watching large flakes layer the windshield.

"It's our turn," Joe said, gesturing with his hand, his voice back to normal.

Sully put on the wipers, drove up to a big plastic chicken, and rolled down his window.

"Get the king-size dinner special," Joe instructed.

"We'll take the king-size special," Sully said to the chicken.

"With extra mashed potatoes and gravy," Joe added. "And plenty of biscuits and butter."

"Pop, why don't you just order?"

"With extra mashed potatoes and gravy," Joe yelled, slurring. "And plenty of biscuits and butter. And extra wings."

Sully said to the chicken, "You get all that?"

"Yep."

"Throw in a pie," Joe yelled. "Apple."

"That'll be thirty-two sixty-five. Pay at the window."

Sully rolled up the window. After a moment's hesitation, he said, "Dad, about Mom—"

"Can't wait to see her," Joe cut in. They were still two cars back. "When's our dang food coming up?"

"Soon. How come Mom never visited you?"

Joe's bony shoulders sagged, and he slumped lower in his seat. "Ain't her fault. It's mine."

Sully waited.

Joe cleared his throat. "That compulsive thing she's got, it's worse. She hasn't left her house since I got the stroke."

Sully tried to digest the news, but it made no sense. "Even to run errands?"

"Nope. Almost losing me, she says, pushed her over the edge. The world outside her door don't feel safe no more. There's a name for it. Agri ... goria ...."

"Agoraphobia."

"That's it. With you fighting a war in some dang foreign country and me half crippled your mom's had plenty to worry about."

Recalling his impatience with Ronnie that morning, Sully felt a sudden rush of guilt. He'd heard about vets who had agoraphobia, a spin-off of PTSD. Prone to terrifying panic attacks, and fearing a meltdown in public, they never left the safety of their home. "It often goes hand in hand with OCD."

"What?"

"Obsessive compulsive disorder. Obsessive behavior, like washing your hands dozens of times a day. Or collecting things, like Mom does." Sully tried to understand his mother's altered view of the world. He thought of the neatly stacked boxes, the perfectly fitted colored labels, the careful documentation of magazines and newspaper articles. Unable to control events outside her door, it seemed Ronnie had resorted to controlling the little universe inside her house; barricading herself in a bomb shelter of information. "Mom had no choice," he thought out loud. "She couldn't visit you."

"Nope. She couldn't." Joe wiped his mouth with the back of his sleeve. "Our lives weren't supposed to turn out this way. We all worked hard. Put money into the ranch, put savings in the bank. We should be set. But now my medical bills ...." He looked down at his fingers tightly twisting Butch's fur, and blinked back tears.

Jesus. "Dad, I'm home now. We'll get it all worked out," Sully said in a confident tone, though anxiety thrashed in his chest like a large bird trapped in a small cage. The ranch was mired in debt. It was going to be mostly on him to pull them out. What if he fell short? What if they lost their home?

"Me and your mom, we talk every day," Joe said absent-mindedly, his blue-veined hands stroking Butch. "She misses the ranch. It's killing her not seeing the animals. It's killing me not seeing her."

"We have to help her come home," Sully said.

Hope flickered in Joe's eyes. "How?"

"We need to help her feel safe. By getting you healthy. Getting the ranch healthy. You need to start treating her better."

"God knows you're right." Butch put his front paws up on the window. Joe followed his gaze then turned back to Sully. "I've been a tough old bastard all these years. Pushed us all too damn hard. I gave your mom a run for her money. Thirty years' worth. Then one day she looks at me and says, 'I'm done.' Just like that. 'I'm done.' It was a shotgun blast to my chest." He swallowed hard, his voice choking up. "She packed up and left me. I couldn't stop her. Look at me now. Hell, I'm paying the price."

Sully waited patiently for more of the story but like Ronnie, Joe didn't reveal the cause of their separation. They sat in the cab watching the wipers clear snow off the window. Sully finally said, "We all make mistakes, Dad."

"I've made mistakes all right. Lying on my back for six months, I had nothing to do but think about mistakes. And how I'd do things different if I ever got the chance. I'm done with smoking and drinking. I promised that to your mom." He reached over and put his hand on Sully's shoulder. "I didn't know if I was gonna live long enough to see you or your mom again. I'm proud as hell that you're a Marine."

Sully throat tightened with emotion. He felt ill-equipped to deal with this new version of his father. He wondered if Joe's meds had affected his mind or if the stroke had caused some brain damage. Something had worn down Joe's thick, thorny hide, and his feelings were leaking out.

The car behind them hit the horn.

"We're up," Joe said, with a little hand gesture.

Sully pulled up to the cashier and paid for three bags of food and the aroma of fried chicken filled the cab. Butch sniffed the bags, nose vibrating. Joe held him tight.

Sully pulled out into the icy street. They both were somber as the Ford weaved through the side streets to Ronnie's rental. He parked in her driveway, helped Joe out of the truck, and wheeled him over the snowy sidewalk with the bags of food bouncing on top of the suitcase. Butch ran ahead, his fuzzy stump of a tail wagging furiously. Sully saw that his mother had been busy in his absence. Stacks of boxes, three rows deep, now lined the porch. Must be from the guest room.

She opened the door before he knocked and stepped aside to let them enter. "Joe," she cried.

"Baby!" Joe shoved the suitcase and bags of food at Sully, stood on shaky legs, and pulled Ronnie into his arms. To Sully's amazement, the hug turned into a kiss, and the kiss just kept on going. Feeling like a third wheel, he retreated to the kitchen and set the bags of food on the table, now cleared of his mother's papers. When he sauntered back into the living room, coughing loudly, they were still locked in a body grip. Ronnie pulled away first, her face flushed with color. Joe sank into the wheelchair, his hand clinging to hers. He looked five years younger.

"Honey," she said to Sully, breathless. "Would you move the boxes on the porch into the garage?"

"Sure thing." Grateful for something to do, Sully moved the boxes and then shoveled the front walk. Clearly, after a six-month separation, his parents needed some time alone. When he reentered the house, he found them sitting in the kitchen, Joe drinking a cold Budweiser and Ronnie pulling food containers from the bags. "Sweet Baby James" by James Taylor spilled from the stereo speakers. Sully grabbed a Bud from the fridge and joined them.

"This is enough fat to land you right back in the hospital, Joe," Ronnie chided, examining the contents of the containers. "If you survive this meal, you're only eating my cooking from now on."

"I dreamt about your cooking every dang day." Joe set his bottle on the table, eyes sparkling with pleasure. "Bring it on."

They opened the cartons and filled their plates, and for a few moments the only noise in the room was the crunching of chicken and Joe's blissful moans. Ronnie looked radiant. Her adoring gaze moved from Sully to Joe, and back to Sully. He saw that she had styled her hair, put on makeup, and was wearing the opal pendant on a gold chain he brought her from Kandahar. It sparkled when it caught the light just right. Inevitably, the conversation turned to ranching and he felt his shoulders bunch up with tension.

"How's Gunner?" Joe asked, holding a half-eaten drumstick. "The brood mares? They should be coming into foal."

Sully's heart skipped a beat. He didn't have the heart to dump the heavy news of theft, murder, and financial gloom on his parents. Not during their happy reunion, not when he had witnessed both of them stressed to the max and in tears today. A lie rolled smoothly off his tongue. "A bull got out of the pasture this morning. He was heading down the driveway toward the highway."

"How'd that happen?" Joe asked.

"Pistol opened the gate."

His parents laughed heartily.

"That mule's name should be Houdini," Ronnie said.

Joe wiped his fingers on a napkin. "Pistol's got twice the smarts of most people."

Sully took a controlled breath, released it, felt his muscles relax. Pistol's exploits were legendary. The mule had an instinct for freeing himself from every gate he'd ever been placed behind, sometimes liberating the donkeys and chickens, too. After successfully skirting the topic of Gunner, Sully proceeded to update his parents on the state of the ranch and the list of repairs needing attention. Joe asked pointed questions and to Sully's surprise, assigned several jobs to himself. No way, Sully thought. His father, weak as a newborn colt, thought he could chop firewood.

After dinner Ronnie put on her reading glasses and examined Joe's bag of meds. "They really go overboard with all this stuff. Antidepressants, sleep aid, stool softener, bladder control. It's a wonder your body can function on its own at all."

"I didn't take nothing but what you told me," Joe assured her.

"Good. These you need tonight." She put three containers aside. "These we ease you off of over time. These we throw out."

Sully felt relieved that his dad was in good hands. "I'm calling it a night," he announced. "I still have chores to do. Dad's okay here for a week, Mom?"

She and Joe exchanged a look. Sully could almost see sparks fly. "Don't worry, dear. I'll take good care of your father."

Joe smiled expectantly. Sully guessed he was getting his hopes up for nothing. Ronnie hadn't told him yet that he was sleeping in the guest room.

Sully stood and stretched. "I'll call in the morning, Mom. Night, Dad."

Joe nodded. "Son."

Ronnie walked him to the door. She touched the opal pendant and smiled. "I love the necklace."

"A jewel for a jewel."

"Here, keep this in your truck." She folded his fingers around a bottle of skin sanitizer. "Use it liberally. Germs are everywhere."

Sully looked at it dubiously, thinking of every shithole he'd crawled through in the last four years. Now he should be afraid of germs? To appease her, he tucked it into his shirt pocket.

Butch started pawing his leg.

"He wants to go with you. Can you take him?" she asked. "I can't walk him."

"Sure, Mom."

"And please, take him to the groomer."

"How 'bout if I just get out my tree clippers?"

"Just don't prune him into a Chihuahua." She laughed. "Your dad would have a fit."

Sully gave her a peck on the forehead and stepped outside into the frigid night. The sky was studded with stars and a sliver of moon was tangled in the bare branches of a tree. Snow had transformed the landscape, burying everything familiar under mounds of white.

While Butch rummaged in the undergrowth, Sully reflected on the day's strange turn of events. He'd discovered both his parents were a bit unhinged. His dad had become a needy invalid and his mom was a hostage in her own home. The ranch was skidding toward bankruptcy and Sully didn't know how to put on the brakes.

On the positive side, he had busted Joe out of the Gulag nursing home, his parents still loved each other, and no one had shot at him today. Tonight he would sleep in a warm bed under his own roof. All in all, not too bad a day. Butch resurfaced from beneath a bush covered in snow. "Let's go, runt." Sully brushed the light powder from his tangled coat and tucked him inside the warmth of his jacket.

CHAPTER FIFTEEN

A WEEK HAD PASSED peacefully since Justin met Avery. He found her to be a generous, tenderhearted woman, content with the small niceties of life. She wasn't looking for a man to take care of her. She had an education, a good job, and was taking care of herself just fine. She didn't mind taking care of him, either. At least for now.

Steering a shopping cart down the brightly lit aisle of the grocery store, Justin smiled as he replayed their first morning together. He had feared she might throw him out when she woke up sober, but to his relief she woke up as sweet and soft as a kitten, practically purring. They made love in the dim morning light, showered together, then cooked breakfast.

Or rather, he cooked. She sat at the table sipping coffee and just looking pretty. Over a mushroom and cheddar cheese omelet, she invited him to stay until he was well enough to rodeo. He showed her his gratitude in the bedroom. Life was good. They settled into a congenial living arrangement. She paid for groceries. He cooked the meals and did the housework. His smile broadened as he made his way to the frozen food section and added a package of chicken breasts to the cart.

It was tax season, Avery's busiest time of year. Every morning at the break of dawn, she tromped off to her accounting job at Acorn Trucking Company. Justin appreciated that she was smart with money, ran the finance department, and authorized every expenditure down to the penny. While she put in a grinding sixty-hour week, he limped around her house doing yard work, handyman chores, and laundry. Every night, Avery came home worn and frazzled. They migrated outside to the shaded patio and ate dinner in the dry desert heat.

He stopped in the produce section and lightly squeezed tomatoes, then avocadoes, and added a couple of each to his cart. Whistling, he picked up a six-pack of Corona and strode up the aisle to the checkout counter.

***

"These enchiladas are delicious," Avery said, red hair glowing in the waning light.

Sitting close together at the patio table, they watched the sun melt into the rooftops beyond the fence line of her small backyard. He was keeping cool in cut-offs and flipflops. She had changed from work clothes to a little gauzy summer dress. Avery, he happily discovered, was a free spirit, confident in her femininity and sexuality. She felt comfortable enough in his company to not fuss with makeup, her hair, or underwear. He loved seeing her nipples pressing against the thin cloth of her dress, and he loved knowing he could touch her whenever he wanted, wherever he wanted, and she would respond playfully, and sensually.

He pushed her fragrant hair aside and kissed the nape of her neck. They shared a lingering gaze, her cheeks flushing prettily, brown eyes shining. "Where'd you learn to cook?" she asked, tucking a strand of hair behind an ear.

"Here and there." Along with chicken enchiladas, he made Spanish rice, refried beans crowned with melted cheese, and spicy guacamole. "I just make simple stuff."

"Yeah, but everything has flavor."

"Fresh herbs. That's the secret. In this case, cilantro and jalapeño peppers."

"So really, Justin, who taught you?"

He took a long chug of his cold Corona. "A summer camp I went to as a kid had a big commercial kitchen. All the boys learned to cook."

"Boy Scouts?"

"Something like that." St. Teresa's Home for Orphaned Youth was a far cry from Boy Scouts, but it was the closest he'd ever come to realizing a safe, secure environment.

"Was your mom a good cook?"

"So-so." He had no idea.

She looked at him over her beer mug. "Why are you so vague about your family?"

He felt his shoulders tense. "I had an ordinary, middle-class upbringing. Boring."

"Where're your folks?"

He usually kept on lying when people asked these questions, but he didn't want to lie to Avery. "Mom died when I was three."

Her face showed surprise, then sympathy, and she continued in a gentle tone. "I'm so sorry. So your dad raised you."

"He's dead, too." As far as he was concerned, the bastard father that deserted him as an infant was as good as dead.

"Who raised you?"

He saw she wasn't going to let it go. This was exactly why he traveled alone. People by nature were nosy. "What's with the fifty questions?" he asked, his tone sharpening.

She sat back, startled. "Hey, I've been an open book all week. I've told you everything about my ex."

Yeah, the guy was a jerk. But the hardships Avery had encountered in her life wouldn't fill a novella. His would fill a whole goddamned library.

"I just want to know a little about you," she said.

"No one raised me."

She looked puzzled. "Are you going to give me a straight answer?"

"Too many foster parents to count," he said in a rough voice. "I lost track after the first five." Not really. He knew exactly. Thirteen foster families in fifteen years, with trips back to St. Teresa in between placements.

"Foster parents? You were an orphan ...."

He felt his face tighten.

"You must have had a few nice families ...."

They sat in strained silence.

"Every nightmare you ever heard about foster parents is true," he finally said.

The look that washed over her face made him cringe. Pity. Which he found intolerable. Instantly, his anger sparked. He wasn't a victim and wouldn't be treated like one. He wouldn't answer any more questions, either, and allow painful, barbed memories to surface. "Excuse me." He scraped his chair back from the table and carried his half-full plate into the kitchen. After scraping his food into the trash, he twisted the cap off another Corona, chugged half of it down and started cleaning up. He needed to calm down. He didn't need to have a row with Avery and jeopardize his living arrangement. He was desperate and would be homeless if not for her. He swallowed the other half of his beer.

Avery had the good sense to give him space. When she came in he wouldn't look at her, just stood furiously scrubbing a stubborn yellow stain in the sink with a scouring pad. She came up behind him and put her arms around his waist. He felt the soft warmth of her body pressing against his back, her breath on his neck.

"I'm sorry I questioned you, Justin. Forget the sink. Let's go to bed."

"Go on in. I'll finish here and then get cleaned up."

When he came out of the bathroom the lights were out and she lay waiting for him. He eased into her arms, felt her smooth hands travel the length of his back, both soothing and arousing. Her touch jolted loose an old memory of Jessica, a foster mother who made a habit of slipping into his bed at night when her husband was out of town.

Skipping foreplay, Justin entered Avery abruptly and moved roughly inside her, losing himself, riding a wave of urgent, irrepressible pleasure until he fell back spent and sweating, his thoughts consumed with Jessica. He could even smell Jessica. That's how they'd had sex. Primitive. Wham bam.

Avery lay motionless beside him. He reached for her, but she turned her back to him. He felt a sudden rush of shame and was catapulted back through time to his bedroom in the McKinley house. After sex, Jessica hurriedly escaped his bed, wrapped herself in a kimono, and disappeared into the house leaving him alone sweating in the dark, feeling like some kind of criminal. Sometimes days and weeks passed when she didn't come to his room. He'd wake in the night, listening for any subtle sound, longing for their few minutes of rough intimacy.

Justin moved over to his side of the bed, giving Avery space, knowing he should apologize, but he felt resentful that she trespassed into his secret world, and tapped into his reservoir of deeply hidden memories. The darkness of Avery's room provided the perfect canvas to project vivid memories of past abuse. Anger stewed in his gut when he thought of some of the misfit foster families he'd been placed with. Mostly hard-working ranchers who used him as free labor, and were overly quick to get physical when he wasn't working hard enough. Seemed he spent half of his childhood hiding welts and bruises beneath his clothes.

His thoughts shifted to St. Teresa, his only childhood refuge. He remembered fondly Father O'Shea, the shuffling, lumbering priest who patiently gave him guidance and his only experience of parenting. The God-fearing staff, nuns and devout volunteers, drilled into him the importance of self-discipline and self-reliance. They taught him good manners, how to cook, clean, and work hard at school. They also tried to persuade him that sex was a sin outside of marriage. How could this be wrong, he wondered? Sex with Avery was the sweetest experience he'd ever known.

Before Avery, everything he knew about sex he'd learned from porn films. Sex with Jessica, his first lover, confused the hell out of him. He felt like he just provided a service. No foreplay, no sexy pillow talk, no affection, just him clumsily bumping under the covers in the dark. During daylight hours, Jessica barely acknowledged his existence, and let her husband and stepsons manage his workload.

With Avery, it was different. Justin liked her. He loved her body, the way it smelled, the way she moved, the way she taught him to move. She had never been shy about murmuring instructions and rewarding him for his efforts with little moans of pleasure. When he was clumsy, she laughed it off, made him laugh, too. Sex didn't have to be so serious. But tonight, it had been. He used it as a weapon, misdirecting his old anger at Jessica. His shame now felt like an ache. Thoughts of the past tunneled through his mind, unrelenting, until he fell into a fitful sleep.

He woke with a start, drenched in sweat. The room was shrinking! Lightheaded and dizzy, his breathing short and rapid, he stumbled through the darkened house out into the yard. He knew what to do.

Inhale deeply for five seconds. Hold for two. Exhale for five.

He repeated the exercise for several long minutes until his heart rate and breathing returned to normal.

Anxiety attacks were nothing new, but they still scared the hell out of him. Each time, he felt as though he was moving underwater, suffocating, moments from death. He'd been experiencing anxiety since the morning he discovered his dead mother lying in bed when he was three. He laid with her corpse all day until a neighbor came to the door. *Mommy won't wake up.* The father he vaguely remembered never came forth to whisk him off to a new life. Instead, he made arrangements for him to live at St. Teresa's. Anger rumbled through his stomach when he thought of the heartless father who deserted him.

There was no going back inside tonight. Justin grabbed his sleeping bag from his camper, rolled it out across the cool lawn, and lay under the black ceiling of night. He distracted himself by connecting lines between the stars and identifying constellations until he drifted into a tormented sleep.

CHAPTER SIXTEEN

SULLY HEARD a truck brake to a halt out in the yard and then the engine died. He scraped the last bite of food off his plate, set the dish in the sink, and glanced out the window.

Christ, Lilah!

He felt blindsided. He had known he couldn't put off seeing her much longer, but he wanted to do it on his own terms, in town on neutral ground. Not here, dressed in his dirty work-clothes, covered in dust from working in the barn all morning. He pulled on his boots at the door and strode out into the yard, Butch hot on his heels.

Lilah waited next to her Dodge Ram pickup, her dark hair lifting and falling in the wind. It was a cold, gray day, yet her warm beauty made him think of nature at the height of summer when everything was fully ripe and blossoming. He parked himself in front of her and tipped his hat back but made no move to touch her. Butch sniffed around her feet, tail wagging with curiosity.

"What's this? A poodle? You gotta be kidding."

Beneath her bulky jacket she wore a short dress over bare legs, and western boots. The wind pressed the fabric against her thighs, accentuating her graceful, athletic build. While he was deployed, the secrets of her body had lived and breathed in his imagination, keeping him sane in an insane country. Under other circumstances, he'd have grabbed her by now, would be kissing her like a thirsty drunk on a bottle.

She picked up Butch, held him like a baby, and peered over his fuzzy head at Sully. "Pretty cold hello, Sully."

"I wasn't expecting company."

"Didn't know I needed an invitation."

Travis came out of the garage in his oil-stained coveralls and smiled ear to ear when he saw Lilah. He caught Sully's expression and his smile withered.

"Hello, Travis," she said.

Travis nodded. "I'll take Butch."

Lilah set him down and the poodle trotted after Travis into the garage. She pulled her jacket tighter against a sharp gust of wind.

"Not a very smart outfit for this weather," Sully said.

"I didn't come here to wow you with my IQ." Her hazel eyes studied him. "What's wrong? You're acting like a stranger."

"I've been gone a long time, Lilah."

"Fifteen very long months." She reached out and touched his face, fingertips caressing the scars.

He flinched and pulled away.

Her eyes narrowed.

"Reflexes," he said.

"You always had great reflexes." Her lips curved into a beautiful smile.

He looked away.

"Am I interrupting something?"

"I've got work to do." His voice was tight. "Fences to mend."

The smile vanished. "You've been home for days, Sully. You haven't called. I had to find out you were here from the bartender at Beamer's last night."

"I haven't called a lot of people." He moved around her and walked into the barn where Dakota, his Tennessee Walker, was groomed and haltered outside the tack room.

She followed.

"Steady, boy." He smoothed a pad across the gelding's back, hoisted the saddle, and centered it over the pad.

"I'm still here, Sully. You plan on just ignoring me?"

He didn't know how to start a conversation where he didn't want to know the outcome.

"We exchanged love letters right up until you got shot. After that, I got one letter. It was like a form letter."

With his back to her, he hooked the stirrup over the saddle horn, and reached under Dakota's belly for the cinch strap.

"Talk to me, Sully. I've been worried sick about you."

He threaded the latigo through the cinch ring and pulled it tight. "Some things shouldn't be taken for granted."

"I'm listening."

"When I was in the hospital, I got a letter from a friend over here." He blew out an angry breath, turned and faced her. "Seems you were seeing other men while I was gone."

Her eyes widened. "Whoa, is that jealousy I'm hearing?"

He didn't trust his voice to speak.

"You know damn well that whenever you were home, I was only with you."

"And when I wasn't?"

"We didn't have a commitment, Sully." She held up her left hand, eyes flashing. "I sure don't see a ring on my finger."

"We had an understanding."

"An understanding doesn't keep a girl warm at night. How many men was I supposed to be seeing?"

"You tell me," he said, barely breathing.

"One."

"Who?"

"Lance."

"Your trainer?" He knew she'd cheated but the admission hit him hard, a sharp jab to the solar plexus. It hurt worse to learn it was Lance Carter, Sully's fiercest competitor in his rodeo days. The two had alternately taken first place at top rodeos. After Sully was deployed, Lance went on to make world champion, then used his fame to launch a career as a top trainer.

"It's because of Lance I ranked state champion in barrel racing last year," she said. "I told you in my letters I was working with him."

"Guess I didn't know what you meant by working." Sully barely kept his anger in check. "He's married."

"Separated."

"Because of you?"

She lowered her eyes, shoved her hands into her pockets.

Despite the cold, he was sweating. He removed the halter and bridled Dakota.

"I like having a man in my life," she said, a note of defiance in her tone. "I'm not gonna pretend otherwise. You made your choice to join the Marines, to go off to some God-forsaken desert, leave me behind with no commitment." She gave him time to reflect and then her voice softened. "You and I always managed to pick up where we left off. Your last leave, you were pretty happy to see me."

"I didn't know about Lance."

"Let's be truthful, Sully. You didn't want to know. You just wanted me to be available when you needed me. I was."

"Is that what you think? Not true. I trusted you." He swallowed, moistening his dry throat. "Are you in love with him?"

"You're the only man I've ever been in love with."

He stopped what he was doing, gave her his full attention.

She approached him, standing close. "That's why I'm here."

He didn't move, trying to suppress the deep longing he felt.

"I waited a long time for you to come home," she said gently, slipping her arms around his waist, tilting her face up to his. "Tell me you're a lil' bit happy to see me."

Sully's whole body tensed and then slowly relaxed into hers. Intimate memories stirred in his mind and he pulled her close. He had dreamt of holding her like this, breathing in the smell of her.

"Now you're home for good. We can be together again." Her voice sounded self-assured, convincing, soft as a breeze. "Let me take care of you."

He could just go with it. Let her do the thinking for him. Enjoy how good she felt, how beautiful she looked. He lowered his head and kissed her with a hunger that ran bone deep. A sweet sensation ferried him away from a world filled with trouble and pain. "Jesus, I've missed you," he murmured.

"I missed you, too. Tell me you love me."

"I love you," he said without hesitation. He kissed her again, feeling weightless, gliding on a current of deepening pleasure. Then the pain of her betrayal sliced into his mind like a sliver of glass. She let Lance kiss her like this. Touch her .... *What am I doing?*

He abruptly pulled away, his arms dropping like dead weight. "I can't do this."

"What's wrong?" Her eyes shone bright in the dim light. Her mouth was flushed with color.

They stood facing each other. The only thing moving were dust motes dancing in columns of slanted light. He wanted to kiss her again, lay her back in the hay, melt her down to raw emotion, but he also wanted to punish her, shake her violently, make her hurt like he was hurting. "I stayed faithful to you, Lilah, for four long years. The thought of coming home to you was the only thing that kept me sane. I watched friends die. Got fucking shot at. It was hard. But I stuck it out because I made a commitment. You had it easy over here. All you had to do was wait."

Silence.

He saw her chin quiver. "Why didn't you marry me?" she whispered.

"I wanted to."

"Why didn't you?"

"Doesn't matter now. You've been with Lance."

"It does matter. I have a right to know."

"I was going to war, Lilah. I could die, or come home different, without limbs, or with a brain injury. It didn't seem fair."

"You never had to go!"

"At the time, it was the right thing to do. Our country was attacked. Innocent people died."

"You could've stayed in rodeo. You were almost at the top."

He said nothing. They'd had these same arguments before he left. Four years later, nothing had changed.

"Sully, let's get past this. I can make it up to you."

"You broke up Lance's marriage. Doesn't that mean anything?"

She stared blankly. "I didn't expect him to fall in love with me."

"You just used him until I came home?"

"He can go back to his wife."

"What?" The callousness of her words felt like ice water in his gut. He tried to grasp the depth of her deceit. Why had he never seen this side of her? Suddenly he felt exhausted. The kind of exhaustion you couldn't sleep off. "Go home, Lilah. I can't deal with this right now. I have other problems. My dad needs help. I have to turn this ranch around. Take care of these animals. Plant hay."

"Let me help you."

"How? You wanna nurse my dad? Give me a big pile of money?"

Her face looked fragile, like she might be on the verge of tears. "You just said you love me."

"I do." He set his jaw, resolute. "But it isn't enough."

Slowly, the muscles tightened in her face. "All right, Sully. Be bull-headed about this, but think real hard about what you're passing up today."

Jesus, he knew.

She pulled her jacket tighter, crossed her arms. "Don't put me aside for too long. I'm just about done waiting for you."

An ache in his chest worked its way up to his throat. His body felt leaden as he placed his boot in the stirrup and mounted Dakota. Glancing down at her, he tipped his hat, something he did out of habit to acquaintances.

Her eyes flashed, angry.

He pressed his heels into Dakota's sides and the gelding moved forward with a start. Sully spurred him into a lope, putting quick distance between himself and Lilah. He heard the Dodge Ram cough once, twice, and then the engine hummed and slowly faded away.

The dreaded confrontation had come and gone. He had resisted Lilah's temptations, but it brought him no relief, just a searing ache inside. He couldn't relate to their former romance. The ease of it. The grace of being in love and sharing passion as exciting as a lightning storm. He was no longer the rodeo star she fell in love with, who lived with a sense of entitlement; who had folks looking up to him like he walked on water. Right now, he needed to stay grounded. He needed to be able to walk around in his own skin. That was something no one could take away.

Sully realized he was heading up to the mountains. Hunkering down in his sheepskin coat with the collar turned up, he concentrated on the stony, narrow trail that snaked through the forest, leading away from the ranch and all its complications. The terrain grew steeper, the shrill wind sandpapered his face. His ears went numb.

Accustomed to discomfort, he welcomed it. It kept his mind clear, his instincts sharp. The Tennessee Walker was the perfect travel horse with its powerful, compact frame and flat walk gait, providing a smooth, gliding ride. Dakota's ears were pricked forward, showing curiosity and good mood. A horse was loyal and would turn on you only if abused. As though in agreement, Dakota snorted, huffing out frozen air.

The forest of ponderosa pine opened to a wide, snowy meadow. Spikes of frozen bunch grass sparkled in the sun like glass. Silence enveloped him except for the cadence of Dakota's hooves and the melody of a gushing stream winding through the grass, its banks encrusted in ice. The surrounding rock formations looked like dwellings from another world, sculpted into icy spires and hoodoos.

Five miles or so passed beneath Dakota's hooves before Sully picked up the mineral odor of wet rock, and he knew he'd reached his destination. He dismounted and led Dakota to the edge of a steaming pool sheltered by smooth granite boulders and the mottled white trunks of aspen trees. Enclosed in rock and warmed from the primal heat of the earth, the hot spring had been a Paiute sanctuary for generations. Travis first brought him here when he was seven. Sully remembered how awed he was by the hot water rising steadily up from the earth. Sully had made the journey here often, seeking solitude and refuge from the burdens of life.

He stripped off his clothes, tested the surface with his toes, then sank into hot water up to his chin. Heaving out a weary sigh, he stretched out his limbs and let the soothing heat penetrate deep into his stiff muscles. He soaked for an hour, occasionally rising from the pool to sit on a frigid boulder to cool down. The subdued color of the landscape and the vapor rising off the water gave the place a serene and mystical quality. Here in the quiet perfection of nature, he felt communion with a higher power, and he reflected on the jagged twists and turns of his life. What was God trying to teach him with these gut-wrenching trials by fire, one after the other?

The old Michael Sullivan—rodeo star, Marine, trusting boyfriend, obedient son—was a fading ghost. After Sully pieced the scattered fragments of his life back together, what would be left? Who would he be? Closing his eyes, he prayed for guidance to live his life purposefully, to make sound decisions, to act with honesty and courage. Then he lay back and listened to the subtle sounds of nature, trying to glean some signal that would be instructive. The stillness of the place seemed to swell with the presence of a transcendent power. He received no definitive message, but he was filled with the inner certainty that he was not alone in this world and he would not be abandoned. The stillness eased his tension and in time his mood came to mirror the calm surface of the pool.

He pulled himself from the steaming water, waited for his skin to dry, then quickly dressed. He mounted Dakota and retraced the horse's hoof prints back down the mountain. After many miles, the lightness faded with the heat from the hot spring. The ranch swept into view in the valley below, and the weight of his problems descended upon him one-by-one.

CHAPTER SEVENTEEN

THE EVENING SUN cresting along the mountain range blinded Justin, who was riding shotgun in the Ford Expedition. He tugged down the brim of his hat while Avery adjusted her visor, the sunset reflected in her sunglasses. She turned into the lot of a shopping mall, maneuvered through rows of parked cars, and pulled up in front of Renegade Rags. Hanging in the windows were posters of fashion models dressed in expensive western wear and staged in front of hay wagons and bleached-out barns.

Avery smiled at him. "Wanna grab your boots?"

Justin looked at the store dubiously. "A hole-in-the-wall shoe repair is all I need. They probably charge twice as much here."

"Come on, Justin. Let's check it out." Avery got out and stood waiting, her sandaled foot tapping the pavement. She wore large sunglasses and a little flowered summer dress that bared her back and legs. Her red hair was pulled back from her pale shoulders and her freckled skin looked blotchy from the heat. At seven o'clock, it was still ninety degrees outside.

With a sigh, he climbed out, took her arm and guided her into the store. Immediately, he was assaulted by a blast of air conditioning and the smell of new leather. The shoe department was right up front. Rows of hand-tooled boots were on display in a spectrum of colors, boasting every kind of inlay: crocodile, ostrich, rattlesnake. A couple of cowboys sat tugging on boots.

Justin picked up a Paul Bond boot similar to the pair stolen by Porky, and he felt sudden anger pulse through his system. He'd saved for a year to buy those boots, kept them immaculate, and only wore them at rodeos and special events. It'd take a serious paycheck to get boots like that again.

Avery led the way to the service window and Justin placed his weathered boots on the polished countertop. They hadn't been worn in months, yet he'd resisted throwing them out. The boots were like an old friend. Rugged and reliable, they had protected him from a storm of mud and manure in their day. Now in desperate need of resoling, they looked as out of place as he was feeling.

"Looks like these boots have walked around the world twice," the florid-faced clerk said with a chuckle, peering at him over his glasses.

"Pretty much." Justin guessed the clerk was thinking the boots weren't worth fixing.

"Here's your ticket. Check back tomorrow. I'll see what I can do."

"Thanks." He stuffed the ticket inside his wallet, which was feeling very lean these days.

"Come try these on, hon." Avery stood examining a pair of sturdy work boots.

Embarrassed by his worn-out running shoes, Justin took her by the elbow and tried to steer her toward the front door. "Time to go."

"Don't be like that." She smiled, her warm eyes making him melt just a little bit. "You could use a few things in here."

He crossed his arms. "Avery, you know my credit card's maxed out."

"My treat."

"Thank you, but no."

"You've earned this. You've fixed my garbage disposal and a bunch of other things." She stared at him earnestly. "You've saved me a lot of money."

"And you're putting me up and feeding me."

"Come on," she said in a honeyed tone that he couldn't refuse. "Just try them on."

The well shod salesman, dressed in creased Wranglers and an embroidered western shirt, now hovered at her elbow. Avery told him to bring a pair of the boots in Justin's size. He left and returned promptly carting a large boot box.

"These will protect your feet from anything," the salesman said. "Steel toes. Waterproof."

Justin sat down and pulled them on. Then he stood and paced the carpet, admiring them in the mirror. Good leather. Well-constructed. Super comfortable.

"The cement in the heel gives steady footing and support," the salesman said.

"How do they feel?" Avery asked after the salesman left to help another customer.

"Expensive." He looked at the price on the box, and whistled. Three hundred dollars. He yanked them off, put his running shoes back on, and escaped down an aisle, hearing her heeled sandals clicking the linoleum behind him. After settling a brown Stetson on his head, he chose another hat with a wide brim and a stuffed rattler hatband, turned and placed it on Avery's head. It fell over her face to the tip of her nose. Fangs bared, the rattler stared ominously at him. She laughed, flashing even white teeth. He tilted her chin and planted a kiss on her mouth, tasted her strawberry-flavored lip-gloss. "You're gorgeous."

She whipped off the hat, her face as bright as a lantern. A constellation of freckles glimmered across her nose and cheeks. Tax season had ended, it was her first weekend off, and the tension had disappeared completely from her face. Not wanting to ruin her fun, he allowed her to take his hand and guide him to the men's clothing section. He looked with interest at the wide variety of shirts and jeans and pulled a blue plaid shirt off the rack. Mother-of-pearl snap buttons, embroidered stitching on the pockets, good cotton. Ninety-eight dollars. It almost burned his fingers as he placed it back on the rack.

"That would look killer on you with your baby blues," Avery said, brown eyes brightening. She pulled the shirt off the rack.

"I've got plenty of shirts." Buck a piece at the thrift store.

"Not this nice. My company's having an end-of-season party next weekend." She looked at him sweetly. "My boss and co-workers will be there. I want you to look nice."

He resisted groaning. Justin liked the quiet life they were living, just the two of them, insulated from the rest of the world. It's what he needed right now. But Avery had her needs, too. He couldn't bail out on her, and she was right, he couldn't show up in worn, faded clothes. "Just the shirt," he said grudgingly. "Maybe jeans."

Moved by her generosity, he felt a lump form in his throat. No one had ever bought him anything new before. All the clothes he got at St. Teresa's were charity hand-me-downs. Distracted, he moved down the aisle until the sound of squeaky wheels made him glance over his shoulder.

Avery was bearing down on him with a shopping cart stockpiled with clothing. A leather jacket, shirts, jeans, the brown Stetson he'd tried on.

"What are you doing?" he asked too loudly. He pulled the hat and leather jacket out of the cart and retraced her steps, placing them back on the racks, the squeaky wheels staying close behind. "Stop stalking me with that thing."

She fished the hat back from the rack and put it in the shopping basket but froze with the jacket when she saw his face. "Don't give me that look, Justin."

He shook his head. "No."

"You need a hat and jacket."

"Let's go," he said testily. "I'm getting hungry."

"I'm having fun," she said, a wistful expression on her face. "Don't spoil it for me."

"Fine. I'm waiting in the car."

He was overcome with guilt as he sat in the Expedition and watched her at the checkout counter through the window. Avery gave so much. He had no way to repay her. She was putting him in her debt, and it was upsetting the balance of their friendship.

In truth, from the start, Justin had viewed their relationship as a temporary gig, no strings attached. He'd never been in a relationship before and he knew he couldn't manage one right now. He was living like a bum: homeless, penniless, ego at an all-time low. He needed to construct a new life out of nothing, and it would be an uphill battle. It came as a painful wake-up call that Avery was building future plans around him. He'd stayed in Phoenix too long, gotten too comfortable, and allowed her to think this could last. Now she wanted to repackage him so she could drag him to her party to meet her working-stiff friends.

He felt like the world's biggest fraud. Avery was sweet and gentle, but she didn't see how small her world was. He, on the other hand, had been traveling to rodeos across the country throughout high school and college, and he'd never had an address longer than a year. He couldn't fathom being corralled into suburban living. That would be like confining a stallion to a barn stall.

A band of anxiety tightened around his chest and, for a minute, he could barely breathe. Jesus. He didn't want to hurt her. She came out of the store with bags piled in the basket, smiling at him, radiant. Feeling like a con man, he got out to help her.

Trying to ease his guilt, Justin cooked Avery her favorite dinner, linguini with prawns in white wine sauce. He lit candles, picked roses from the yard and stuck them in a vase in the center of the table. In the flickering light they ate slowly, savoring the food and each other. Occasionally he lifted her hand to his mouth and kissed her palm, her wrist, leaned over and kissed the warm groove of her neck. Emotionally he should be pulling away, but he was drawn to her. The wine warmed his blood. He wanted the fringe benefits without the demands.

After dinner she grabbed the wine and glasses. "Let's finish this on the patio."

Relaxing together on the swinging chair with the velvety night settling around them, she sipped wine, and he strummed his old Gibson. Justin knew his voice wasn't much, but he could do a decent western twang and a pretty good yodel, imitating Sourdough Slim. Avery loved the cowboy songs and blushed prettily when he slipped her name into the lyrics. Tonight it seemed appropriate to sing "The Colorado Trail" with its haunting lost-love theme.

"What a beautiful song," Avery said after he finished three verses. "So full of longing."

"It's a hundred years old," he said, finger-picking his guitar. "Came from an anonymous cowboy who'd been trampled by a horse. Multiple broken bones and lacerations. He spent several weeks in the hospital and sang that song to the other patients."

"What happened to him?"

"No one knows."

"Will you sing another song?"

"For you darlin', anything." He sang a couple more tunes and then laid the Gibson to rest in its battered case. The pressing heat of the night and the wine made him drowsy. "Let's sleep out here tonight."

"Sounds nice," she said. "But I need to get cleaned up and I like my bed."

Feeling amorous, he reached over and caressed her belly.

"Don't Justin, I'm still full." She moved his hand away and pinned him with her soft brown eyes. "I've been doing a lot of thinking about us. How well we get along and all. Everything you own is in my garage. Why don't we make this living situation official?"

"You mean permanent?"

"Yes, you dweeb." She flashed a beautiful smile.

"Like, be a couple?"

"Yeah. What do you think we're doing now?"

Justin's good mood plummeted like a kite falling from the sky. Thoughts of captivity flickered through his mind.

"Babe?"

Her voice invaded his thoughts. She was looking at him with a curious expression. "What's wrong? You're grimacing."

He shifted his weight and the porch swing groaned on its chains.

"Are you going to give me an answer?" she asked.

"I'm not ready to be having this conversation." Justin felt her body stiffen. "Avery, we've only known each other three weeks."

"And we're living together as man and wife."

"You're still married."

"Not in my heart. We've settled into a relationship, Justin. We're happy together. What more do you want?"

"I haven't been an adult long enough to answer that question." He knew he wanted more than this. He wanted property with good pastureland, a solid house, quality livestock. That dream materializing might be years away. "I'm not old enough to legally drink. I'm sure not mature enough to settle down."

"You're more mature than men twice your age. I know. I'm divorcing a forty-year-old juvenile delinquent."

"Avery, until I can offer a woman something of worth, I have no right to be in a relationship. Right now, I'm penniless, with no prospects, and I still can't rodeo." He needed at least a good couple of weeks.

"I make a decent salary," she said. "I can put you on my health plan. You won't have to worry about money."

"I want to earn my own way," he said fiercely.

She looked away with a hurt expression.

For several long seconds they sat in strained silence. Somewhere a car backfired. The chorus of crickets grew louder.

"Face facts, Justin. The odds of you making a living off rodeo are slim to none." Her tone sounded reasonable, calm. "If you stay with me, you could go back to school. I know people in town. I could get you a part-time job."

"And work for minimum wage? Christ, Avery, I can't quit rodeo. Not now. I'm getting to the top. It's my only chance to earn big money, fast."

"Most bull riders barely break even."

"True, most bull riders earn shit for money. But now I'm in the PBR. Last year, the top twenty-three riders took in over a million each. The number one rider topped out at five million. I expect to be making six figures within the next couple years."

"If you don't kill yourself first," she said, an excited edge to her voice. "The risk for injury is higher for PBR. Bulls are bigger. It's not called the most dangerous sport on dirt for nothing."

"Every sport is dangerous," he said.

"The linemen that crush each other in football weigh three hundred pounds," she said. "Bulls weigh two thousand. Most cowboys weigh in at around one fifty. Those odds seem even to you? Riders get trampled, get concussions. It's David versus Goliath every time you sit on a bull."

"Hell, Avery, living off you is injuring me more than any bull ever could. I've every intention of paying you back for everything once I'm on my feet."

"You're planning on leaving me, then?" Her voice became quiet. She sat very still.

The fuzzy concept of leaving hadn't crystallized until she spoke it aloud. He was comfortable here and would have stayed another two weeks, but now he saw clearly it was time to go. Before she got even more attached. It would be better for her, too, in the long run. After she got to know him better, she'd be disappointed. He wasn't an easy man to love. The thought of seeing the bright light dim in her eyes when she looked at him filled him with sorrow. He was gripped by a keen sense of aloneness, like a stone falling down a dark well with no bottom in sight. "I'm sorry, Avery."

"Will you come back?" Her eyes, big in the moonlight, brimmed with tears.

He nodded.

"When?"

"I'll be passing through here for rodeo all the time." His voice caught and he said hoarsely, "Come here." He framed her face with his hands and wiped the tears away with his thumbs, wishing he could patch up the hurt he caused. He kissed the top of her head and cradled her in his arms.

"You've been so good to me. I don't deserve a woman like you."

For a long time he felt her tears seeping into his shirt and the occasional spasm of a sob, but eventually her body relaxed and her familiar soft snores rumbled against his shoulder. His thoughts time-traveled backwards over his troubled life and the long years of indentured slavery. By the time he reached eighteen and was free of social services, he'd had his fill of pseudo-families, where things appeared hunky-dory on the surface, but in the shadows, ugly secrets festered.

He'd grown a tough hide, a preference for his own company, and an understanding that there was something inherently wrong with him. Trust was weaned out of him at an early age and he had never learned how to forge close bonds with other people. He'd had plenty of acquaintances in his life, but no real friends. He doubted he had the emotional capacity to cement his soul to a woman's. Sure, he wanted a wife one day, but even then he knew he'd always have a desire to bust loose and hit the road for a spell. One thing he learned the hard way was that it was a mistake to get too comfortable. Nothing good ever lasted.

The sound of Avery's rhythmic breathing filtered into his thoughts. The familiarity of her body conforming to his own soothed something raw and wild in his nature. For a long time he studied the simple world within her fenced backyard, wanting to remember these untroubled moments of suburban life; the smell of fresh-cut grass, the faint buzz of June bugs dive-bombing the porch light, the distant barking of a dog as a car turned into a driveway, the smoky aroma of barbequed steak lingering in the air from a neighbor's grill.

She stirred. He stroked her hair and memorized her face in the moonlight. He knew he would dream of her body often and the many joys he'd discovered in her arms.

***

Justin didn't sleep well. Normally he slept past eight, but he rose at dawn, filled with restless energy. After an hour of calisthenics, avoiding pressure to his ribs, he showered and made himself breakfast. Coffee and a mushroom omelet were waiting for Avery when she made a sleepy appearance in the kitchen. Her face looked solemn, resolute.

As usual, she talked about the headlines in the paper—the distant war, local politics, their horoscopes—but her voice sounded flat, distant. Despite her coolness, he wanted to be near her. He shadowed her as she dressed for work and watched attentively as she brushed mascara onto her lashes and put on lipstick. After running a brush through her hair, she turned off the light, leaving him perched on the edge of the tub in the darkness. There was no fire in her goodbye hug, no lingering kiss, no promise of future intimacy. She merely pecked his cheek and flew out the door. He stood staring after her, acutely aware that something essential had been ripped away from his soul.

After the sound of her SUV faded down the street he tried to lose himself in household chores; vacuuming and scrubbing down the kitchen, but nothing relieved the pressure building in his chest. The everyday sameness of Avery's existence felt suffocating. He missed the intensity of rodeo: the in-your-face threat of death, the respect of hardened cowboys who bore injuries like badges of courage, the admiration of buckle bunnies who wanted to taste danger by riding a cowboy. He was seized with a longing to be on the road heading for some vague destination, speeding past busted-down ranches that spoke of failure and broken dreams. He wanted to disappear into the horizon. No expectations. No disappointments.

His desire for freedom filled him with misery.

CHAPTER EIGHTEEN

SULLY AND TRAVIS had been up for hours when the sheriff's volunteer group arrived. Sully was constructing a wheelchair ramp up to the back porch, his carpenter tools holstered around his hips. He crossed the driveway to meet the men piling out of the Yukon; Sheriff Matterson, a couple deputies, two neighbors, Pastor Cooper.

A van pulled in behind the truck and the wives got out, bundled against the cold in wool scarves and down jackets. Wearing big smiles, everyone gathered around Sully. Hugs from the women, claps on the back from the men. The small talk was cheerful and polite, catching him up on bits of local gossip. Everyone avoided the topic of the war he'd left behind. The conversation drifted to Monty's murder and stolen horses. Sully recognized fear in the women's voices, anger on the faces of the men.

"Cain't believe I didn't see nothing, or hear gunshots." Bob Stevens was a lean man with sharp features and a thin mouth. He owned the property next to Monty's and still had six good cow horses in his barn.

"How'd they get Gunner outta here without making a stir?" his wife Eva asked. She was as round as Bob was lean, with small eyes peering over plump red cheeks.

"Wish I knew, Eva," Sully said, hearing anger seep into his words.

"Forensics turn up anything, Carl?" Pastor Cooper asked.

The sheriff pushed his hat back, revealing a deeply creased brow. He looked haggard, eyes puffy, stress lines around his mouth. "We combed every inch of his house and barn. Whatever forensics found, it's at the lab. The M.E. hasn't released any info on the body yet." He hooked his thumbs into his belt. "We go to the bottom of their active case files."

Sully saw his own disappointment mirrored on the faces around him.

"Okay, enough with the gruesome talk," the sheriff said. "We came here to lend a hand. Let's get to work. It's too cold to paint outside but we can start indoors. Jim, Pete, you two start upstairs. Ladies, find things to do in the house."

Even in civilian clothes, Carl Matterson looked like a cop and acted like one. Sully spotted Travis coming out of the barn, Butch trotting close behind. Sully had cropped the poodle short and Travis had fashioned a little red sweater for him out of an old turtleneck. Pulling iPod buds from his ears, Travis looked surprised at the party of people milling in the yard.

"Hey, Travis. How about making these guys useful?" Matterson said. "Think you can dig up some projects for them?"

Travis looked puzzled. "What kinda projects?"

"Sorry, Travis," Sully said. "I forgot to mention these folks were coming out to give us a hand. General repairs, clean up."

"Well, I'll be a son of a gun." Travis grinned. "How much time you got?" He escorted Bob and Evan back into the barn.

The women loaded up casseroles from the van, followed Sully into the house, and spread their dishes across the kitchen counters. Sully peeked under foil and lifted lids, releasing the aromas of chicken enchiladas, lasagna, and tuna casserole.

"We'll have a potluck at noon. Everyone meet back here in the kitchen," Sue Matterson said. She was a pretty woman; tall, well-proportioned, blond hair turning gray, no-nonsense brown eyes. A good match for a tough cop like Carl. She'd kept their three boys in line with a firm hand until they left for college. "Let's get this food put away." She opened the fridge and stood motionless, frowning. It was empty except for a bowl of eggs Sully had gathered from the hens, leftover beans still in the pot they'd been cooked in, and a half-defrosted chunk of meat sitting on a plate, bleeding.

"What the heck?" She pulled out the meat, wrinkled her nose, and held it at arm's length. "This stinks."

All eyes in the room turned to Sully.

"I believe that's the last of the elk Travis shot before my first deployment. He was gonna grill it for dinner."

"Eek!" The disgusted faces of the women forced Sully to stifle a grin. Travis would douse it in hot sauce. He could eat anything.

Sue looked at Sully like he was utterly incompetent and tossed the mound of meat into the trash, then set the can out on the porch. The women started stuffing the fridge with casseroles. He sure wasn't gonna go hungry anytime soon. He peeled back foil on a pan and caught Sue's eye, his hand hovering over a blueberry corn muffin.

"Go ahead, Sully." She smiled. "Eat up. That's what they're here for."

Carl also reached for one, but Sue gave him a look and slapped his hand away. "Forgetting your diet already? Go on. Get. There's no room in the kitchen for you."

The two men strode into the living room, Sully guiltily stuffing his mouth. Matterson removed his hat and ran a sunburned hand through his thinning hair. "Time to roll up our sleeves. I'll start taping. Wanna take down everything on the walls and start spackling?"

"Sounds like a plan." Sully started in his bedroom, pulling down old posters and packing his trophies and buckles into boxes, then moving them to the garage. Returning to his room, he pulled all the furniture into the middle of the floor, covered everything with drop cloths, and stood in the doorway viewing his handiwork. Ghostly images remained on the walls. Decades of his life had just been stripped away. His new identity would soon take shape in this space, starting with a fresh coat of paint.

Carl was taping the oak doorframe in the living room. He had turned on the radio and was singing "Digging Up Bones" along with Randy Travis, making up in volume what he lacked in harmony.

"I hate to break up the music fest but what color paint did you get?" Sully knew he was stuck with whatever it was, considering it was free.

"Macadamia nut."

"What the hell kinda color is that?"

"Brent at the Depot said this is what they're painting all the model homes." He pried the top off a can, stirred, dipped in a brush, and slapped a few strokes across the wall. It was a warm cream color that made the yellowed white beneath it look dirty. "You approve?"

"Damn straight. Why didn't you just say it was buckskin?" Sully smiled. "Let's get 'er done."

The rhythm of painting and the buzz of women's voices went uninterrupted for several hours. Sully took a coffee break and saw the women had taken down the curtains and pulled up all the throw rugs. All morning he heard the rumble of the washer and dryer coming from the laundry room. Women were dusting and scrubbing crevices and light fixtures and other places he never thought to clean. With good cheer and efficiency, they moved through the house like a military brigade. He caught snippets of conversation coming from all corners.

Just before noon Travis appeared in the doorway looking indignant. Carl and Sully were painting the last wall. "Who threw my elk in the trash?"

"Hell, Travis," Carl said. "That thing's got freezer burn. Must be four years old."

Travis put his hands on his hips. "I was gonna eat that elk. Paiutes eat different from white people. We like frozen shit, sometimes for years."

"I'm sure you do, but you've got casseroles now." Sue came up behind Travis from the kitchen. "Any of which is better than that elk."

She and Travis locked eyes. Sully saw his shoulders slightly sag and then muttering something in Paiute, he turned on his heel and backtracked through the kitchen.

"Tell the guys we're eating in fifteen minutes," Sue called out to him before the kitchen door shut behind him.

Sue and Carl looked at Sully.

He shrugged, feigning innocence. "I'll replace it with steak. He'll be fine."

CHAPTER NINETEEN

THE PHONE RANG seven times, eight. No answer. It was blazing hot standing inside the grimy phone booth at the local Speedy Mart. A few feet away a gang of local lowlifes stood smoking on the curb, their baggy shorts sliding halfway off their asses. He was just about to hang up when a familiar baritone voice answered.

"Hank Sterling here."

"Hey, Hank. This is Alex."

Silence.

"We met at Chester's in Red Rock a few weeks back. I'm the bull rider. Rode your bull."

"Of course. I remember. Alexander Hamilton." He chuckled. "You in town?"

"No, but I'd like to be. I'm in Phoenix. You said you could give me a job. Does that offer still hold?"

There was a long silence. Justin shifted his weight from one foot to the other. He could smell something dead in the air. His finger traced the phone number of a girl named Fanny etched into the chrome.

"If you come work for me Alex, it's on my terms. You need to be serious and committed. No skipping out on me to join the traveling circus."

"You have my word on that." Justin pushed his hat back and wiped sweat off his forehead with his sleeve. What kinda work you talking about? What kinda pay?"

"One step at a time. Show me what you're capable of. If it works out, you'll learn a lot about running a ranch. A successful ranch." He paused, letting his words sink in. "Your paycheck depends on you. How fast you learn, how hard you work."

Indentured servitude, Justin thought. Images of desperate men ignited in his brain. Dried up men who worked hard their whole lives for other people and had shit to show for it. Justin wanted to say he had a better offer, but he didn't. "All right, Hank, you've got a deal. But I need an advance."

Sterling broke into laughter.

"What's so funny?" Justin asked.

"Your audacity. Okay, Alex. How much you need?"

"Enough for gas to get to Beaverhead."

"Where do you want it sent?"

Justin gave him the phone number of the closest Western Union. "I'll leave as soon as I get it."

"I'll send it today. Don't even think about cheating me." The humor had dropped out of Hank's tone. Justin felt the heat of his piercing gray eyes streaming through the telephone wire.

Cheat you? As if that were even possible. There'd be nowhere to hide. Hank Sterling was an institution. World champion bull rider twice over. Big landowner. Filthy rich. Anyone who knew anything about rodeo knew of Hank Sterling. "I won't cheat you, Hank."

"Good. See you soon, Alex."

CHAPTER TWENTY

THE RINGTONE of his cell startled Sully out of a deep sleep. He groped for the phone and mumbled hoarsely. "Sully, here."

"Sully, you gotta come get me."

He bolted upright in bed. "Dad, are you all right?"

Joe launched into an unintelligible rant, slurring his words.

"Dad, slow down. What's wrong?" Sully glanced at the clock: five a.m.

"Ain't nothing wrong. I just wanna come home."

Sully's mind was dull with sleep. "Okay Dad. After I get my chores done."

"Come get me now. A man's got a right to be in his own home." The line went dead.

Sully hung up and fell back on his pillow. He wasn't ready to bring Joe home. There was work he wanted to finish. He threw the covers aside and padded to the kitchen, filled the coffeepot with water, and measured the coffee. From his dad's feisty mood, it sounded like the old Joe was back and headed for home, ready to get everyone up before dawn and start running the show. He felt a sad longing for the dad he'd known too briefly, the one who cried and told Sully he was proud of him.

***

He found his father sitting in his wheelchair on Ronnie's front porch. Clean shaven, thick hair brushed back from his gaunt face, blue eyes clear and glinting. His clothes looked oversized on his scrawny frame and his knees and elbows were bent into sharp angles. He looked as if he might be going to church if it wasn't for the hard line of his jaw, which said he was not to be messed with this morning.

"Looking good, Dad." Sully flashed his mother a smile as she joined them on the porch.

"Morning, son." A green wool shawl was draped over her flannel nightgown. Sheepskin boots covered her feet and her red hair was blowing around her face. With a tense expression, she pressed a grocery bag into Sully's arms. "Corn muffins and turkey chili. It'll get you through the next few days."

"Thanks, Mom." He thought of all the casseroles stuffed in his fridge and wondered where he'd put it.

"Don't let him eat red meat or anything fried," Ronnie clipped. "No butter and watch his sugar intake."

"Will do." He pecked her on the forehead and looked at her closely, but she offered no explanation for Joe's sudden departure after only four days. Obviously the golden glow of their honeymoon had faded. Their farewell was colder than the morning. Joe's face tightened when she kissed his cheek.

Sully steered the wheelchair over the icy paving stones, loaded Joe inside the cab, and folded the chair into the back seat. The on-again conflict between his parents made his stomach churn. After winding through side streets and merging into traffic on the parkway, he tested the waters. "How'd things go with Mom?"

Joe shrugged, staring out the side window.

After his few attempts at conversation sputtered out, Sully turned on the radio. Music pulsed into the cab and Sully kept beat by slapping his hands on the steering wheel. There was good reason to be cheerful. The sheriff's clean-up squad had been a blessing. The inside of the house was painted, hay money had come in, and his long list of ranch repairs had been cut in half. The sheriff bought one of the bulls and a beautiful papered brood mare, which meant money in their bank account and two less animals to feed.

The weatherman said it was going to be a sunny day, a sparkling forty degrees. The snow would start melting and it'd be easier to work outside. Nice way to slip into the month of April. Though still a few months away, the promise of hot summer days teased his brain, softening the impact of his father's sullen mood.

As they approached the ranch, Joe started looking around and sat forward in his seat. By the time Sully pulled up behind the house, he was vibrating with impatience. He opened the door before the truck came to a full stop. "Get me my wheelchair."

Sully barely got him into the chair before Joe started wheeling himself across the yard toward the corral, his body bouncing as he rolled over the icy ground. Sully followed.

"Gus! Whiskey!" he croaked.

At the sound of Joe's voice, the two donkeys started honking like taxi cab drivers stuck in traffic. One high, one low, heads cranked skyward. The excitement was contagious. Horses started whinnying, chickens strutted out of the barn clucking and ruffling feathers, and Pistol the mule rattled the pasture gate, beaming his long-toothed grin.

Though determined to cover the distance himself, Joe's glacial progress was painful to watch. "Dad, let me help." Sully grabbed the black rubber handgrips.

"Let me be," Joe barked. "I can do it myself." His face was flushed almost purple. The veins in his neck bulged out like cords.

Oh, shit! His father was going to have another stroke then and there. Sully pulled the chair back into a wheelie and expedited his father's journey to the corral, ignoring his slew of angry curses. Fenced inside with the donkeys was Whistler, Joe's champion roping palomino, now twenty-seven years old.

"Whistler," his father squawked, as though begging to be rescued.

The Palomino's ears shot straight up, and he lost no time trotting to the gate. Neighing loudly, he stretched his long neck over the rail and blew softly into Joe's hair. Joe stood shakily, one wobbly hand anchored to the rail, and pressed his face into the gelding's silver mane. The two huddled together and Sully heard his father murmur a magical language only decipherable to equines. Joe then greeted the donkeys and mule and appeared to be having a meaningful four-way conversation while scrubbing their necks with his fingertips.

The open affection Joe gave to animals always puzzled Sully, considering his inability to connect with people. Watching Joe's emotional reunion with his four-legged friends touched a soft spot in his heart. It must have been agony being imprisoned in the nursing home with only humans for company.

"Son, get me my saddle," Joe clipped, no-nonsense.

Sully stood stunned for a moment. "No way, Dad."

As though on cue, Travis peeked out of the bunkhouse door, unshaven face rumpled from sleep, fingers still buttoning his shirt. He broke into a broad grin at the sight of Joe. "Well, I'll be damned." Butch's head popped out between his legs. Travis hopped from one foot to the other, pulling on his boots, then hoofed it across the frozen yard and clapped Joe on the back, almost knocking him over. "Goddamn, Joe. Didn't know you'd be home today. Shit. You're skinnier than a scarecrow."

His father grinned back. The old Paiute was one of the few men Joe thoroughly respected.

"Yeah, they woulda killed me soon enough if Sully hadn't busted me out. Shit for food. Men giving me sponge baths." Joe looked around, sucked in a lungful of air, and exhaled. "Hell, I missed this spread."

He turned his attention to Butch, who was neatly trimmed and decked out in the little red sweater. Joe's mouth stretched into a wide, lopsided grin. He sank into his chair and reached out. "Come here to your ol' man, Butch."

The poodle sat back on his haunches, indifferent, showing no sign of recognition.

"Come."

No response.

"What the hell?" Joe shot Travis a look. "What'd you do to my dog?"

Travis shrugged. "Been taking care of him, is all." He snatched Butch off the ground and sat him on Joe's lap. The poodle put his paws on Joe's chest, gave his face a couple licks, then promptly jumped off and trotted back to the bunkhouse.

"He's cold," Travis said. "Give him time. He'll come 'round."

Disgruntled, Joe turned to Sully. "Where's that saddle?"

Travis and Sully exchanged a look. "He wants to ride," Sully said sourly.

Travis sized up the situation. "I'll take care of it. Find something to do, Sully. Maybe cook breakfast?" He grinned at Joe and stepped into the corral with a halter in hand. "I'll have Whistler saddled in no time."

"I don't think that's a good idea," Sully said, crossing his arms.

"No one asked you." Joe's tone matched the tough determination in his eyes.

"Just saying ...."

"I ain't no cripple," Joe banged his fist on the arm of his wheelchair. "You ain't gonna turn me into one."

Travis led Whistler to the barn.

Damn. "Make sure he stays in the arena."

"Make sure he stays in the arena," Joe mimicked in a singsong voice. Sully wanted to cuff him.

Joe steered himself toward the barn, the effort straining every muscle in his frail body. Sully watched him stop every few feet and pant. It was all he could do to not intervene.

He retreated to the kitchen. Rummaging through the fridge and cupboards, he got out a mixing bowl, Bisquick, milk, and eggs, and starting whipping up the batter, all the while stealing glances out the window. After a few minutes, Whistler came sauntering out of the barn with Joe confidently mounted in the saddle. The pair looked like ghosts of the show-stopping performers they'd been in their heyday. Joe leaned over, opened the gate, and rode into the arena.

Sully poured batter into a large cast-iron skillet forming three pancakes, then he laid strips of bacon on the grill pan. Out in the arena, Joe had Whistler making circles at a nice slow walk, warming him up. Sensible. Sully breathed easier.

Travis came out of the barn carrying a saddle and leading his mother's high-performance horse, Gracie, intending no doubt to get in the arena and stay close to Joe.

Fresh coffee dripped into the pot, bacon popped and sizzled. Sully flipped the pancakes, set the table, got out butter and maple syrup, and started a second batch of pancakes. In the arena, he saw Joe signaling commands to the palomino with subtle movements of the reins, which made the need to use his frail legs unnecessary. An inexperienced eye would miss them entirely.

Travis was bent over, cinching Gracie's saddle. The gray-dappled mare stood eagerly waiting to cut loose in the arena. Now there was a horse that could move!

Breakfast was ready. Sully turned off the burners, set the covered pans aside, and went out on the porch to lure in the men. He watched his father expertly back Whistler into reverse, then turn him in circles, his back hooves almost stationary, his front legs crossing over one another in a wide pivot. Sully couldn't help but be impressed. Even disabled, his

Linda Berry   143   *Hidden Part 1* father was one of the most talented horse trainers in the country. All the same, he wanted Joe off that horse. He'd done plenty for one day. "Time to eat," he yelled.

Sully pulled his eyes away from Whistler's fancy footwork. Joe hadn't latched the gate securely and it was swinging open. Alarmed, he raced to get to the gate, and noticed Joe had frozen in the saddle, face pale, looking ready to faint. He suddenly slumped forward, giving Whistler the wrong signal. The palomino broke into a trot, bouncing Joe in the saddle like a rag doll. Sully reached the gate. Whistler streaked past him like hell on wheels, shot across the yard, and galloped up the snow-covered trail leading off the property.

Adrenaline spiking, Sully snatched the reins from a surprised Travis, leapt onto Gracie's back, and whipped the mare into a full-throttle gallop, targeting the renegade palomino kicking up snow up ahead. As Gracie strained to close the gap, Sully saw that Joe's weak leg was flapping uncontrollably against Whistler's ribs, prompting the horse into a more frenzied gallop. Joe's hands gripped the pommel and his body lurched from side to side. He was moments from disaster.

Gracie came alongside Whistler at blinding speed, matching the thunderous rhythm of the palomino's hooves stride for stride. Sully edged the fearless mare closer still. He leaned into the palomino and tried to snatch the reins. Whistler pulled away, widening the gap. Sully inched closer, tried again, fingers skimming the leather straps. The palomino pulled away.

Joe's hands were white-knuckled, the strain showing on his face.

"Hang on, Dad!"

Gracie inched closer. Sully's leg brushed his father's. Stretching his arm as far as he could, his fingertips brushed leather and hooked the reins. Careful. Careful. He applied subtle pressure, then slightly more. If Whistler braked too soon, his father would be catapulted from the saddle like a rock from a slingshot. "Whoa. Whoooooooa."

Sully slowed both horses to a trot, then into an ambling gait, but before he could ease Whistler into a four-beat walk, Joe leaned away from him, falling from the saddle. Sully snagged his belt and held his weight precariously with one hand while managing Whistler's reins with the other. Not until the world rushing past came to a complete standstill did he pull his father back toward him and lower him safely to the ground. Joe sank into a crusty snowdrift and lay in a crumpled heap, motionless.

Panting heavily, blood pounding in his ears, Sully dismounted and knelt beside his father. He pressed his fingers to his carotid artery, looking for a sign of life in the bloodless face.

Joe gasped. His eyes fluttered open. "I'm okay," he wheezed.

Sully momentarily scanned the terrain around them, waiting for his racing heart to slow down. They were in a meadow blanketed by snow and ringed by ponderosa forest. Tracks of deer, rabbits, and birds were stamped into the smooth glistening surface. A peaceful scene, but Sully knew that hidden beneath the snow the ground was booby-trapped with ruts and gopher holes. It was a miracle neither of the horses hit one of those deathtraps and broke a leg, which would have meant a violent tumble, and the likelihood of death to both horse and rider.

Feeling both relieved and angry, Sully helped his father to his feet, brushed the snow off his clothes, and supported his meager weight against his own. Joe was trembling uncontrollably, his lips turning blue. Lathered in sweat, the horses stood nervously, blowing steam, rib cages heaving. Gracie comforted the older horse who stood licking his lips, no doubt stunned by this sudden demand for warp speed after being left in pasture for six months. Both horses needed rubdowns and bowls of grain to calm them down.

Sully heard the sound of the four-wheeler coming over the ridge and saw a cloud of exhaust, Travis leaning forward in the driver's seat. He pulled up alongside them.

Joe's swagger vanished as he sagged into the passenger seat, teeth chattering. "It wasn't my fault Whistler took off. I had him under control. Who left that dang gate opened?"

"You did," Sully said.

"The latch must be broken."

Yeah, right.

They started for home, Sully mounted on Gracie with Whistler following behind. He looked at his watch. Not quite eight a.m. and already all hell had broken loose. Travis took the horses to the barn. Sully wheeled Joe up the new ramp into the house.

Hunched over, his father didn't notice the transformation: everything freshly painted, windows sparkling, old wood floors shimmering under a new coat of wax. He insisted on rolling himself straight back to the master bedroom where he struggled to get himself out of the chair. Energy spent, he sat passively on the edge of the king-size bed and allowed Sully to pull off his boots, peel off his wet clothes, and help him into flannel pajamas.

"Lay down, Dad."

Joe curled up under the covers, shivering, his limbs sorely lacking muscle and flesh. Sully tucked another blanket around him, then a thick quilt on top of that. His anger dissipated at the sight of his father's modest presence on the big mattress. He knew Joe associated being back on the ranch with his former strength and endurance, but he wasn't going to barrel through his recovery with bull-headed determination alone. He'd have to put in the time, and it was going to be an uphill struggle. Sooner or later, he'd have to accept that he would never again be the robust, strapping cowboy he used to be.

"The remote's here on the nightstand with the phone," Sully said. "I'll bring in breakfast. If you need anything in the meantime, use the phone. Don't yell."

Joe turned on his side and faced the wall. "Coffee."

"Sure, Dad."

"And bring me my dog."

CHAPTER TWENTY-ONE

FOR THIRTEEN HOURS straight, revved up on coffee, Justin drove through northwestern Arizona into Nevada, barreling through hundreds of miles of arid desert, aiming to get to Oregon before nightfall. The drive was long and monotonous. He barely noticed the landscape. Listening to tormented love songs by Patsy Kline and Hank Williams, he tried to sort through his emotions, which were as snarled as a nest of rattlers. Nagging questions hammered his brain. Why did he leave Avery so abruptly? Why didn't he give the relationship a chance?

He'd been racing away from Phoenix all day, yet the further he got, the stronger Avery's presence grew inside the cab. All his senses seemed wide open. Out of the corner of his eye, he saw sunlight catching her hair, heard her lilting laughter, and smelled her rose-scented body lotion. At every truck stop, Avery's gravitational pull threatened to derail him. The hollow-eyed, blank faces of men who lived alone in their semis gnawed at him. Nomads. Like him. Only one thin thread kept him on course. He was driving on someone else's dime, and he had given Hank Sterling his word.

The desert climbed in elevation and he saw the outline of conifer forest in the moonlight. Snow started falling. He slipped the truck into four-wheel drive and lowered his speed as he moved through the thickening drift. He drove slowly, the wipers rhythmically moving the snow into little heaps off to the sides of the windshield.

Six hours shy of Central Oregon, he pulled into a rest stop and parked across from a dozen big rigs. Their orange and yellow markers were barely visible behind the curtain of blowing snow. White powder coated everything and lent the night a dreamlike quality. His stomach swirled with acid from too much coffee. After chewing a few antacids, he burrowed into his sleeping bag and listened to the wind batter the truck, and his thoughts drifted to Avery. The smell and feel of her skin haunted him. If he were in Phoenix, he'd be holding her close, her flesh warm and soft against his own.

When Justin woke, there was an icy chill in the camper. Frost glazed the windows. He unpacked a down jacket and stepped out into the frozen landscape, sinking several inches into new snow. Stinging cold. The brightness of the sun was startling, and his breath puffed out like steam. His truck was the sole vehicle in the lot, a mound of white, looking like some hunched-over Arctic animal. Shivering in the unheated restroom, he shaved, brushed his teeth, and ran a comb through his hair. Skidding on ice in his running shoes he made his way back to the camper.

Time to dig out his old, resoled boots. He opened a cardboard box, removed some work clothes and instantly smelled new leather. Holy shit. There sat the boots he'd tried on with Avery at Renegade Rags. She had gone back and bought them, hid them in the truck. A pang of guilt sliced through him. Should he keep them, or send them back? Out of necessity, he had kept the hat, the jacket, a shirt and one pair of the jeans she bought him. The rest he had left behind, price tags still intact.

He decided to keep the boots. He was going to be working a ranch, which meant mud, manure, and dangerous hooves to dodge, not always successfully.

Pressure built up behind his eyes. A few tears squeezed out while he pulled on the boots. Now a part of Avery would be with him every day. When he stepped out into the cold to scrape ice off the windows, the grooved soles provided excellent traction. He felt more competent, more mentally prepared to meet the demands that lay ahead. Boots were a point of pride for a cowboy. Avery had restored some of his dignity.

CHAPTER TWENTY-TWO

SULLY WAS RELIEVED when Joe put away an enormous breakfast. Five pancakes smothered in butter and syrup, four strips of bacon, two eggs. Afterwards, he lay in bed reading the paper. When Sully checked on him an hour later, he was passed out, mouth slack, snoring loudly, Butch curled into the groove of his hip.

Sully called his mother from the barn and related the high drama of the morning. Joe hanging on for his life on his runaway palomino. She expressed no surprise. After thirty years of marriage, she'd seen everything. "I'm sorry, son. I was afraid he'd be a burden to you."

Too late for regrets. "He's feistier than a wild boar. Did he stop taking his anti-depressants?"

"I put out his pills every night, but I didn't police him. He's a grown man."

After a long moment of silence, he said, "I have some bad news about Gunner."

"Is he okay?" she asked, voice wary.

"He was stolen."

He heard her sharp intake of breath. "What in God's name are you talking about?"

Sully gave her an abbreviated version of the horse thefts and Monty's murder, and heard her gasp a few times.

"Poor old Monty." Her voice wavered and he knew she was close to tears. "That man was always kind to everyone. I can't believe our Gunner is gone. Murder. Horse theft. What's the world coming to?"

Stomach twisting, Sully listened to her muffled sobs. He sure wasn't going to add to her misery by bringing up the missed insurance payment.

Enough grief for one day.

"Does your dad know about Gunner?" she asked, when she was able to talk.

"Not yet."

"You tell him when the time is right."

"What's going on between you two, Mom? You both looked super stressed this morning."

Another long silence.

"You'll have to wait till he's ready to tell you himself."

Sully huffed out his exasperation. "Okay, Mom. You need anything?"

"No, son, I'm okay. Right now, just focus on your dad."

"I'll come see you soon."

"I'd like that," she sniffed.

After Sully helped Travis groom Gracie and Whistler, the two men parted company to do their various chores. They met back in the kitchen for lunch. Joe showed no interest in leaving the bedroom. While watching TV, he ravenously put away three cornbread muffins and two bowls of chili. When he finished, his stomach protruded like a basketball.

Pack on those calories, Dad.

CHAPTER TWENTY-THREE

JUSTIN'S FIRST GLIMPSE of his hometown was a towering wall of rim rock rising up like an amphitheater, sheltering the valley below. The snow-capped Cascades were reflected in the rearview mirror and whitewashed clouds hung in a brilliant blue sky. The town itself encompassed about seven square miles and he knew every street and alley and most of the surrounding ranches.

People and events flooded his memory as he passed the fairgrounds, historic courthouse, and high school. Though he grew up here, he'd been something of a loner, and if it wasn't for his status as a track star, he would've been invisible. Good memories of track events, fishing the Crooked River, and trail riding in the Ochoco were shadowed by memories of abuse. He didn't want to be here, and he was putting himself in grave danger by taking the risk. Some violent people here in Beaverhead wouldn't mind dragging him into the woods and beating the holy crap out of him. He swallowed and glanced at the rearview mirror, almost expecting to see a blue Dodge Ram bearing down on him. This gig at Sterling O was temporary. The sooner he was gone, the better.

Justin drove through town and felt relief when the stands of lodgepole pine gave way to arid soil and endless miles of sagebrush. The stark, open beauty of the high desert stretched out before him, then buckled into moss colored buttes and jagged mountains on the horizon line. Out here, a body could breathe.

It wasn't hard to find Sterling O Ranch. Hank owned fifty thousand acres. Any road that was an offshoot of the highway eventually led to his ranch. He drove through immense stone pillars crested with the ranch name in wrought-iron letters. Justin followed the road through conifer forest, and past meadows, rocky bluffs, a handful of small lakes, and acres of hayfields. Angus cattle grazed in fenced pastureland, the cows shadowed by calves.

As the truck gained elevation, Justin spotted a sprawling ranch house perched up on a ridge like an eagle's nest. He passed indoor and outdoor arenas, round pens, two large gabled barns, outbuildings, and a few cottages. Everything was well-constructed and immaculately maintained. Nice piece of paradise.

He parked in the spacious driveway in front of the house, climbed out and stretched his cramped legs. The view was stunning, spanning a hundred miles. The cost of a ranch this size, with plenty of fresh water and good grazing land, was beyond his accounting ability. The dry air was scented with sage, the temperature in the high forties.

Two Labs and two border collies loped across the driveway to greet him. "Hey boys, hey." Justin grinned, petting all four in turn. He loved dogs.

The sound of a screen door banging shut directed his eyes to the big porch encircling the house. A young woman with a tumble of dark red hair stepped out into the sunlight. "What can I do for you, cowboy?"

The four dogs dashed up the stairs and danced around her, whining and licking her hands.

Justin pushed his hat back from his face and removed his shades. "I'm Alex Hamilton. I'm here to see Hank."

"He's out of town," she said with a suspicious tone. "He expecting you?"

"Yes, ma'am. He offered me a job."

"You the bull rider?" she asked, coming down the stairs.

"Yes, ma'am."

"Didn't think you'd get here till tomorrow."

She was a looker, with beautiful curves and a generous bustline, accentuated by tight jeans and a low-cut top. Her turquoise boots looked better suited for dancing the two-step than dodging mud pies.

"I'm Sarah, Hank's daughter."

Up close, he got a good look at her. Wide set green eyes, full mouth, too much makeup, a couple inches taller than him, mid-twenties, hair a wild concoction of waves bouncing around her shoulders. The sweet scent of cinnamon ghosted around her. Gold bangles jingled on her wrists as she shook his hand. Her long fingernails were painted purple.

"Heck of a drive from Phoenix," she said, watching him with an expression that seemed to be caught between boredom and amusement. "You tired, Alex, or would you like to take a look around?"

"Look around, if you have time."

"Time's about all a woman has out here." She drawled in a fake Texas accent, as though mimicking a line from a movie. She motioned with her arm like a game show hostess. "This is the house. Dad likes things big."

Justin admired the two-story ranch house, around five thousand square feet, solidly built, lots of ponderosa and river rock trim.

"Let's head out back, Alex," she said, losing the drawl. "We'll take the Cruiser."

They circled the house, wound through a stand of Aspens, and came to a five-car garage. The dogs trotted ahead and waited eagerly by a silver Land Cruiser parked in the semi-circular driveway. They all piled in, dogs panting over their shoulders. Pausing to light a brown-papered cigarette, Sarah inhaled deeply then blew out cinnamon-scented smoke. Now he understood where her personalized scent came from. He waved smoke from his face.

"Sorry." She opened all the windows and started driving slowly up the road, wheels crunching gravel. "Let me give you a little history about Sterling O," she said, holding the cigarette out the window and sounding like a tour guide. "We've been a cattle ranch since 1879. Mom's side of the family. Dad married into the business." She took a long drag from her cigarette and crushed it in the ashtray as she exhaled. "The O in Sterling O is named after Mom. Her name was Olivia. She died last year. Cancer." Her voice wavered and she looked out the window. "Sorry. I still have a hard time talking about her."

"Sorry for your loss," he said gently.

Sarah drove silently for a few seconds before diving back into her story. "We've got fifteen hundred head of cattle on thousands of acres of grassland. Dad likes his meat organic. We supply a specialized market. We produce five thousand tons of hay a year and keep the range in quality condition." She pushed strands of hair from her eyes. "Dad's a nut about being a good steward of the land."

"I respect that," Justin said. "So you're a cow n' calf operation. I thought rodeo bulls was your thing."

"Who can support themselves on a handful of bulls?" She shot him a sidelong glance that clearly said he was an idiot. "You can't live on rodeo alone. Bulls are just a side hobby of Dad's. He breeds the best rodeo bulls in the world."

"The meanest, for sure," Justin said.

"Dad says you rode Cyclone. That true?" She looked at him with skepticism.

"Yeah."

"Really?"

"Really."

"I thought Dad was joking. No shit?"

"No shit."

"You gotta be one bad-ass cowboy to stay on a Sterling bull." Her voice was suddenly full of awe, eyes shiny with excitement. "Seriously? You rode Cyclone? Holy fucking shit."

He'd seen that look of adulation plenty of times before on rodeo groupies who hung out in cowboy bars hoping to meet the real deal. He looked away from her gaze. What gives? She's in the business and should be more professional.

Through the side mirror he saw dust rising in a steady plume behind the vehicle. The fragrant odor of grass and warm manure came through the window. He breathed in deeply. Hell, he missed the smell of a ranch. They passed white-fenced pastures occupied by appaloosas, paints, Arabians, and quarter horses, grazing and drowsing in the sun. "You got some fine animals here."

"Best money can buy." She wrinkled her nose. "I have nothing to do with the livestock. I stay in the office all day, handle day-to-day operations."

"You don't ride?"

"Nope. Cows, bulls, horses. They're all the same. Big, dirty, smelly."

Not the conversation he expected to be having with Hank Sterling's daughter. A ruckus of hooves, whistles and bawling cattle suddenly caught his attention.

Sarah pulled over and parked. Accompanied by the dogs, they walked to the fence and watched two cowhands herding cattle into a fresh pasture. One cowhand in particular was an ace rider, sitting balanced and instinct-ready on the bay quarter horse beneath him. The bay's well-muscled body and powerful hindquarters made him perfectly suited to the quick maneuvers needed to outsmart a cow. A calf split off from the herd and the bay shot into action, blocking its path with short, precise movements that mirrored those of the calf, steering it back to its mother.

The two riders secured the gate and dismounted behind the Land Cruiser. Outfitted in chaps, jeans, work shirts, and wide-brimmed hats, the two stood together talking. Justin sauntered over to the talented rider who stood as tall as him and had a similar build. "That bay of yours has some serious cow sense," he said in a congenial tone.

The rider turned and Justin found himself staring into the face of a pretty woman about his own age. No makeup, tanned face, hair tucked up under her hat, gray-blue eyes.

"That cow sense comes with years of training," she said without smiling. "And excellent breeding."

"You're about as good at cutting as any rider I've seen," Justin said, caught off guard, and sounding more ingratiating than he intended.

She looked past him as though he were invisible.

He caught a whiff of cinnamon as Sarah jingled up and wrapped an arm around his shoulder. He stiffened, but not wanting to appear impolite, he didn't pull away.

"This is my lil' sis, Cody. Cowgirl extraordinaire." Sarah's voice was tinged with sarcasm. "She'd live on a horse, if she could. We can hardly get her to come in for meals."

Cody's features tightened.

"This is Alex Hamilton. The bull rider Dad hired."

"Alex, huh?" Cody's gaze met his and anger flickered in her eyes. "If he's on the payroll, stop chatting him up and put him to work. We're wasting daylight." She turned to her partner. "Let's get down to bottom pasture. Check on those new calves." Without so much as a glance in Justin's direction, she mounted her horse and rode off with the cowhand. She whistled, and all four dogs bounded after her.

"Nice to meet you, too," Justin said under his breath.

"Don't mind her," Sarah said, pressing her breasts against his arm. "She's gun shy. Especially 'round good-looking guys with gorgeous blue eyes."

He stepped away from her, his face warming. Sarah was sexy as hell, but he wasn't about to encourage a come on from the boss's daughter. Shit, she was gonna be trouble.

Unruffled, Sarah steered him back to the car, lighting a cigarette and shooting out a cloud of smoke. "Cody just got divorced," she said, strapping herself in. "Her ex is a piece of work, I'll tell you. Real psycho. In prison for life, I hope." She continued up the road. "Wanna see the view from the bluff?"

"Sure." He didn't want to be alone with her.

"Ever been married?" She laughed. "No, of course not. You're too young. How old are you?"

"Twenty."

"That all? You look twenty-five. It's the way you carry yourself. Real confident."

"I guess."

Sarah rambled all the way up to the bluff, sharing personal details about the ranch hands that he didn't want to know, and then detouring back to her sister. "You notice how Cody treated me, Alex? Cold, huh?"

He shrugged.

"That's how she's been since moving back home four months ago. We used to be close. Now she's angry all the time. Her claws out in seconds. Granted, she went through hell, but she doesn't have to take it out on me."

Justin listened with detachment. Gossip made him uneasy, and he didn't want to be Sarah's confidante. He planned on leaving this ranch soon enough, collecting nothing for his trouble but a few paychecks.

At the top of the cliff, the view was breathtaking. Untamed earth stretching out for hundreds of miles, spotted with lakes. Spires of pine trees cleaved the blue sky, and two white tailed hawks lazily rode the thermals. The quiet peace of the place filled him. He made an obligatory comment about the view, but Sarah was looking blindly into space, oblivious.

With a brooding expression, she revved the engine and headed back down the hill, picking up her harangue where she left off. "Cody ruined the peace around here, for sure. Dad was thrilled to have her back, though. Even though I do all the bookkeeping and administration. I keep this place running like clockwork, but Cody is his pet. Always has been. Next best thing to the son he always wanted." Sarah wore a deep scowl as she parked the car in the driveway. "We were tomboys for Dad. She and I gave it up when we discovered boys in high school, but now she's back, looking and acting like a man."

Justin wondered if Cody was gay. He hoped so. He didn't need two pretty girls distracting him. Sarah was going to be a handful as it was. "That why he named her Cody?"

"Hell, he didn't name her Cody. Her name's Katie. I don't know what her game is. She doesn't talk to me. I'm alone in the office all day. She's out here with the guys." Her mind seemed to come into sudden focus, and she gave him her full attention, features softening, her knee pressing against his. "Come have coffee with me sometime, Alex."

"Sure thing," he said, finding her abrupt personality changes unsettling. He climbed out, feeling safer with the Cruiser between them.

"Well, I better get you working, or Cody will take my head off later. Can you drive a tractor?"

"I can drive anything with wheels."

She looked at him with appreciation. "Follow me."

Sarah started him out on a tractor mounted with a harrow. He went to work churning manure clods into the fields. Best fertilizer in the world. It'd push up a fertile crop of new grass. For the next few hours, he was content to work alone, breathing in the smell of upturned earth, listening to the gentle sounds of livestock braying, watching the sun travel across the sky. This was his Holy Grail. He knew his soul was tied to land and animals. It's how he intended to live his life until the day he dropped dead out of the saddle.

CHAPTER TWENTY-FOUR

BY TWILIGHT, Justin had loaded the flatbed truck half a dozen times and dropped hay bales in pastures and paddocks across the property. The sky had clouded over and an icy wind came out of the west, cutting through his flannel shirt. Chilled and feeling soreness in muscles not used in a while, he drove back to the barn. By the time the dinner bell echoed across the fields, he was starving, having worked all day without eating. Sarah had told him to enter the dining room through the back door.

On the porch, he slapped dust and hay from his clothes and wiped dirt from the soles of his boots. His hands were numb, and he felt light-headed with hunger. Footsteps came up behind him. He turned and saw Cody, her face flushed from the cold. A tangle of straw-colored hair fell loose around her shoulders. Up close, he saw that her slate-blue eyes were fringed with dark lashes, and her full mouth looked soft and sensitive. Somehow, she looked familiar. "I think we've met somewhere before."

"We never met," she said, eyeing him critically. "But we went to the same high school. I was two years ahead of you." Her face tightened, a faint movement of muscles around her jaw.

"Sorry, don't recall …."

"That's not surprising. You hung out with jocks. A pretty conceited bunch."

Her words stung him, catching him off guard. True, he had hung out with his track mates, but they were mostly shy, not conceited.

"Back then you went by your real name, Justin Powell. You like starting off a new job lying about who you are? You got something to hide, Justin?" Looking at him as though he just climbed out of a manhole, Cody brushed past him, opened the door, and made her way across the floor of a spacious dining room to the head of a long oak table.

He entered the room feeling disoriented, accused of some nebulous crime. The four dogs rushed past him and settled themselves by the big stone hearth where a bright fire roared. Sarah and three rugged cowhands were already seated at the table passing around steaming platters of food. The aroma made his mouth water. Sarah flashed a big smile, the bangles jingling on her wrists as she patted the chair next to her own. Justin moved into her cinnamon scented sphere, grateful for a friendly face, even Sarah's.

"Hi, I'm Justin," he said hurriedly to the men before Sarah could introduce him as Alex. "Justin Powell." He glanced at Cody, saw the merest flicker of expression in her eyes.

Sarah shot him a questioning look. "Justin …" she said, going with it. "This is Roth, Billy, and Nelson, our hard-working ranch hands."

The three tough-looking, sunbaked men staring back at him looked as though they lived in the saddle. They greeted Justin in a friendly manner.

"Sarah says Hank pulled you off the rodeo circuit," Roth said out of the side of his mouth, chewing. He was middle-aged, with a wind-burned face and neck, chapped lips, and thinning gray hair.

"Yep," Justin said.

"Bull rider?" Roth's knife sawed smoothly through a thick, juicy steak.

"Yep." Justin took a bowl of mashed potatoes from Sarah and heaped a good portion on his plate, followed by a grilled steak and roasted asparagus. He wasted no time cutting up the beef, stabbing a piece, and getting it into his mouth.

"I rodeoed when I was your age." Without putting down his flatware, Roth pushed back his left sleeve, revealing long raised scars on his muscled forearm. "Compound fracture. Here and my femur. Got tossed off a maniac bronc. We were miles from a hospital. Nearly bled to death bouncing around in the back of a pickup."

"My uncle rode bulls, too," Billy piped up with a subtle Mexican accent. He was around Justin's age, lean with chiseled features, eyes black as obsidian, a sheath of shaggy hair hanging low on his brow. "Ain't a bone in his body ain't been broke. Now he's held together with nuts and bolts. Walks like Robocop."

All three men laughed, watching Justin's face, waiting for a reaction. He kept eating.

"My cousin got throwed a coupla years back," Nelson said, tearing off half a crescent roll with his teeth. Thirtyish, stocky build, bull neck, over-sized ears poking out of curly red hair, thick red mustache that bobbed when he spoke. "Bull stomped on his head. Squished it like a grape. Now he works for the Salvation Army."

Justin couldn't help but smile at their antics. "Gotta be tough to make it in rodeo. Cowboys compete all the time with injuries that sideline athletes in other sports."

"We've sure seen it all," Roth said. "Busted bones, concussions, torn rotator cuffs, smashed faces …."

"That's enough with the war stories," Sarah interrupted. "I'm eating here."

"Doesn't say much for the intelligence of those cowboys," Cody said dryly. "Considering rodeo doesn't provide health insurance."

"Can't let fear stop you from competing," Justin said.

"Didn't stop you from getting on Cyclone." She looked at him with an expression he interpreted as disapproval.

"Justin rode Cyclone in Arizona," Sarah explained to the men, who were looking bewildered. "For eight seconds."

There was a hushed silence around the table. Eyes widened.

"Fuck that. Cyclone's never been ridden," Roth said. "Who's bullshitting who?"

"Watch your mouth," Cody said.

"It's not bullshit," Sarah said, ignoring her sister. "Tell 'em, Justin."

All eyes turned to Justin. He shrugged. "Dumb luck is all."

"Nothing to do with luck," Nelson said, tone indignant. "You ruined our bull's perfect record. He's thrown thirty riders right outta the chute."

Roth and Billy were looking at Justin with new appreciation.

"All riders want the same thing," Roth said, holding a fork laden with mashed potatoes midway to his mouth. "To ride the rankest bulls in the world. The badder the bull, the higher the rider scores, and the better his paycheck. If the rider gets tossed, the bull scores, and the better our paycheck. Around here, we root for the bull."

"I respect that," Justin said, spreading butter on a crescent roll.

"Our bulls are stars. They know their job," Cody said in a heated tone, gesturing with her knife. "When that chute opens, they're gonna drop a cowboy in the dirt in seconds flat. You're the enemy in *our* camp."

"Cut him some slack," Sarah said. She tucked a loose strand of hair behind her ear and smiled sweetly at Justin.

"I know the reputation of your bulls," Justin said. "World class. Apache's buck-off rate is eighty-four percent. Dumps a rider in three seconds or less."

"Crash-Course has thrown seventy cowboys out of a hundred rides," Roth said with unmistakable pride.

"Crash-Course is a terror for such a compact bull," Justin said. "He's younger and more aggressive."

"Cyclone has now been ridden once, by you, out of thirty-one tries," Nelson said, wiping his mustache with his napkin, still indignant.

"A damn good percentage, if he hangs on to it," Justin said, taking a bite of the warm, buttery roll.

Roth cleared his throat, studied Justin with narrowed eyes. "I don't get why you're here. You gotta be good. Why leave rodeo?"

"Taking a break." Justin kept chewing, satisfying the rumbling in his stomach.

"I saw you on the tractor this afternoon, and later dropping feed," Roth said. "You know what you're doing. You here to do ranch work?"

Justin shrugged. "Whatever needs to be done, I guess. I grew up working spreads around here. Blue Moon, Dickerson, Big T cattle ...."

"Know 'em all," Roth said. "Good people."

Good people unless you were a ward of the state, Justin thought with bitterness. Then it was slave labor and poor living conditions. He didn't like being the center of attention. "This Sterling beef we're eating?"

"Damn straight," Nelson said. "Won't taste nothing finer."

"Most tender steak I've ever had." Justin jabbed another bite into his mouth.

"Grass fed, free range," Sarah said. "No antibiotics. No hormones."

"Just meat the way God made it," Roth said.

Everyone was quiet for a moment, forks and knifes clicking on plates. The fire crackled in the hearth, burning low and sending long flickering shadows up the walls and ceiling. The dogs had rolled over on their sides and were soaking up heat. Roth placed another log on the flames and stoked the embers with a poker, shooting a constellation of sparks up the chimney.

"Wonder where Hank and Bear are," Nelson said. "Bear never misses a meal."

"Looking at bulls in Culver." Cody poured coffee from a carafe into her cup.

"He called," Sarah said. "They're running late. Should be flying back in a couple hours."

It occurred to Justin that the huge building he'd seen down in the flats was a hanger. Hank had a private plane and airstrip. Sweet.

"Where's Justin bunking?" Roth asked, pushing his empty plate away. "It's crowded in the bunkhouse, but we can make room."

"No problem." Justin assumed the biggest cottage he'd seen was the bunkhouse. No doubt, each hand had his own room, but he had no desire to be forced into close quarters with strangers. "I'm used to sleeping in my truck."

"That ain't gonna happen," Cody said. "Can't have you whizzing on Dad's daffodils in the middle of the night."

The hands got some chuckles out of that.

"You can sleep here in one of the guest rooms for now." Cody leaned back into the shadows, her eyes as gray as a wolf's and just as unfriendly. "Sarah can get you settled."

He nodded his thanks.

"Anyone for poker?" Roth asked. "You owe me, Cody."

"Count me out." Cradling her cup, she glanced at Justin and he felt a crackle of toughness coming out of her. She emptied her cup, pushed herself away from the table, and left the room.

"Not much of a talker, is she?" Justin asked.

"Used to be," Nelson said. "Before she married Buddy Jack."

"Jack the Ripper." Sarah said the name as though the words burned her tongue. "Did you know him?"

"No. He graduated two years ahead of me." But Justin knew of the Jack family. Big ranch, big money, politically connected. Buddy, he recalled, had a badass reputation; flirted with everything that had ovaries, smashed up a brand new BMW sports car. His DUI got thrown out in court. Family clout, the rumor went. Cody ended up with him?

"Psycho bastard," Sarah muttered, unaware of the sudden cool temperature at the table. No one caught Justin's eyes. Clearly, the topic of

Cody's marriage made the hands uncomfortable.

"Nelson, Billy, poker?" Roth's words cut through the taut silence.

"Hell no," Billy said. "Last time, you took me for everything but my whitey tighties."

"Me neither. I'm tired of being skinned. You never lose." Nelson looked at Justin. "You've been warned. He don't take prisoners."

Roth looked at Justin.

Justin put up his hands. "I've been warned."

"Well, if we ain't doing poker, I'm done." Roth stood up and stretched. The three hands left the table together with a loud scraping of chairs and boots scuffing the floor. Then the room fell silent, except for the fire popping and hissing in the grate.

CHAPTER TWENTY-FIVE

SULLY PARKED his truck in Maggie's driveway and sat for a moment, his mind jumping from the violent images of Eric's death to the beautiful custom home nestled in the forested hills above Bend. It was easy to imagine Eric as a carefree teenager in baggy shorts and sneakers, rushing from the house with golf clubs or a tennis racket. He could almost hear the wheels of his skateboard coursing down the driveway.

Then he pictured Eric as he had known him, dressed in cammies, riding shotgun in an armored Humvee, a grin ever ready on his face. The sensation of Eric sitting next to him suddenly felt so real the hair rose on his forearms. The setting sun streaming through the windshield felt warm on his skin, as near a touch from a ghost as he could imagine. Sully fingered the St. Christopher medal hanging from his neck. Hope you're at peace, Lil' Bro.

He grabbed the grocery bag and strode up to Maggie's door, feeling Eric's presence shadowing him. The wind was kicking up and cumulous clouds the size of schooners drifted across the darkening sky. Snow melting from the eaves of the roof pattered a melodic rhythm on the saturated earth. He rang the bell, removed his hat.

Maggie opened the door, a chef apron tied around her waist and a smudge of flour whitening one cheek. The dimming sunlight caught her eyes just right and they sparkled like opals. He was taken by how pretty she looked.

"Hey, Sully," she smiled. "Come on in."

He matched her smile, not sure whether to give her a hug or a hand shake. He did neither. An awkward moment passed between them. He tapped the bag. "I brought dessert."

"Great. Just about time to eat." She turned and he followed, his eyes taking in her shapely figure. Dressed in jeans and a t-shirt with her hair in a ponytail, she looked as lithe as a teenager.

"I'm trying something new," she said as they entered the kitchen. "Hope you're hungry."

"I can always eat."

Bowls, canisters, and measuring cups were strewn across the counters and a shapeless mound of dough was plunked on a cutting board. Something cooking in a pot on the stove smelled delicious. Suddenly he was starving. "I thought you didn't cook."

"This isn't cooking, Sully," she said. "It's following a recipe. It's not creative but I'm tired of frozen dinners."

"Beef stew in Burgundy sauce," he read from the open cookbook. "Fancy."

"And buttermilk biscuits, I hope." Blowing a loose wisp of hair from her face, she assaulted the dough on the board with the rolling pin. The gluey mixture stuck to both the roller and her fingers.

With amusement, Sully watched her struggle. "My mom always puts flour on the rolling pin first, and sprinkles some on the dough." His attention was diverted to the stove, where the contents of the pot began to bubble over and hiss into the burner.

Maggie gasped. "Oh, my stew."

She and Sully reached for the pot at the same time. Their hands met, shooting off a little spark between them. "Allow me," he mused, lifting the lid with a potholder and turning down the flame. "Crisis over. Hmmm. Smells good."

"Thanks. As you can see, I'm a bit of a terror in the kitchen."

"The terrorist chef. Catchy. Maybe fodder for a new TV show. Let me help with those biscuits." He rolled up his sleeves, washed and dried his hands, and held them up like a surgeon. "Step aside, Madam. Watch and learn."

She chuckled, handing him the roller.

After scraping off the rolling pin, he dusted it with flour, sprinkled more on the cutting board, then executed his mother's technique which he had observed since he was knee high, standing on a chair at the counter. The dough spread smoothly across the board.

"Good job. You're a genius."

"Runs in the family. How thick do you want it?"

She looked up at him over the cookbook, her reading glasses low on her nose. "The recipe says half an inch."

"Got a ruler, or do you trust me?"

Her eyes sparkled with good humor. "Trust you."

Using an upside-down glass, he cut out the biscuits and lined them on the oiled cooking sheet. Once they were safely in the oven, he helped her clean the kitchen. "Seems you found a use for every dish you own."

"No, there's still a bowl in the cabinet." She washed and he dried, then she removed her apron and ushered him to the barstools lining the island. "Enough work. Sit, drink, relax." They sat and she gestured to two bottles of wine sitting on the counter. "Merlot, or Cabernet?"

"Hmmm. Tough choice," Sully said, mystified. "You choose, and I'll pretend I know the difference."

"Cabernet it is." She expertly removed the cork and filled two long stemmed glasses.

He sipped, enjoying the rich blend of flavors in his mouth. "Nice. I'm really starting to like this stuff."

"We'll make a connoisseur of you yet." Maggie swirled the wine in her glass. "This aged really well. My husband put it in the wine cellar twenty years ago." She took a sip, nodded toward his grocery bag. "What's for dessert?"

He reached into the bag and pulled out a bottle of root beer and vanilla ice cream. "Floats."

Her eyes brightened. "I love root beer floats. Aha. Eric told you."

"Guilty as charged." He crossed the room, put the contents in the fridge, and reseated himself. "Alcohol was nixed in Afghanistan, but root beer and ice cream were unlimited, and it was cold. A plus, when the temperature was spiking at a hundred and ten. The heat could melt the tread on your Nikes."

She had put out salsa and chips. They both dipped and crunched.

"Eric and I drank floats and watched movies on our days off," he said. "We had a limited collection. We watched the same movies dozens of times." He crunched, swallowed. "He said you were both movie buffs."

"Understatement. We've seen every movie ever made at least twice." She sipped her wine. "We used to quiz each other on movie quotes."

"He did that with me, too. I didn't know half of them." He smiled, remembering how Eric acted out the characters, mimicking their tone and inflection to perfection.

"Try one on me." Her eyes lit up.

"Okay." He thought for a moment. "'I love the smell of napalm in the morning.'"

"Too easy. *Apocalypse Now*." She thought for a moment. "Here's one for you." Her face got tense and she said in a belligerent tone, "You want the truth? You can't handle the truth!"

"Jack Nicholson. *A Few Good Men*."

She raised a brow. "I thought you weren't good at this."

"That's one of the movies we watched over and over. Here's a quote that's more obscure. 'Badges? We ain't got no badges. We don't need no badges.'"

"That's the worst Mexican accent I ever heard," she laughed. "You were going for the guy in *The Treasure of the Sierra Madre*. One of Eric's favorites."

"Correctamundo. No one did accents better than Eric." A sudden memory of Eric on patrol made him chuckle.

"What?"

"One night we had to deal with some unfriendly elders in a remote village. They wouldn't let us drive through town without showing credentials. Eric did the whole Sierra Madre shtick. *Badges? We ain't got no badges. We don't need no badges. I don't have to show you any stinking badges.* Our translator looked at Eric like he was nuts. The guys in my squad were falling over laughing."

Maggie laughed, too. "Did they let you pass?"

"Yeah, for five packs of chewing gum." He was happy to make her laugh, and to share memories of Eric.

The oven buzzer went off.

"Time to eat. Wanna grab the biscuits? I'll ladle the stew."

"Teamwork." He slid the biscuits from the baking pan onto a platter and they sat at the counter with steaming bowls of stew. Maggie refilled their glasses.

"I really missed my mom's biscuits over there. They were a staple at our house." He picked a biscuit off the platter, dropped it on his plate. "Hot." He cut it in half, slathered on butter, took a bite.

"What's the verdict?" she asked, watching him closely.

"Hmmm." He brushed crumbs from his shirt. "Mom, forgive me. These are just as good."

Maggie beamed. "Try the stew."

He blew on a spoonful, tasted it. "Good. This beef's really tender. You must've beaten the hell out of it."

"Aren't you supposed to? I used a hammer." Her face was flushed with pleasure. "Actually, it's the Burgundy. I added extra. When in doubt, douse."

"Can't go wrong." He buttered another biscuit, ate half in one bite.

He and Maggie made easy small talk while they ate. She was a good listener, and she encouraged him to talk about what he loved most. Everything horses. He rambled on through two bowls of stew, sharing how much he loved being back in the saddle, and how rewarding it was to work with horses. "I have a half dozen reining horses that need serious attention. Before I left, they were like Marines fresh out of boot camp, obeying hand gestures and voice commands instantaneously. Now they're fat and lazy. From a full lope, Amigo used to stop on a dime, two feet in front of my face. Now he'd kill me if I didn't jump out of the way."

She looked impressed. "Wow, horse whisperer."

"Actually, that would be my dad. He's a rodeo legend. The Horse Whisperer is mute next to him."

She pushed her empty bowl away, moved her wine glass closer. "You learned a lot from him, didn't you?"

"Everything. Especially discipline. Dad made me practice, practice, practice. Seems I spent most of my life in the saddle. Even eating and sleeping."

She emptied the last of the wine into their glasses and opened the other bottle. "Sorry to bring this up Sully, but I heard on the news last week that some champion horses were stolen in your county. A rancher was murdered. Pretty scary stuff."

"He was my neighbor." Sully cleared his throat. "I found the body."

Maggie's eyes widened. Her hand froze with her glass halfway to her mouth. She set it back down on the table.

"Monty Blanchert. I knew him all my life. Did chores for him when I was a kid."

"Are you okay?" She touched him lightly on the arm. "Are your horses safe?"

His gut tightened. "My best stud was stolen the night before I came home."

"I'm so sorry to hear that," she said, her features softening. "It's frightening, bad people targeting your community."

Sully wasn't afraid, just angry as hell.

"How are your parents?" she asked. "They must be so glad you're home."

"They separated. Mom lives here in town. Dad had a stroke six months ago. I just brought him home from a nursing home." Sully shifted his weight and released a breath that sounded world weary, even to him. "I'm taking care of him."

"That's a lot on your plate," she said gently. Her eyes fixed on his, infinitely compassionate.

"Yeah ... well ... life throws curveballs. You just keep on playing."

They were both quiet. He was sorry the conversation took a bad turn. He wanted to take a break from his troubles, park them outside her door and not burden her. She didn't need any more sadness in her life. He polished off the rest of his stew, wondering if he was overstaying his welcome. Maybe it was time to go.

"Time for root beer floats," she said in a lighter tone.

"Sure." He was in no hurry to get back to the ranch.

"How about you do the floats and I'll make popcorn, then we can plop in front of the big screen. I have hundreds of DVDs."

He smiled. "Chances are I could find one I like."

Sully picked *Something about Mary*, a light, corny comedy he'd seen dozens of times with other homesick Marines lusting after Cameron Diaz.

Maggie put another log in the fireplace and stoked up the flames. He settled into the recliner, she nested on the sofa with a quilt thrown over her legs. They started watching the movie, munching popcorn and drinking floats, and soon they were both laughing out loud. Sully knew the script by heart. When he mimicked the voices during the funniest lines, Maggie burst out laughing. She was an easy audience.

He enjoyed the heat of the crackling fire and the warmth of Maggie's company. His gaze shifted from the TV to photos of Eric and his father smiling down from the mantle. He felt safe and comfortable in the surroundings that had shaped Eric's character, and instilled in him the courage to go to a war zone to help his country and injured Marines. In his absence, Sully knew Eric would appreciate him watching out for his mom. He stole a glance at Maggie. Her eyes were locked on the screen and she looked relaxed, her cares transported far away. She laughed suddenly and met his eyes. He smiled back, barely aware he was doing it.

During the second movie, Sully passed out. Maggie let him sleep and woke him after midnight with a gentle hand on his shoulder.

"You work too hard, Sully," she said at the door.

He shrugged, shaking off the cobwebs.

She gave him a warm hug and tucked a bag under his arm. "Biscuits and beef stew for lunch tomorrow. Same time next week?"

"Sure thing. Thanks for a great evening, Maggie."

CHAPTER TWENTY-SIX

"CAN I HELP YOU with the dishes?" Justin asked Sarah, even though he was dead tired.

"Hell, no." She let out a rich, throaty laugh that lit up her pretty face. "Billy's parents do the cooking and cleaning. They go to mass on Sunday night, but they'll take care of it when they get home."

"How long have they worked here?" he asked, making conversation.

"Forever. Billy was born on the ranch. Now he's eighteen. They have their own cottage."

"Maybe you could show me to my room," he said politely.

"Happy to." Her lips spread into a sultry smile, as though he'd made an intimate suggestion.

"Then I'll pull my truck around back and unload my stuff."

When she stood, he saw Sarah had gained a couple inches in height since the afternoon. Her long legs now ended in four-inch heels. How women walked in those things, he had no idea. She had somehow managed to squeeze into a sprayed on red dress that accentuated her curvy figure. He followed her down the hall, a little hypnotized by the sway of her hips.

Sarah turned into a doorway and stepped aside to let him enter. The bedroom, he saw with a rush of pleasure, was spacious and handsomely furnished. Knotty pine furniture, over-stuffed leather chairs, Navajo rugs on the walls, handmade quilts folded across the bed. Through an open door, he saw brass fixtures and granite countertops in the adjoining bathroom. This kind of luxury he'd only seen in magazines. Too nice for a ranch hand. Maybe tomorrow they'd put him in the barn.

Feeling the tightness in his muscles, he couldn't wait to take a hot shower and get horizontal between the sheets. "This is great, Sarah." He turned and felt a jolt of annoyance. Sarah had planted herself on the bed, looking relaxed and in no hurry to leave. *Shit.*

"You don't talk much, do you?" she said, that lazy drawl returning to her voice.

"Not much to talk about."

"I'm sure that's not true." She pulled a pack of cigarettes from her pocket, shook one out, tucked it between her teeth, and lit it. She inhaled deeply, exhaled from her nose and mouth. The way she looked up at him through her lowered lashes, the way she smoked, reminded him of Lauren Bacall in her early movies. Cinnamon smoke drifted into the room. Feeling bushwhacked, he thought for a moment, considering how to politely extract her and her cigarette from his room.

"So what's with the name change from Alex to Justin?" she asked.

"I use Alex as a rodeo name."

"Why?"

"What are those things you're smoking?"

"They're French. Less nicotine."

His eyes stung. "Do you mind not smoking in here? I'm allergic."

"Oh, sorry." She sucked in a drag as she walked into the bathroom, then she tossed the cigarette into the toilet. His gut tightened as she resettled herself on the bed lying on her side, head propped on a fist. She watched him like a cat, docile, all curves, brows arched expectantly. He felt himself getting aroused at the prospect of what she was offering. She seemed to know what he was feeling. He looked away.

"We all went to Beaverhead High. Small world, huh?" she said.

"Yeah, small."

"Your name really Justin?"

From down the hall, Justin heard the door open and shut in the dining room, followed by heavy footsteps. "Sarah?" A man's voice boomed. "Sarah, you here?"

"Back here." She stood quickly, smoothed the surface of the bed, yanked down her dress, and reached the door the same time as a man in the hallway.

"Hey, baby," he said, pulling her into his arms. "You all dolled up for me?"

"Just for you, darlin'."

He wrapped his arms around her waist and lowered his lips to hers.

Even in the dim light, Justin saw that the man was a hulk, around six-foot-six, built like a lineman. In her heels, the top of Sarah's head brushed his earlobe, and his bulk gave the impression that her curvy frame was reed slender.

"Thought you weren't coming home for a couple hours," Sarah purred. "Didn't hear you fly over."

"We came in from the north."

The man's posture grew rigid as he spied Justin over her shoulder.

"Oh, this is Justin Powell," she said, pulling away. "The bull rider Dad hired. Justin, this is Todd Behr, our livestock foreman, and my fiancé. We all call him Bear, as in grizzly." She looked up at him. "I was just showing him his room."

Bear's eyes traveled down her body, then scanned the room, the bed, and came back to Justin, giving him a good look over. Justin could read his thoughts. The man's cold expression made the hair rise on his arms. Justin stared back in equal measure. It was a pissing contest, each telegraphing his disdain for the other. Bear blinked first.

"So, you're the bull rider?" He stepped into the light of the room, his voice matching his bulk. A low rumble.

"Yep."

"You up from Arizona?"

"Yep."

"We weren't expecting you today."

Justin shrugged.

"Hank said you handled yourself pretty decent. Rode Cyclone, huh?"

"Did my best."

"Not something that makes us too happy around here, but we respect talent." The big man crossed the floor and held out a paw the size of a frying pan. The two shook hands. Bear squeezed. Justin didn't wince, though it hurt like hell. It was meant as a warning.

"If you're here to work with livestock, you'll be working under me," Bear said with a slightly menacing tone

Great. If that were the case, this job would be hell. Justin had worked for men like Bear before, men who liked to throw their weight around and intimidate people. He wondered what Sarah saw in him. The hulk was handsome in a hollow-cheeked, bull-necked sort of way, all muscle and attitude. If she got off on brute strength, this was the guy. He envisioned

Bear slapping hay bales together like cymbals while Sarah swooned. Justin didn't foresee himself knocking back a few cold ones with the couple anytime soon. He wanted them gone.

"Let me get you some dinner, darlin'," Sarah crooned. "You must be starving."

"Food sounds good." He gave a curt nod to Justin and followed Sarah out of the room.

Justin left the door open a couple inches, listening to their voices drift down the hall.

"What the hell were you doing in his room dressed like that?"

"I dressed up for you."

"Where's your ring?"

"I forgot it." Sarah's tone was indignant.

"What's he doing sleeping in the house?"

"That was Cody's decision," Sarah said. "The bunkhouse is full."

"Cody's, huh?" His tone warmed a bit.

"Yeah, Cody. Why don't you give her the fifth degree?"

A pause.

"Sorry, babe. Come here."

Justin closed the door, relieved to put a barricade between himself and the high-strung personalities he'd encountered today. It was crystal clear what Sarah's intentions had been. She figured she'd have a couple hours to romp in the sack with Justin before her fiancé showed up. Justin would not have let that happen, but if he had, and Bear walked in on them, he figured he'd be ripped into flank steaks before any questions were asked. Though engaged, Sarah hadn't worn her ring. Helluva thing, cheating on her man like that.

He stripped off his dirty clothes and got into the shower. The hot water felt good on his sore muscles and the thick lather of soap washed away the dust, but it didn't wash away the bad feeling festering in his gut. Seemed he'd be navigating a minefield on this job, trying to avoid conflicts with his nut-job co-workers—something he'd had to do a good part of his life, moving from home to home. Chalk it up to human nature. Seemed there were always one or two jackasses who were determined to make his life miserable. He could practice civil disobedience for only so long before he fought back and raised some holy hell. Thankfully, he could always count on doing a stint back at St. Teresa's before his next placement.

Temporary refuge.

As he toweled dry, Justin's thoughts turned to rodeo. He felt a keen longing to be back on the circuit where he didn't have to put up with people's bullshit. Only one thing prevented him from jumping into his truck and hightailing it out of there. Hank Sterling. In Red Rock, Hank had taken the time to single him out, give him some sage advice, and offer him a job, even though he was a total stranger mixed up with bad company. Hank had seen something in him that he didn't see in himself and had fronted him money when he was dead broke. Justin had given Hank his word that he wouldn't bail. He aimed to keep that promise.

CHAPTER TWENTY-SEVEN

AFTER WHISTLER'S STAMPEDE, Joe kept to himself, eating in his room, lying in the darkness watching TV, his expression sullen. Sully checked on him regularly and helped him make his slow journey down the hall to the bathroom. He insisted on using his walker. Click, scoot, click, scoot.

Sully admired his father's determination to build up his strength, but he resented taking an eternity to walk down the hall when he could be getting work done. Patience.

After dinner, Sully spotted his father's anti-depressant prescription in the bathroom trashcan. He fished it out, spilled the pills on the countertop, and counted them. All thirty pills were there. It had been obvious that Joe was deeply depressed and now he knew why. He stopped by Joe's room and found his father propped up in bed watching the news with the volume turned up high. Butch lay beside him gnawing on a chew toy.

After waiting for a commercial, Sully picked up the remote and muted the sound.

Joe glanced up, eyebrows coming together in a scowl. "Whatcha want?"

Sully held up the pills.

Joe glared.

"Why aren't you taking them?" Sully saw the strong jaw and hardness around Joe's eyes.

"Gimme back my remote."

"In a minute. First, talk to me."

"You the Gestapo now?"

"Dad, you can have bad side effects quitting these, cold turkey."

"I ain't taking that shit." Throwing the bedcovers aside, Joe stood, holding on to the edge of the nightstand. He snatched the container from Sully's hand and threw it forcefully into the trashcan. Butch jumped to his feet at the sharp clatter and watched them nervously.

Trying to keep his cool, Sully reached into the can, retrieved the container, and placed it on the nightstand. "Try taking a half tablet. I'll cut them up for you."

"You take those zombie pills yourself if you like 'em so much," Joe barked, voice vibrating. "Don't try drugging me so you can take over the ranch."

"What're you talking about?"

"You think I didn't notice you painted the place?" Red blotches appeared on Joe's neck, worked their way up to his face. "What was wrong with it before? Your mom 'n me picked that paint together."

"It wasn't white anymore. It looked dirty."

"You didn't ask me first, did you?"

"I wanted to surprise you."

"I was surprised, all right." His whole body tightened up, neck veins bulging. "Where's Jasper? You think I'm crazy? You think I can't see the bull pasture from the window? You think I can't tell a bull's missing?"

Sully's gut tightened. "He's sold, Dad. Sorry, but we needed to pay bills."

"What else did you sell?"

"Bella, one of the brood mares."

"Jesus Christ Almighty! You sold my Bella?" He looked stricken. "That mare throws perfect colts."

"They got a good home. The sheriff bought them."

"Why didn't you ask me first?" Joe's words were now almost indecipherable. Spit foamed in the corner of his mouth. "I call the shots around here, not you!"

Sully stood frozen.

"Don't make any more fucking decisions about anything. You understand me?"

"It had to be done."

"Get outta here."

Sully stood there stupidly.

"Get out!" Joe jabbed him sharply in the chest, pushing him out of the room. The door slammed shut in Sully's face so hard the walls vibrated. Butch started barking. He heard his father's muffled voice consoling him and then the TV blared back on.

Travis rushed into the hallway from the kitchen. "What the hell?"

"Dad's pissed that we painted the house and sold Jasper and Bella." Sully suddenly felt twelve years old, blindsided by his father's hair-trigger temper. Only back then the angry words were accompanied by a cuff to the ear or a boot to the seat of his pants. His father's idea of child rearing was to knock sense into Sully first and ask questions later. Anger swelled in his chest. His hand balled into a fist. He felt like smashing something.

"Easy, Sully."

Sully unclenched his hand.

"Follow me. You need a beer." Travis led the way to the kitchen.

The room still smelled like the onions, fish, and potatoes they'd had for dinner. Travis had done the dishes and they were stacked high in the dish rack, an intricate balancing act. He didn't like using the dishwasher. Sully sank into a chair, eyes studying the worn tabletop as he resurrected a slew of past injuries inflicted by his father. "I'd like to pack him up and dump him off at the nursing home. Let him rot there."

Still dressed in his work clothes, sleeves rolled up to the elbow, Travis opened the fridge, pulled out two Millers, twisted off the caps, placed one in front of Sully, sat down with the other. "Drink."

Sully took a long pull of beer. The act of doing something normal had a neutralizing effect. He met the old Paiute's patient brown eyes. Fatherly concern. No judgment. He felt his anger taper off a notch.

"Your intentions were good Sully, bringing Joe home. But I agree, we brought him back too soon. We shoulda given you more time to adjust, to make your own imprint on the ranch."

Sully listened, his fingers picking at the corner of the label on the bottle.

"Joe's always been top dog, demanding everything be done his way, pretty much ignoring anyone else's opinion." Travis shifted in his chair, his expression solemn. "Probably one of the reasons you left home and joined the Corps."

Sully nodded.

"You've changed, Sully. He hasn't. You became a Marine. Moved up the ranks. Commanded men. Made all the decisions." Travis sipped his beer, his manner thoughtful. "Now you're home, and you're not going to go back to being second man down."

"Maybe I should've consulted him before I sold the livestock," Sully said, feeling a stab of guilt. No one could push him into a tailspin of insecurity like his father.

"You were trying to spare him grief. Tough decisions had to be made. Bills had to be paid. This ranch strayed off course. You're getting us all back to center." Travis leaned back in his chair, his knotty fingers relaxed around his bottle. "Your dad's gonna be messed up for a while until he kicks that medication. Ignore him. Keep doing what you're doing. Don't back down."

Travis had always been the voice of reason in the tumult of every storm. This was their pattern. Joe hit. Travis soothed.

"You and Joe are gonna butt heads from now on. Get used to it." There was a touch of humor in his eyes. "Joe needs to learn to share the power."

Travis was right. Things had changed and would never revert to the old ways. "He doesn't know about Gunner yet. All hell's gonna break loose when he finds out."

"He'll blame me for that. Not the first time, not the last." Surprisingly, Travis smiled, his eyes crinkling into deep lines. "I'll tell him about Gunner. You just stay clear of the fallout."

Joe's wrath never fazed Travis. As far back as Sully could remember nothing much ever fazed Travis. Only once had he seen the old Paiute break down. It took a hell of a tragedy. After twenty-one years of marriage, his wife Chenoah died in a car crash while returning home from the reservation after visiting her family. It had been a snowy night. Icy roads. Steep grades. An eighteen-wheeler veered across the highway into her lane and hit her head on, crushing her Jeep into an accordion. The news of her death devastated everyone, especially Travis, who turned into a dead man walking. He hid out in his cottage by the creek, looked like hell when he emerged with a few packed bags. With no explanation, he left the ranch and went to live with Chenoah's family on the rez. Sully was thirteen.

Without Travis to act as a buffer between himself and Joe, it proved to be the toughest year of Sully's young life. Joe's abuse knew no bounds. Travis returned a year later with no fanfare and moved into the old bunkhouse. He had changed into a solemn man, but his Teflon shield was fitted back in place, repelling "bad vibes" like water off polished glass.

Travis's words broke into Sully's thoughts. "Wanna play cards?"

"Sure. Why not." Sully got up to get the cards out of the junk drawer. Next to the paperclips and pencils sat a stack of worn postcards held together by a rubber band. He removed the rubber band and sorted through them. They were the cards he'd sent home during his two deployments. The edges were dog-eared and frayed as though they'd been read countless times. "Who put these in here? Mom?"

"Joe. He took them out all the time. Read them over and over."

Confounded, Sully replaced them as they were. He felt a touch of resentment that his father was incapable of showing affection openly. The dog-eared postcards testified that he had a tender streak hidden beneath the gruffness, but finding it was like drilling for oil. Hit or miss.

Sully got out two more Millers, passed one to Travis, and took his seat at the table. After shuffling the cards, he and Travis played gin rummy for an hour or so, drank more beer, and shared some laughs. Sully's mood lightened. Neither won at gin.

"I'm done," Sully said, slapping his cards on the table. The beer and the weight of the day brought on a heavy feeling of fatigue. He tossed the empty bottles in the trash, slapped Travis on the back, and shuffled down the hall to get cleaned up. He heard loud noises erupting from his father's TV. Guns shooting, tires squealing. Every night, Joe fell asleep with the TV blaring. Sully made it a habit to turn it off and take Butch out for his last potty run.

Pausing outside Joe's door, he felt a hardness creep into his heart. He was tempted to go to his own room and let Travis take over Joe's caretaking. But he recognized that he was indebted to his father. Though their temperaments were vastly different, he had inherited traits from Joe that had served him well in life. A strong work ethic, and a commitment to duty. Floating beneath his anger and resentment, he knew he loved his father, and respected him. They were as intertwined as the roots of a gnarly old tree.

Sully opened the door. Butch jumped off the bed and frantically pawed his legs, tail wagging at high speed. Sully turned off the TV and took Butch out into the crisp night air. They hiked above the hayfields following the trail along the edge of the forest. Hillocks of snow glistened in the darkness, the sky was choked with stars, and the luminous moon winked at him through tree branches. From the deep velvet tunnels between the trees, the forest gave off a blue-black chill. Sully heard the scuffling of animals and wondered what creatures were silently watching. Deer, owl, raccoon, skunk, fox?

Butch scurried on top of the snow like a bird, barely making an imprint, while Sully's boots crunched deeply. The wind carried the soft sound of horses neighing, and he could hear the rush of Wild Horse Creek cascading over rocks. The peace of the country seeped into his soul, and it felt healing to be out of the house, away from his father's sense of ownership. His lingering feelings of resentment shifted to pragmatism and his thoughts turned to projects needing his attention in the morning.

CHAPTER TWENTY-EIGHT

HARD-WORKING MEN needed fuel and Justin was happy to see that the hands at Silver O were well fed. Standing in line at the buffet table in the dining room he covered two plates with eggs, bacon, sausage, potatoes, pancakes, fresh fruit, biscuits and gravy. Carafes of strong coffee waited on the table.

"You're allowed to get seconds," Roth chuckled, sitting down across from him.

"Wanted to save myself a trip." After smothering his pancakes in butter and syrup, he ate heartily, listening to the small talk of the cowhands. He was scraping the last bite off his plate when he heard the jingle of bracelets, caught a whiff of cinnamon, and felt a hand land firmly on his shoulder. Feeling his muscles tense beneath her fingers, he looked up at Sarah's painted-on face. Today she had the good sense to camouflage her sexy figure beneath a baggy work shirt, and he didn't have to work so hard to keep his eyes above her neckline. He scanned the room, but the hulking foreman was nowhere in sight.

"Morning, boys," she said, chipper.

"Morning," Roth and Nelson said in chorus. Billy nodded, cheeks packed with food.

"You done, Justin? Dad wants to see you."

"Sure thing." Justin gulped down the last of his coffee, placed his hat on his head and grabbed his jacket from the back of the chair. He walked with Sarah through a spacious lodge-style living room that featured a cavernous fireplace, oversize furniture, large western paintings, Navajo rugs, and an antler chandelier that must've weighed a ton. Sarah wasn't kidding when she said Hank liked things big. She walked him down a polished hardwood hallway, opened half a double door, and motioned him inside. With a flirtatious smile, she closed it behind him.

Hank stood talking on his phone in front of a huge picture window that offered a spectacular view of his property. In the distance, the white peaks of the Cascades cut into a turquoise sky. Trying not to eavesdrop, Justin removed his hat and gazed around the room. Masculine. Stone fireplace, big leather chairs, bookshelves lined with rodeo trophies and buckles. Photos on the walls depicted Hank riding bulls and posing with famous cowboys and politicians, while his daughters, from toddlers to adults, were posed mostly on horseback dressed as cowgirls. Hank's desktop held two computer monitors, a sculpted bronze stallion, and stacks of folders and books. A framed photo of a beautiful woman with long red hair and green eyes commanded the space in the middle of the desk. From her resemblance to Cody and Sarah, Justin knew it was Olivia.

"Good to hear from you, too, Chuck. See ya in Boise." Hank stuffed his phone into his breast pocket and shot Justin a dazzling smile. A deep blue chambray shirt brought out the steel gray of his eyes, his silver hair was brushed in a youthful style, and he moved with an air of easy authority. Hank was that rare man, Justin thought, who looked comfortable in his own skin.

"See you made it here in record time," Hank said.

"I'm a goal-oriented guy."

"How's it feel to be back in Oregon?"

"Good."

Hank rounded his desk and sat on the edge. "Have a seat."

Justin sank into a mahogany-colored leather chair and admired Hank's hand-tooled boots.

"I talked to Cody this morning. Seems she stripped away your alias last night."

Justin sized him up. The man looked relaxed and cheerful. He decided to go with the mood, matching Hank's light tone, "Yeah, looks like I've been busted."

"I don't know what you're dodging, Justin, but your secret's safe here."

Justin studied him, suspicious.

"It might surprise you that I already knew who you were back in Red Rock."

"No way."

"If I hadn't, I wouldn't have offered you a job. You were messing with some real slime. I imagine from your long stay in Arizona, Porky caught up with you."

Hell. Justin felt the heat rush up to his face. Crossing one ankle over a knee, he picked at the frayed hem of his jeans. He was thankful when Hank started talking again.

"As a matter of fact, the first time I saw you, you were just a freshman in high school."

Justin looked up, surprised. He waited to see where this was going.

"Someone with your athletic ability isn't easily forgotten. I went to most of the games at Beaverhead High with the girls. From the very beginning, you stood out. I watched your skill as a sprinter progress through high school."

Wow. Hank had been at his track meets.

"You were fast. You had that special quality that separates winners from losers."

Justin's coaches said as much. They called it drive. Justin called it desperation. A need to pull himself out of his hardscrabble existence and cast a good light on his family name. He owed his mother that much.

"You put in a helluva lot of practice," Hank said. "Not many young people have focus at that age. They party, scrape by."

"My life was pretty much ranch work, homework, and sports. I didn't have time to hang out much with anyone beside my teammates."

"Good discipline. Builds mental toughness. Hones your instincts."

Justin worked his fingers around the brim of his hat, feeling self-conscious under the glow of Hank's warm praise. Since the beating and his forced departure from rodeo, he'd felt demoralized. Hank's words were like a shot of oxygen, pumping up his deflated ego. A world-class champion himself, Hank understood what it took to be a winner: the personal sacrifice, long hours, and pushing yourself beyond the point where your body wanted to quit.

"Let's take a walk, Justin. I'll show you around." Hank grabbed a denim jacket off the coat rack, wrestled into it, then settled a black Stetson on his head and adjusted it to the correct angle. Justin followed suit. They left the house and walked up the dirt road leading to the barn. Immediately their path was crisscrossed by the four dogs, their noses alternately sniffing the breeze and mowing the earth. The crisp morning air was seasoned with sage and juniper, and the braying of cows and twittering birds provided melodic background music. Nut-job personalities aside, Justin determined there was no ranch on earth more beautiful than Sterling O.

"After high school, you dropped off the radar screen," Hank said, picking up the conversation where it had left off. "I heard you went off to college on a sports scholarship."

"That's right."

"I was pleased to hear that. Then I'll be doggoned if you didn't start popping up again last year at small rodeos throughout the west." Hank glanced over at him, watching his expression. "You decided to drop out of school. Turn pro."

Justin kicked a rock up the road in front of him. He didn't like talking about himself. "I didn't want to drop out. My scholarship lasted two years. I didn't have the money to continue. My plan was—"

"Make some quick money and continue your education?"

"Pretty much."

"How's that been working for you?"

Justin looked away, embarrassed.

They reached an enclosed pasture and several horses trotted over to meet them at the fence. Justin and Hank reached out and stroked their long silky necks. A red dun mustang with a deep chest and short back blew softly into Justin's hand as he stroked the velvety underside of his mouth. "Man, you're one handsome animal."

In response, the mustang pawed the ground with one leg and tossed back his head, dark mane flying. Justin laughed. "He's got spirit."

"I see you like horses," Hank said.

"Yeah. Grew up with 'em. Never owned one though." He sighed. "Someday …."

"This is Porter."

"He a Kiger?"

"He is." Hank looked at Justin with appreciation.

"A herd of Kigers was discovered in southeastern Oregon in 1977. Their lineage can be traced back to the Spaniards in the seventeenth century." Justin combed his fingers through the mustang's dark mane. "Left alone in the wild for hundreds of years toughened them up. They're sure-footed and fearless."

"You know your mustangs."

"I trained a few."

"At the Cotter ranch?"

Justin nodded, not inviting further conversation. Neil Cotter had worked Justin to the bone. He lost ten pounds in the eight months he lived there, part from hard labor and part from depression. Neil wanted to officially adopt him, but Justin's track coach became concerned and fought Social Services to get him out of there. Justin went back to St. Teresa to await his next sentence to foster care, not knowing the worst was yet to come. The McKinley clan, and Jessica.

Hank dragged a hand over his jaw. "Neil's old school. A tough old cowboy."

"Nice way of putting it."

Hank studied him carefully, his eyes narrowing as though reading Justin's thoughts. "How many foster homes were you in?"

Justin looked at him sharply. "How'd you know that?"

"I make it my business to know who works for me, Justin. How many families?"

"Thirteen." He tugged his hat lower on his forehead

"More than me." Hank's expression shadowed and his jaw tightened for a moment. "Tough life, isn't it?"

"You an orphan, too?"

Hank nodded, looking straight ahead over the heads of the horses. He turned to Justin, half smiled. "Porter's yours while you're here."

Justin blinked. Deeply pleased, he tried not to show it. "He's really fine. Needs some grooming. That winter coat needs brushing off."

"You own a saddle?"

"No sir."

"We got plenty in the tack room. Look for the one decorated with pieces of beaten silver. It'll fit Porter well."

"Thank you. I'll keep it in good condition."

"Good."

They stood in comfortable silence, continuing to give the animals affection.

"Wanna see our bulls?" Hank asked.

Justin grinned. "Just waiting for you to ask."

Hank led him past the barn to a large corral that was configured to mimic a rodeo arena. Two of the cowhands sat mounted in the center and Bear was up on the rail overlooking the chute.

Hank signaled.

Bear released a bull.

Justin immediately recognized Crash Course, the Sterling claim to fame. Big-league rodeo star, three-time PBA Best Bull of the Year. The bull burst into the arena bucking furiously, propelling his two-thousand-pound frame into the air as though weightless, crashing back down. With spectacular speed and force, the bull spun to the left, then the right, executing maneuvers that would force a rider to make instantaneous, difficult adjustments. Justin had seen many skilled riders fly off his back inside of three seconds. Out of a hundred tries, seventy cowboys had been tossed in the dirt. Justin's adrenaline spiked as he watched the bull's performance. "Man, that reverse spin is a killer."

"Spinning is bred into our bulls," Hank said with unmistakable pride. "It's what makes them hard to ride. Comes with decades of breeding specific genetic factors."

Mounted on first-rate quarter horses, Billy and Nelson galloped into the center of the arena and steered Crash Course out of the corral.

"I'd love to give that bull a shot," Justin said, hearing the yearning in his voice.

"That idea entered my mind after you rode Cyclone." Hank put one foot on the bottom rung and rested his forearms on the top rail. Justin did the same.

"Cyclone's a young bull with a lot of potential, that's why I'm testing him at smaller rodeos. I butted into your business at Red Rock, Justin, because I saw your talent, knew your background, something of your character, and thought we could help each other out."

"I appreciate the loan," Justin said sincerely. "I intend to work it off."

"I like your enthusiasm. I heard Cody really piled it on yesterday."

"No complaints."

He turned to Justin, somber gray eyes holding his gaze. "Manual labor isn't what you're here for. You're too valuable, and too smart, to be spending your time thickening your calluses."

Justin drew in a breath. "What am I here for?"

"There're lots of opportunities if you apply yourself." Hank turned to watch Bear herd another bull into the chute. "You could learn to run a ranch from the ground up. Ranching is a complex business with lots of facets, all equally important." Hank pressed his fingertips together. "It's impossible to sustain a ranch and make a profit without understanding the management side, as well as the livestock side, the hay-making side, the rodeo side."

"It's a corporation with lots of divisions."

Hank nodded at him, his tone passionate. "You bet it is. We both know that a bull rider's career is short. Like me, you'll probably be out of the game in ten years or less, due to injuries. It's important to learn how to earn a living that will sustain you beyond your rodeo years."

"I majored in business, Hank," Justin said. "I plan to have my own spread someday. But I can't lie to you and pretend I'm ready to give up bull riding."

"Our thinking is aligned in that department. You're also here for training."

"Bull riding?" Justin's voice held an edge of excitement.

"Bingo." A wide smile creased Hank's tanned face.

Justin felt a surge of adrenaline. Hank Sterling, world champion bull rider two times over. He'd be the best trainer in the world!

"So, you ready to take a shot?"

Justin didn't want to act too eager. "What're you getting out of this partnership?"

"I'll take a percentage of your winnings. As your sponsor, our reputation as a breeder would get a boost. Down the road, maybe you'll be my ranch manager. My daughters won't be around forever."

"Bear said last night I'd be working under him." Justin scowled.

Hank's gaze traveled across the arena and settled on Bear, a deep frown creasing his brow. The look in his eyes was unmistakable. Dislike, plain and simple. Surely Bear had expectations of moving into the manager position once he married Sarah. Bringing Justin into the mix would throw a nasty wrench into the natural order of things. No wonder Bear had given him the evil eye last night.

"Nah, he was mistaken. You work for me," Hank said firmly.

Justin felt relief.

"If you can ride my bulls, you can ride anything out there. My goal is to get you competing at top rodeos. A decade of wins should give you a pile of trophies and plenty of money."

Justin felt a roller coaster mix of excitement and fear. It was a hell of a tall order, going from small rodeos to the big leagues. Could he do it?

Hank signaled Bear. The chute opened and Cyclone shot out like a force of nature. The bull's agility and athletic performance made the hair rise on Justin's arms. Cyclone went into a spin, a reverse spin, and then launched himself into the air, kicking all four legs to one side before coming back down. Justin's hands tingled as he relived his moments of glory mounted on the bull's back.

Hank turned to him, read his expression, and flashed a toothy grin. Justin knew the two were sharing a unique experience—an adrenaline rush only those who'd ridden a champion bull to the sound of the buzzer could possibly understand.

"You ever lose the urge to ride again?" Justin asked.

"Never." Hank tapped his hip. "Artificial hip. Haven't ridden a bull in fifteen years." He tipped his hat back from his forehead. Sunlight caught and brightened his gray eyes. "So, you game to stay on board?"

"Hell yeah, I'm game."

"Then let's get something straight right up front." Hank's tone turned serious. "You're gonna put in long hours. You'll get tossed in the dirt more times than you stay on board. We're gonna toughen you up where it counts." Hank tapped his temple. "Up here. The guys at the top got there by being smart. You get lazy on me, Justin, you're outta here in a heartbeat. I won't deal with anything less than you at one hundred percent. Do we have an understanding?"

Justin met Hank's stern expression, grinned. "When do we start?"

"Tomorrow," Hank grinned back. "You start earning your keep today. Cleaning stalls."

Justin didn't blink. Cleaning stalls was menial labor, but it was honest work, critical to the health of the animals. In fairness to the other hands who were putting in long days of labor, he wanted to do his part. He recognized the potential here, but he also saw a heap of trouble waiting in the shadows. Best take it one day at a time. Focus on the bull riding.

CHAPTER TWENTY-NINE

SULLY SPENT the next few days doing what he did best, what he had doggedly dreamt of doing every day while he was lugging combat gear around the dust bins of Afghanistan—training horses. His trainees included two colts who were so full of combustible energy all they wanted to do was kick and buck and use the corral as a playpen. Training inexperienced horses took time and patience, but Joe had taught him well.

In his earliest memories, Sully remembered sitting in a saddle, his little western hat strapped under his chin, his cowboy boots barely skimming the length of the saddle-skirt, listening to his father giving instructions. Sully's determination to become a good cowboy, just like Joe, had been fierce. His father's instructions were deeply implanted and still sprouted in Sully's head like green shoots in fertile earth. *Teach a horse to operate on feel, son, not force. Invite the horse to work with you. Don't threaten it.* If Sully lost patience and mistreated an animal there was always a sharp reprimand and a whack to the back of his head. *There's a difference between firm and force, dammit! Don't bully a horse to save yourself some time. Give the animal all the time it needs. Now get back in there and do it right.*

Joe's training methods, though stern and demanding, instilled in Sully an intuitive, gentle way of working with animals. At the risk of a horse suddenly spooking and running him over, he learned to focus his attention moment to moment on what the horse was doing, anticipating his every move. He developed the sensitivity to feel that sudden change when a horse got what he was trying to say, and then a little magic happened. *It's a dance, son. Listen to the music. Tune in to the rhythm of the horse. Let him become your dance partner. Don't step on his toes.*

After grooming his last horse and cleaning his tack, Sully strolled out of the barn hungry and exhausted. It felt good to be making progress. In a few weeks, he would put one of the geldings up for sale and pay off some more bills. He spotted Joe cautiously wheeling himself down the ramp from the porch wearing work clothes and his old high-crowned, wide-brimmed Stetson. Good sign. Maybe getting out of his dark bedroom would improve his disposition.

Joe stopped wheeling and let gravity pull his chair to the bottom of the ramp. He raised his head as Sully approached. A bath towel was folded across his lap. "Good job on the ramp."

"Thanks," Sully said, wary. He hadn't spoken more than ten words to Joe since his angry explosion three days ago.

"Where's my dog?"

"Sleeping on a pile of hay." Sully whistled, and Butch came tearing out of the barn with bits of hay flying behind him. He braked to a stop at their feet, tail wagging, head cranked back, waiting to see which one would give him a treat. Sully picked him up and plopped him on Joe's lap. Butch balanced himself on his hind legs and licked the old man's stubbly chin.

Joe grinned, eyes sparkling.

The dog did have magical powers. Sully noticed Joe's face looked fuller. Shoveling hefty meals down his throat all day was getting good returns.

"Mind pushing me down to the creek?" Joe asked. "I'd appreciate it."

Sully wanted to eat and relax, but Joe's unusual politeness stoked his curiosity. "Sure, Dad. I'm up for a walk."

They took the path that ran above the hay fields, now thawing under the warming sun. Rivulets of water cut through the ice and a crop of puddles reflected the turquoise sky like bits of mirrors. Buds unfurled on the apple trees and islands of brown earth emerged as the snow receded. Sully's thoughts turned to the planting of hay. The irrigation would soon be turned on and Shankle would be laying down spring seed. The trail followed the contours of the creek, meandering through stands of junipers and aspens, and sometimes intercepted by pathways of water.

"I should get snow tires for this thing," Sully said, panting as he maneuvered the wheelchair through mud and slush. He brought the wheelchair to a stop at a large clearing that sloped gently down to the water's edge, his favorite spot on the ranch.

During the summer, the water was calm, and the animals would wade up to their shoulders to cool off. Sully remembered swinging out over the creek on a rope with his friends, seeing who could make the biggest splash. Tracks of mule deer and jackrabbits crisscrossed the muddy shore and the piercing chirp of red-winged blackbirds mingled with the gurgle of water. Afternoon sun filtered through the branches, turning the creek into liquid gold.

Joe wore the expression of a thirsty man taking in a long, cool drink. Nature and sunlight acted as an elixir.

"Hand me that stick over there, son," Joe said, pointing a gnarly finger.

Sully picked it up, wiped off the mud, and handed it over.

Joe threw it a short distance. "Get it!"

Butch flew out of his lap, pounced, and trotted back dragging the stick from his mouth. This ritual continued for several minutes with the stick going further out until it was splashing in the creek. Sully seated himself on a damp stump and watched the entertainment, impressed by Butch's tenacity. The dog paddled dutifully in and out of the water, oblivious of the cold.

"That right there, that's loyalty," Joe said.

When Butch ran out of steam and was panting on Joe's lap, the old man rubbed him down with the towel and wrapped him up like a burrito, with only his eyes and nose poking out. Joe turned his attention to Sully. "I need to tell you what's going on with me and your mom."

Sully met his father's piercing blue eyes. He leaned forward, his attention rapt.

Joe's gaze seemed to withdraw as though he was visiting distant memories. His blue-veined hands absent-mindedly stroked Butch's head.

Waiting, Sully listened to snowmelt drip from tree branches. "Dad?"

"Twenty years ago, your mom and I were going through a rough spell." Joe's eyes returned to him. "Money was tight. My rodeo days were coming to an end. You were just a boy." Joe suddenly coughed. Looked away. Coughed again.

Sully could hardly contain his impatience. "Yeah. So?"

Joe looked at him, face reddening. "I met another woman."

The bluntness of the words caught Sully like a sharp rap to the head. "You cheated on Mom?"

Joe leaned forward in his seat as though not wanting to say the words too loud. "It was more than an affair. It lasted five years."

Sully sat motionless, his body tense, waiting to feel something.

Joe watched him intently, as though trying to place his words in some secret, safe place. He was hoping, Sully knew, for some sign of acceptance.

"You cheated on Mom for five years?"

Joe nodded, his face haggard. "Your mom never should've found out. What was she cleaning the attic for? No one had been up there in fifteen years. She found some old letters I'd hidden. Threw them in my face when I walked in the door."

"You kept letters?" Sully sat quietly, absorbing the impact of Joe's confession. A spark of anger ignited, and flared. "Maybe you should have just hit Mom on the head with a shovel."

"I should've burnt those dang letters."

"That's all you have to say?" Sully walked to the edge of the water, thinking of the pain and shock his mother must have endured. He now understood why she left the ranch. He faced his father. "I can't believe Mom took you in last week."

Joe looked away from Sully's accusing stare. "That's your mom. She's a good woman. Better than I deserve. I thought she forgave me, but as you can see, I ain't at her place no more."

"No wonder she's all messed up."

Joe gave him a sharp look. "Look Sully, this happened a long time ago. I stayed faithful the last fifteen years. Don't that count for something?"

"Sure, Dad. You deserve a fucking medal."

"The way you feel about a woman ain't something you can control. I loved your mom. But I loved another woman, too. I took care of them both, and you." Joe's voice choked. "Her name was Hannah."

Sully didn't want to know her name. He didn't want to humanize the woman who was the wedge that pushed his parents apart. "Where did Mom think you were when you were cheating?"

"On the road."

"What ended it?"

"She died."

Sully thought about that for a moment. "What would've happened if she lived? Would you have kept seeing her?"

"That's what your mother asked."

"Would you have left us for her?"

Joe looked away, said nothing. He inhaled sharply as though from a sudden pain, then he dropped his head in his hands and covered his face.

Sully turned away, picked up a stone, threw it across the surface of the water, watched it skip to the other side. He stood there for a long time, trying to stifle his anger. Didn't work. He turned and walked back to Joe. "You son of a bitch. I'd beat the holy crap out of you if you weren't in that wheelchair."

Joe went limp and he slouched in his chair. For a moment, Sully thought he was having another stroke. He slowly recovered, squared his shoulders, looked at Sully with sharp eyes and a clenched jaw. Butch watched Sully, too, ears twitching.

Sully released the brake, spun the chair around and began pushing it home. Too fast, too furious. Mud and ice flying. He took pleasure in watching Joe's body bounce around like a jack-in-the-box. Butch emitted long, low growls.

"Stop it. Stop pushing me."

Sully ignored him, anger boiling in his chest.

"Let me go. I'm not done telling you yet."

"I'm done listening."

Joe's arms flailed above him, fists trying to land a good one. Sully thought it pitiful how easily he could dodge them. It wasn't that easy when he was a boy. When Joe got ticked, he beat Sully with whatever he could get his hands on—a horse whip, leather belt, electrical cord. Sully nursed welts for days. Miraculously, at fourteen, he came to match Joe's height and strength. He fought back in a storm of unleashed fury. Broke Joe's nose, blackened his eye. It was the last time his father ever laid a hand on him. Instead of whining about it, Joe treated Sully with new respect. In Joe's world, a man didn't waste words, but fought with his fists to prove his manhood.

When they reached the house, Sully left him sitting in the chair at the bottom of the ramp. "Gunner was stolen," he said sharply. "And Monty Blanchert was murdered." He stormed into the kitchen past Travis who stood over the stove stirring a pot of chili.

"Where're ya going? You gonna leave Joe at the bottom of that ramp?"

Sully shut himself in the bathroom and turned on the shower full blast. He stripped off his clothes and stepped under the steaming water trying to still the thoughts ricocheting in his head. He had spent his whole life trying to please his father. Copying his cowboy tactics, becoming an ace rider, tackling rodeo and excelling at it, all the while trying to squeeze a little affection out of the man.

Now he discovered that all along, Joe had lied and cheated and led a double life. He found plenty of affection to give to some loose woman while meagerly rationing it out to Ronnie and him. Sully fixated on packing Joe up and dropping him off at the nursing home in the morning. Letting him rot there, eating their pig slop food and getting sponge baths from the ex-gang member, Frank.

Sully waited until Travis and Joe finished dinner before he left his room. He could hear canned laughter coming from Joe's TV. He went into the kitchen and warmed up a can of mushroom soup and was dishing it into a bowl when Travis walked in.

"What the hell were you thinking?" The old Paiute's normal air of self-possession had vanished. The tone of his voice was a shade below furious. "Telling Joe about Gunner and Monty like that? You trying to give him another stroke?"

Sully sat down to eat, felt the heat of anger rise up the back of his neck.

"We agreed to let me tell him," Travis said.

"How'd he take it?" Sully knew anger showed raw on his face.

"Bad."

"Good."

Travis stood silently watching him. He opened the fridge, twisted off the cap of a Miller and leaned against the counter drinking it. When he finally spoke his voice was tight, but Sully was no longer the target of his wrath. "Judging from your face right now, I don't think I wanna know what's going on between you two."

It was an indirect invitation from Travis to confide in him. Sully simmered, chewed.

Travis waited.

"All I'm gonna say on the subject is that you can stop blaming Mom for Dad's stroke, and for the state of the ranch. I know you and Dad are tight, but he brought this whole mess on himself. He gave Mom no choice. She had to leave. If Dad wants to confess his sins to you, that's up to him. You ain't getting nothing from me."

Travis turned the information over in his mind as Sully got up for a second bowl of soup and the rest of the cornbread. They both heard the sound of a truck crunching gravel outside.

"That's the sheriff," Travis said. "He called while you were in the shower."

"Why didn't you say so?"

"Just did."

Travis opened the door before Matterson knocked. The sheriff's big frame was momentarily silhouetted against the sunset. He took his hat off and entered.

"You off work?" Travis asked.

"On my way home. That beer looks good, if you're asking."

"Already got it out." Travis put a frosted bottle in his hand and the sheriff sat across from Sully, his leather holster squeaking. He chugged a quarter bottle. "Man that tastes good." He wiped his mouth with the back of his hand. "So Joe's home. You must be relieved."

Strained silence.

"He got Whistler out his first day back," Travis said.

"I'll be a son of a gun," Matterson said. "Joe's always been a force of nature. With that kind of determination, he'll recover fast."

Or kill himself trying, Sully thought.

"He around?" Matterson asked. "I'd like to say hello."

"No," Sully said.

Matterson's eyes narrowed.

Ignoring Sully, Travis and Matterson made small talk.

Sully ate his cornbread and soup, trying not to glare. Travis asked about Bella and Jasper. Matterson said his kids were riding the gentle mare, and the bull was eyeing the heifers in the adjoining field. Both men laughed. Matterson turned to Sully. "Got some news about Monty."

Sully pushed his empty bowl away. "I'm listening."

"With the snow melting, forensics went back out and scoured his property. Retrieved bullets. A .223-caliber rifle killed the dogs. Monty was shot with a .45 auto. Died instantly."

"After being beaten," Sully said.

The sheriff looked down at his beer, then back up. "The lab processed the bullets. They were a match to firearms reported stolen months ago. Breaking and entering. Unrelated to horse theft. These guys added Monty's arsenal to what they already had."

"Crime pays well," Sully said.

"Not for long." Matterson's voice roughened. "We'll get them. They're gonna screw up. One of those firearms will show up in a pawnshop."

"They find any prints?" Sully asked.

"They wore gloves." He drained his bottle, then stood and adjusted his hat. "Thanks for the beer. Gotta run. Sue's holding dinner."

"Stop by any time you have more good news," Sully said.

The sheriff's jaw tightened for a second then he nodded to Travis and was out the door.

They listened to his truck pull away from the house.

"No need to give Carl a hard time," Travis said.

"We're at a dead-end," Sully snapped.

"It's only been a week and a half," Travis said.

"Long enough to ship Gunner to the other end of the world." Unable to sit still, Sully put his bowl in the dishwasher, said goodnight to Travis, and headed for the barn. He stood in Gunner's empty stall, feeling helpless and sick.

Chico and Buck watched him from their neighboring stalls, dark eyes large and liquid, heads beautifully sculpted just like Gunner, their sire. They nickered to him. He gave them both a treat. Chico had been gelded. Buck was still a stallion and could carry on the champion bloodline, but he needed a shitload of training.

Sully haltered Buck and took him out of his stall and started vigorously brushing him down. He lost track of time, ranting to the stallion about the betrayal of his father and the injustice of horse theft and murder. Buck listened attentively, ears flicking back and forth to the tempo of Sully's voice. He returned Buck to his stall and took out Chico and brushed him down just as energetically, continuing his harangue. After wringing out the blackest strains of his anger, he shifted his thoughts to the other pressing business at hand. The finances. Unless Sully won the lottery, he figured it would take a good eight months to dig his way out of debt. But if he stuck to his guns and worked hard, he could probably do it by

Thanksgiving.

The cold wind scoured his face as he walked back to the house. Dead tired, he fell into bed. He looked at the photo of Eric and Maggie before turning out the light. He had promised Maggie the first night they met that he'd do something purposeful with his life. He owed that much to Eric, who would never have the chance. Touching the St. Christopher medal, he silently recited the Marine prayer that had given him courage every day in Afghanistan.

If I am inclined to doubt, steady my faith; if I am tempted, make me strong to resist; if I should miss the mark, give me courage to try again. Guide me with the light of truth and grant me the wisdom by which I may understand the answer to my prayer.

CHAPTER THIRTY

THE DOOR to Justin's bedroom burst open and Billy's silhouette was captured inside the frame of light from the hallway. "Time to rise and shine."

Justin groaned.

"Up and at 'em."

Justin blinked when Billy turned on the overhead light.

"Outside. Five minutes." Billy set a mug of coffee on the nightstand and left the room.

Justin reached for the java, drank half a cup, staggered to his feet and started yanking on his running clothes. This was the routine. His new life. Two weeks ago, he thought Hank would get him on a bull immediately, but the closest he'd come to a bovine was viewing one from the sideline as the ranch hands put it through its paces in the arena. Instead, Hank put Justin on a rigorous workout schedule. Hank must've read his mind because there was no way he was gonna get out of a warm bed voluntarily to freeze his ass off at the crack of dawn. Billy was assigned the duty of getting him going.

Outside in the brisk morning chill, Justin started off stiffly, settling into the lowland trail leading from the house. He pushed one heavy leg in front of the other until he broke out in a good sweat and his warmed muscles moved fluidly. He reached the first switchback climbing the hill up to the bluff. Long, easy strides. Good rhythm. Breathing well. Alert, energy-charged.

Astride his quarter horse, Billy took his job seriously, trotting behind, moving up ahead and circling back, herding him like a wayward calf. Justin dug in, relaxed but pushing himself, his jogging clothes damp, sweat dripping down his face. He gave it all he had, long strides, fast cadence, arms pumping, lungs burning until he reached the top. His muscles trembled with exhaustion. He bent down, hands on knees, gulping air. Then he started back down.

When he reached the house, he showered and gorged himself on breakfast, went out to muck stalls, and then met Hank in the well-equipped home gym for his daily workout. Thankfully, power lifting wasn't the game plan. Hank isolated muscle groups and pushed Justin through multiple repetitions using lighter weights. "You're building strength and flexibility," Hank told him, working right alongside him. "When you're on a bull, you're holding every ounce of your weight, so you want as little body fat as possible."

Hank set the bar high for stamina and endurance. Justin was impressed that a man in his fifties was in such prime condition—six-pack abs, sculpted legs, arms, and shoulders. No way was Justin going to be out-matched by a man more than twice his age. Justin's brain was getting a workout, too. After weightlifting, he joined Hank in the state-of-the-art home theater to study rodeo footage. The room had reclining leather chairs, a full bar, shelves of rodeo paraphernalia, and hundreds of DVDs of top-ranking riders. Hank was teaching him how to size up the competition.

Frequently, Hank slowed down a video or froze a frame to point out characteristics of an individual bull or technique of a rider. Justin hung on every word.

"Watch this," Hank said sitting forward in his chair, his remote aimed at the big screen.

Justin focused on the rider coming out of the chute in slow motion.

"Know who this is?" Hank asked.

"Derek Moser. Two time PBR World Champion. He rides the unrideable bulls."

"He's the first professional bull rider to earn six million in the course of his career," Hank said.

Justin whistled.

"He's number one in the world. He's your competition." He turned to Justin. "With your natural talent, you can beat Derek. You just need to get smart about it."

Justin studied the screen with new intensity. His desire to beat Moser was so strong it felt like an ache.

"That's Rock n' Roll he's riding," Hank said. "This bull's long and powerful, and wild as a lightning bolt. See how hard he kicks out his hind legs? Then he turns back underneath himself." He reversed the footage and replayed it. "Watch Derek adjust. Not a single mistake. He's thinking right along with the bull."

The hair rose on Justin's arms.

"He knows where his body weight is every second," Hank continued. "Watch the bull spin to the right. Look at his adjustment. He's settled in."

Justin sat riveted. Derek's instincts were flawless, the equal to any NFL quarterback.

"It's all about basics," Hank said. "That's what keeps a rider consistent. Derek's doing the same thing, over and over."

They watched the same ride repeatedly. Justin noticed something different every time, in every shift in balance, leg and arm positioning, angle of his head. After twenty minutes he'd memorized even the flapping of the rope. Since his training began, bucking bulls had been charging through Justin's brain every waking minute, dominating his dreams at night. "So when do I get on a bull, Hank?"

Hank walked to the bar, pulled a single malt scotch off the shelf, reached into the freezer and tossed some ice cubes into a tumbler. "When you have the right attitude." Hank poured two fingers of whiskey and returned to his seat.

"What's wrong with my attitude?"

Hank took a long sip, sat back relaxed. "What drives you, Justin?"

There was no hesitancy in his answer. "Adrenaline charge. Best high in the world."

Hank's expression sobered.

Justin knew he'd given the wrong answer.

Hank took another sip, ice cubes clinking. "There's nothing more insane than hopping onto the back of a bull. In fact, most crazy people wouldn't do it. You have to be alert and clear-headed to even consider it. It's called the most dangerous eight seconds in sports for a reason. If the rush is all that drives you, you're gonna get dead in a hurry."

"I want to be the best in the world," Justin added with passion.

"Do you?" Hank drained his glass, leveled his steely gaze at him. "I'm not convinced."

Justin hated that piercing gaze, as though Hank were looking into his soul and coming up short. Some wild emotion shot up from his gut. He heard the frustration in his voice. "Damn it, Hank, put me on a freakin' bull. I'll show you how badly I want to win."

Hank broke into a grin, laughed out loud.

Justin stared, incredulous. "You were playing me."

"You're too damn serious for a kid." Hank reached over and slapped Justin on his knee. "Lighten up. We're starting in the arena tomorrow." Hank nodded toward the bar. "Grab a beer."

Justin got out a Growler, twisted off the cap and took a swig. He knew Hank was right. He was too damn serious. Having fun for fun's sake was something he never learned how to do. Maybe Hank could teach him that, too.

Hank gestured toward the large screen with the remote. "Here's the toughest bull in the business. You ever hear of Helter Skelter?"

"Who hasn't? He's the bovine version of Jaws." Justin leaned forward in his chair.

Hank chuckled. "A holy terror under a cowboy." He pressed a button on the remote. Heavily muscled in the loin and quarters, a cream-colored Charbray launched from the chute like a wayward missile, seemingly right into the room.

Justin's gut tightened. This video clip was legendary. Every cowboy's nightmare. He didn't want to watch but Hank wanted him to see it. Initiating his signature move, Helter Skelter jerked his rump high off the ground, forcing the rider to shift his weight forward, his head and torso low. This signaled the bull to snap his head upwards, meeting the rider's face in a violent collision. Knocked unconscious instantly, the cowboy's body flopped like a rag doll and catapulted to the ground where it lay crumpled in a heap.

Sickened, Justin turned away.

"The bones in that cowboy's face were shattered," Hank said with gravity. "He underwent several reconstructive surgeries to implant titanium plates. I've met him several times. Nice kid, good cowboy. Continued riding with just one eye."

"Yeah, I know." Justin avoided watching bull wrecks on YouTube. What was the point?

"In a hundred and twenty rides, only eight cowboys stayed on Helter Skelter for eight seconds," Hank said. "The last time was a year ago, by

Derek. Since then, nobody's heard that eight-second buzzer that wasn't lying in the dirt, hurting bad. This bull gets smarter as he matures." Hank froze the clip, looked at Justin. "Now, what would you do if you happened to draw Helter Skelter during a competition?"

Justin rubbed his hand over his jaw, thinking, wanting to come up with the right answer. He decided to speak frankly. "I'd tip my hat and say no thank you. I'd walk away from the prize." He met Hank's eyes. "Sorry. I'd rather live with my face intact. Bull riding isn't the only game in town. I have a life coming later, I hope."

Hank's expression relaxed. "Good. Sensible kid. You have fear. You can't perform well without it."

"Is that what was missing from my attitude?"

"Bingo. I've seen your dedication Justin, and your willingness to work at peak capacity, but I've also seen cockiness. No trace of fear."

All of which seemed ironic to Justin. He was no stranger to fear but he'd become an ace at hiding it. He looked at Hank. "That cockiness is a cover, Hank. It helped me survive abusive situations. I get cocky when I'm getting close to shitting my pants."

Hank's gray eyes softened. "I've been there myself, son, many times. Who hasn't in this business?" He swallowed. "I know all about rough treatment in foster homes. Trust me on that."

They shared a look that said each fully understood the other.

Hank pressed the remote and the screen went black. "Enough for today. Time for dinner."

"So, tomorrow in the arena? What time?"

"After breakfast. Keep your impatience in check. To start with, it's gonna be all about technique. You seen Daisy, my milk cow? Tomorrow it's just you and her, up close and personal."

They both shared a laugh.

"You'll be riding rank bulls before you know it, Justin. At which point you won't have time to think about technique. It'll be ingrained." Hank casually placed an arm around Justin's shoulder as they walked out of the room. A lump formed in Justin's throat and he fought back the sudden pressure of tears. *This is what it feels like to have a father. A man willing to devote his attention to my needs, not just his own. A man who wouldn't hurt me.*

CHAPTER THIRTY-ONE

EXHAUSTED AFTER PUTTING in a hard day's work, Sully pulled off his boots on the porch, went into the bathroom and showered, then lay down on his bed waiting for Travis and Joe to finish dinner in the kitchen. He passed out almost immediately. When he woke, the house was quiet. Joe's TV was turned off. The house was dark except for the dim light above the stove in the kitchen. He wolfed down two ham and cheese sandwiches, a large piece of peach pie, and half a quart of milk and then padded softly down the hall to his bedroom. Butch started barking.

"Sully?" Joe called out, sounding half asleep. The light came on in his bedroom.

Damn. He had managed to avoid Joe the last few days except at breakfast, which Sully ate quickly, his eyes glued to the paper. He walked to Joe's door and pushed it open. His father was pulling himself into a sitting position on the bed, his pajamas twisted around his torso, hair sticking out like a thatch of hay. Butch took one look at Sully and burrowed under the covers, a moving lump until he reached the middle of the bed.

"Need a bathroom break?"

"I get myself to the bathroom just fine. Don't need your help."

"What do you want?"

"I wanna talk."

"I'm tired, Dad."

"You been ignoring me. That don't make a problem go away."

"It's two in the morning."

"I brung you up right, to respect your father," Joe said sharply, eyes flashing. "Sit down."

Sully considered walking out on him but instead he sank wearily into the wheelchair. He studied the handful of medications on the nightstand, the walls, anything but Joe. After the room was painted, Sully had carefully replaced the pictures that had hung on the walls for decades—photos of his parents as young sweethearts and rodeo posters featuring Joe in his prime as a bare back rider. In Sully's favorite picture, his father stood lean and handsome in his rodeo gear. At age five, Sully sat on Whistler's back dressed just like Joe; white hat, leather chaps, tiny boots and spurs. He remembered the exact moment a newspaper photographer shot that picture. It appeared on the front page the next morning. Brimming with pride, Sully had taken the paper to school for show and tell. He finally met his father's gaze and noticed his haggard expression, the blue shadows beneath his eyes. "Did you take your pills?"

"Yeah, 'cept my sleeping pill."

"Here, take it now." Sully opened the container, shook out a blue pill, handed it to him with his glass of water.

Joe obediently swallowed. "I got something else to tell you. You ain't gonna like it. But it needs to be said. I can't live with these secrets no more."

Sully sighed. Joe wanted to confess more sins. What was it going to be now? Sully fixed his gaze back on the photo. Back then, Joe was a big star, especially popular with female fans. Was that how he met the other woman? Did she fall for him while watching him perform his slick moves on his golden palomino? Did she wait in line to get his autograph, then bat her lashes and flirt up a storm? Sully knew a lot about that. He could have slept with dozens of women but he remained loyal to Lilah.

Joe cleared his throat, shifted his position against the pillows. "There's no easy way to tell you … so I'm just gonna say it. The woman I was with … her name was Hannah …." Joe started coughing. He reached for his water, took a sip.

Sully felt the muscles tighten in his face. "Just tell me, Dad."

"Hannah got pregnant … she had a son … I'm the father."

Sully responded with a cold, steady stare.

"You have a brother. He was three years old when Hannah died."

"You had a son with her?"

Joe nodded. "He was a beautiful boy. Looked just like you when you was a baby." His voice choked, and tears welled in his eyes.

"Did you live with Hannah?"

"Yeah. An apartment in Beaverhead. I paid for it."

"How often were you there?"

Joe squinted, thinking back. "Guess 'bout a week every month."

"Did she know about us?"

"Yeah, she knew everything. She even seen you once. Came to the kiddie rodeo when you was riding. She wanted to get your autograph, just so she could meet you. I wouldn't let her." Joe looked at Sully with a desperate urgency, as though waiting for some kind of understanding, or forgiveness.

He wasn't getting it tonight. Sully sat glaring, said nothing.

"Go ahead," Joe said. "Be hard on me. I got it coming."

"What kind of woman sets up house with a married man? Has his child?" Sully said ruthlessly. The anger rose like a launched missile, uncontrollable. "Hannah was a liar and a cheat, just like you. She betrayed Mom and me, too."

Joe flinched, mouth slack.

"Mom and I weren't enough for you, were we Dad? You had to have another goddamned family on the side. I don't even know who you are. Who Mom and I lived with all those years. Maybe everything you ever told us was a lie." Unable to sit still any longer, Sully got up and stormed out of the room.

"Sully!"

Feeling disconnected from his life, Sully paced the dark hallway, listening to the rustling of Joe getting out of bed and into his wheelchair. Sully circled the island in the kitchen twice, then left the house in his pickup, peeling out of the driveway. Where the hell was he going? Anywhere. Just away from Joe. He needed time to think, to cool the white-hot anger consuming him. He drove randomly down narrow country roads, some unpaved and mined with potholes, his headlights bouncing. His thoughts were sprinting back and forth through time, trapped in an endless maze of memories. What kept resurfacing was the keen sense of loneliness he felt in his childhood during his father's absences. When Joe returned home, Sully eagerly raced to the door to meet him, clinging to his leg, ecstatic, but his father typically brushed him off after a mandatory hug. Joe, he remembered, seemed always to be in a hurry. He had hayfields to plant, fences to mend, horses to train, a rodeo to get to. *Or Hannah.*

It riled Sully to no end to think that Joe bestowed affection on some other woman, some other son, while leaving him and Ronnie behind. His stomach churned with the acid of resentment. He drove aimlessly until the pink colors of dawn filtered into the sky and his gas tank was nearing empty. He realized he had driven to his mother's neighborhood. He pulled into her driveway, got out, and strode to her door.

Looking dazed from sleep, Ronnie opened the door in her bathrobe, a crease from her pillow scarring one cheek. She took one look at his face and said simply, "He told you."

"Yeah, he told me." Seeing sadness darken her eyes, he pulled her into his arms, now understanding fully how lonely she must have been these last six months, harboring Joe's secrets alone. She pulled away, eyes moist. "Let me make you breakfast."

"Sounds good, Mom."

They both got busy in the kitchen. He made coffee, she cooked French toast and apple sausage. They sat at the table eating and making small talk. After two mugs of coffee, he felt renewed energy. Morning sun slanted through the blinds, striping his mother's face in golden light and shadow. "Good coffee, Mom."

"French roast."

They'd avoided the topic of Joe. He wanted to soften her hurt, console her, but he didn't know how. "I'm sorry about Dad."

"Me, too."

"You should've told me. I never would've pushed him on you."

She sipped her coffee and looked at him over the brim of her cup. "Seeing him was good for me. It snapped me out of my coma. Made me realize I've been hibernating, thinking only of myself. I saw that he was going to be okay. He didn't need me to take care of him. I could let him go. He needs to be home now. That's his best medicine."

There was no bitterness in her words and he sensed her quiet courage. Sully placed his hand over hers. His mother was recovering from the shock of leaving Joe, and her reasonable nature seemed to be returning. He'd always loved her deliberation and decisiveness, her kindness and gentleness with animals. He sorely missed her presence at home; the fresh cut flowers spilling over mason jars, homemade pies cooling on the windowsill, the faint scent of lavender lingering in a room after she'd passed through. Ronnie had always been his ally, a refined counter balance to the sharp, ragged edges of his father.

"We both need to forgive him, Michael." Her gentle, steady gaze met his.

"I don't know if I can."

"You will in time." Smiling faintly, she carried their dirty dishes to the sink, brought back the coffee pot, refilled their cups. Both stirred in cream and sugar. "He told you about Hannah? The boy?"

"Yeah," he said bitterly. "The tramp and her bastard son."

Ronnie's face blanched and her freckles stood out like dark splashes. "Michael, don't. That isn't fair. He's your half-brother. None of this was his fault. If I had known about this poor, motherless boy, I would have insisted Joe bring him home. I would have raised him as my own." She pushed shaggy bangs from her eyes. "Your father told me all about Hannah when he was here. They met in a bar where she worked as a waitress. I found pictures with the letters. She was beautiful. I think she was the true love of his life. Not me."

He felt for her as he watched the grief wash back into her face. Sully remembered when he discovered Lilah's unfaithfulness, how the hurt gushed up like a geyser, washed over him and through him, never completely seeping away. "*You* were Dad's true love, Mom. That was obvious when I picked him up from the nursing home. He couldn't wait to see you."

She seemed not to hear. "Hannah was so beautiful. She was going to college, studying to be a nurse. Your dad paid for her education."

"While we were struggling."

Her face shadowed. "We did okay, Michael. We didn't have a lot of luxuries, but we had a good life."

"That's what Dad said. Like that makes it okay."

"Would you have traded anything? Living on the land, our animals?"

"No. The only thing I would have exchanged was Dad." He stopped, hearing anger leech into his words.

"I knew he was pushing you too hard to be a rodeo star. That was so important to him." She looked at him with a sad expression. "I should have left him years ago. Taken you with me."

"Mom, none of this was your fault."

She squared her shoulders and gave him an adoring look. He never had to be exceptional to win her favor. Being himself had been enough.

"You're every bit as tough as your father. But you also have heart, and a gentle spirit."

He saw the strong line of her jaw, the pride in her green eyes. "I got that from you," he said.

"I often wondered why you went off to join the Marines." She raised a brow, a question in her words. "Just when your career was taking off. I blamed your father."

Sully sat quietly for a moment. They'd never talked about this. He remembered the stress he'd been under trying to realize his father's dream. He'd felt like a pressure cooker ready to explode. "I needed to be my own man. I couldn't do that under Dad's thumb. When 9/11 happened, I wanted to do my part. It gave me a greater sense of purpose than being a rodeo champion."

"I'm proud you went, son. You came back different. Stronger." The lines around her mouth softened. "The ranch is your heritage. We always meant for it to be passed on to you. I thought when you and Lilah married, we'd build another house on the property so you could have your privacy."

Sully looked out the window, then back at Ronnie. "Mom, Lilah and I aren't getting back together. I've moved on."

She looked surprised for a moment, but she gave him a tender smile and didn't question him. He was thankful for that. He leaned back in his chair, stretching his legs under the table. "Where's my half-brother now? What's his name?"

"Joe wouldn't tell me," she sighed. "It's a painful subject. He put him in some kind of boy's home after Hannah died. He sent a monthly check for his care for several years, until he got adopted."

"He gave away his own son?" Sully's face flushed hot with renewed anger. "Heartless son of a bitch."

Ronnie didn't defend Joe's actions. They sat in silence. Sully tried to imagine what life would have been like if Joe had been honest and they had taken in his half-brother. He'd always yearned for a sibling. Ronnie got up and started cleaning the kitchen. He looked at his watch. "I've gotta run, Mom. Chores." He stood and pecked the top of her head.

She leaned into him for a moment. "I love you, son."

"I love you, too, Mom."

"Wait, I have something for you." She pulled a white envelope out of a kitchen drawer, handed it to him as though it were fragile. "Take this."

"Okay." He left the house, got into his truck and opened the envelope. He pulled out a colored photo of a small boy wearing a white cowboy hat, boots, and spurs. It looked like a twin to the picture of Sully sitting on Whistler in his father's bedroom. Blue eyes staring at the camera, little smile lighting up his face, almost the spitting image of Sully. Sully turned it over. No name. Just a date scrawled in the upper right corner. June 1990.

"I hope you got a good home." Tears welled in his eyes, hot and swift. Ashamed to cry, he covered his face with one hand, felt his shoulders shudder as he tried to suppress a sob. He felt deeply the loss of the brother he never got to know, a little boy who had been given away like a piece of garbage, never knowing he had family just forty miles away. Sully wiped his tears with the back of his sleeve, put the truck into gear, and pulled away from the curb.

CHAPTER THIRTY-TWO

SETTLING INTO a comfortable routine at Sterling O, Justin kept to himself, didn't say much, worked hard, and retired to his room immediately following dinner. He spent his evenings reading Ranch Management magazine, writing letters to Avery, and finger-picking his guitar. Each night before dinner, he took twenty minutes to groom Porter in the barn. After shedding his winter hair, muscles rippled beneath the mustang's shimmering coat, his mane and tail shone like silk, and his polished hooves gleamed like tap shoes. Sarah and the hands teased Justin relentlessly at the dinner table.

"What'd you do with Porter, and who's that Dapper Dan in his pasture?" Roth asked.

"He's ready for his GQ close up," Nelson said.

"We're gonna have to lay down red carpet to get him out of the barn," Sarah said.

"You ever gonna ride him?" Billy asked, "or just dress him up for the prom?"

Cody said nothing, just looked at him with her unreadable expression.

**

The sun was low in the sky. Late afternoon shadows stretched lazily across the ranch. Justin had worked an hour of free time into his schedule before dinner so he could at last ride Porter. He saddled the mustang and led him into the arena. Before he got his boot planted firmly in the stirrup, Porter jerked away and bucked vigorously. Justin figured the ill-mannered mustang had been out to pasture too long, and could benefit from some ground exercise. He put the horse on a lunge rope, stood in the center of the arena, and directed the animal with a crop, trotting him in circles, then reverse circles. He saw that Porter was steady, had impulsion, and stayed in his gait. After siphoning off some restless energy, the mustang revealed a calm willingness to please, and he plodded over to Justin when instructed, affectionately blowing into his hand. Feeling a presence behind him, Justin turned to find Cody at the gate, hands on her hips, squinting, evening sun on her face. She was dressed in men's Wranglers and a work shirt buttoned up to her neck, both a couple sizes too big. He tipped his hat, wondering what critical comment she was preparing to make.

She posted herself on the top railing, blocking the sun with her hand. "It's about time you took that mustang for a ride. I was wondering if you had it in you."

"What's that supposed to mean?"

"Dad said you've never owned a horse. Maybe this one's too much for you."

"You have to be patient with a horse. The payoff is, it'll be patient with you."

"How do you know when it's ready?"

"Instinct. The same instinct you use when you're working that cow horse of yours."

She surprised the hell out of him by smiling, and he caught a look of amusement in her eyes that reminded him of her father. Her blond hair rose and fell softly on the breeze, a feminine contrast to the hard expression she usually wore. Up until now, he'd successfully avoided both Sterling sisters and life here had been pretty peaceful. Maybe by ignoring her, she'd get the message and go about her business. He placed his boot in the stirrup and hoisted himself into the saddle. Porter bucked two, three times, then settled down and responded respectfully to his signal to walk. Smooth and rhythmic. Justin gave short, brisk squeezes with his legs, signaling a slow, steady trot. Porter ignored him, obviously wanting to test the skill of his new rider.

He heard Cody snigger. Clenching his jaw, he popped Porter on the rump with the reins with just enough firmness to tell the horse who was boss. Porter responded by moving into the slow relaxed lope Justin wanted. Controlling the animal mostly with his legs and weight and a light touch of the reins, he rode him in large circles, then reversed direction and rode in small, precise circles. The horse was nimble and quick, and he allowed Justin to guide him through a number of reining patterns required for competitions; backing up, pivoting, sidestepping, fast spins.

Impressed as hell by the amount of training that had gone into the animal, Justin found himself grinning broadly. Porter was rock solid, with a lot of power and collected balance. Occasionally, he glanced at Cody, who watched his every move with a strange intensity.

He and Porter finished off with a couple of short bursts of high speed with long, sliding stops. The horse was a little rusty, but he understood all the basics, and in time, with more practice, he'd perform fluidly. He rode Porter to the gate, dismounted and led him out of the arena heading for the barn. Cody jumped down from the railing, caught up with him, and matched his gait.

"Porter's a really solid horse," he said, feeling tense from her presence. "Quick and responsive."

"Yeah, I know. I raised him from birth. Did most of his training."

"You're a top-notch trainer," he said, not disguising his respect.

The compliment didn't register. She didn't even blink. He noticed she had the same high cheekbones and full mouth as her beautiful mother. He felt a twinge of attraction to her, but then her mouth compressed into a hard line and her face tightened into its usual stony expression. Unapproachable. "That why you came out to watch? You wanna make sure your baby's in good hands?"

"Of course," she said in a haughty tone. "He's a valuable horse."

"I appreciate that. I know Kigers. They're tough. In the wild, they can go forty, fifty miles a day, eating nothing but bitter grass. Hardly any water."

She glanced at him, said nothing.

"Some Kigers can be traced back to a single stallion named Mesteño," Justin said. "He was captured with the original herd in 1977 in Harney County. Is Porter related to him?"

"Yes."

He endured an awkward silence as they entered the coolness of the spacious barn. The smell of pine shavings and oiled leather reached his nostrils. What was she up to? Cody parked herself against a stall door and crossed her arms, hands clutching her elbows. Shafts of light fell through the tall, angular windows, brightening her blue-gray eyes and giving her skin a golden luster. Dust motes danced in the air around her like tiny galaxies. She watched in silence as Justin tied Porter to a ring with a quick-release knot, then lifted the saddle and pad off his back and set them on a saddle stand. If she was trying to annoy him, it was working. "Is there something I can do for you?" He pushed up the brim of his hat.

"Yeah. How about talking?" she said with a slight flaring of nostrils.

He gave her a sideward glance, trying to figure out her motive for tailing him.

"You've been here for three weeks, and you've managed to say absolutely nothing about your personal life. You don't tell stories, which is pretty damned unusual for a cowboy who's done years of road trips."

He hadn't known she was paying attention. "I like to listen. More interesting. You learn stuff."

She looked at him with suspicion, lines tightening around her mouth.

"What do you wanna know?" he asked, on guard.

"What you're hiding."

His whole body tensed. He grabbed a brush from the tack box and started giving Porter a good grooming, using short, firm strokes, loosening dirt and hair.

"Where've you been since high school?" Tone like a homicide detective.

"Doing rodeo for the last six months. Before that, college."

"College?"

"Business major. That surprise you?"

"Why'd you quit?"

Justin looked at her over the mustang's withers. "I didn't quit. I ran out of money."

She studied him. "Bear said you got beat up in Arizona. That true?"

"How the hell did Bear know that?" he asked, fuming.

"He was down there with Dad. They were sitting in the motorhome and saw some cowboys go psycho on you. Dad went out to help, but then some dude on a horse rode in and broke up the fight. Bear said they were bad-assed lowlifes, just itching to beat your brains in. That true?"

Christ. Did the whole ranch know his business? Did this female have any tact? Feeling his face heat up, he leveled a hard look at her, the brush suspended in his hand. "Is talking about my private life a job requirement?"

"I don't want any trouble here," she said tersely. "Those cowboys you messed with in Red Rock are known felons. Jeb Waters, and a scumbag named Porky. They have rap sheets from here to Texas. Got into some trouble in town a couple years back. Arrested for murder. Charges were dropped. Lack of evidence." She was watching him closely. "I don't want them coming here looking for you."

"I'd never messed with Waters and Porky before Red Rock. Never will again." He was brushing so hard, Porter stepped away from him.

"What're you hiding from?" She eyed him coldly.

He felt the old fear and anxiety swirl in his chest.

"Maybe you're wanted by the law. In three weeks, you've never left the ranch. You afraid of being spotted in town?"

"I'm not a criminal," he said irritably, tossing the brush into the tack box. "I've done nothing that could get anyone here into trouble. Now if you don't mind, I'd like to keep my personal life private."

"What's your problem, Justin?" Her eyes flashed and anger flickered over her face. "Do you even know how to be social?"

"You're not exactly one to give lessons. You think this was a fun conversation?"

She pinched her mouth, jammed her hands into her pockets.

He picked Porter's hooves in silence. She didn't leave. It dawned on him that it wasn't a good idea to be on bad terms with Hank's daughter. "I'm sorry," he said, forcing his voice to sound friendlier. "I don't mean to be rude. Guess I could use some etiquette lessons." He gazed at the set edge of her chin and decided to give her a little of what she wanted. "Yeah, I got beat up in Red Rock. Bad, okay? Those bastards stole my rodeo winnings, fractured my ribs, put me out of work. I took this job because I needed money." Now he was rambling. "I never owned a horse because I was an orphan. I didn't have rich parents like you, who gave me things."

Silence.

"I grew up living with foster families. Everything I know about horses and bulls I learned from working my ass off on other people's ranches." Memories of abuse crowded his mind, stoking his anger. "If you really want to hear some stories, I could tell you a lot about some of the asshole ranchers around here, and the shit that goes on behind closed doors …." His voice drifted into silence as he watched her. She now stood perfectly still, her face pale, and he interpreted the downward thrust of her mouth as an expression of pity. He felt his face burn with embarrassment, and he felt the old irrepressible ache—the loneliness of being shiftless in life, with no moorings that tied him to family and friends, with no direction that pointed home.

A strong gust of wind swept through the open door, stirring up dust that carried the scent of sweet wild grass, then it settled down again.

Cody's face colored, too. Bright pink blotches on both cheeks. A strained silence stretched between them. She unhooked her gaze from his and stared out the doorway of the barn toward the house. "Dinner started fifteen minutes ago. We better get a move on."

"I'll get Porter back to his pasture." He added as she turned to leave, "I'm glad I took this job. Your dad's been really good to me. I've had better treatment here than any place I've ever lived. I'd never do anything to hurt Hank."

She gave him a funny look, like an attempt at smiling, but her eyes looked uneasy. "My dad's very trusting. I'm not."

Justin watched her walk away, trying to sort out the baffling mix of feelings she stirred inside him.

CHAPTER THIRTY-THREE

BOTH JUSTIN AND HANK were late for dinner. Cody watched as the screen door opened and Justin walked in. He looked beat as he shrugged out of his coat and hat, hung them by the door, and made his way to the chair he'd claimed as his own. As always, he carried himself well, with athletic grace, his back straight, hands strong and square, nails always clean. He didn't look at her. After her interrogation in the barn, she wasn't surprised.

"Who spit-and-shined you guys?" Justin grinned at the three hands.

The room seemed to come into sharper focus and she noticed that all three men were clean-shaven and dressed in their going-to-town clothes. Good jeans, clean shirts. She was sure that under the table, boots were polished. Billy's dark hair was slicked down and shone like lacquer.

"You coming with us, Justin?" Roth was wearing his Friday night happy-face in anticipation of seeing his girlfriend who lived in town.

"Yeah, man. Come knock back a few. Dance with the ladies," Nelson raised his brows up and down, a wicked look in his eye. His sunburned face looked well-scrubbed, and his bushy mustache was neatly trimmed.

"Can't do it," Justin said. Carlos and Maresol had grilled thick burgers for dinner with all the trimmings, and Justin busily assembled his burger with lettuce, tomatoes, onion slices, pickles and condiments. "I'm dog-tired. I'll go into town tomorrow to pick up some personal items."

"Listen to him," Bear said with a smirk. "He gets paid to exercise and watch videos. We work our asses off. He wears down running shoes."

The hands laughed but Cody thought the remark tasteless. She found herself defending Justin. "He keeps the stables and paddocks clean. Anyone else want that job?"

"Shoveling shit?" Nelson grinned at Justin. "It's all yours, dude."

"I'll pass," Roth chimed in.

Each of the hands had started out with stable duty as a rite of passage. Now Justin was low man on the totem pole, fair game for badgering. Cody saw he took it in stride.

Talking on his cell phone, Hank strode into the room in full business mode and seated himself at the head of the table opposite Cody. He pocketed the phone, nodded to everyone and got busy preparing his food. She saw the tension leave his shoulders as he put his workday behind him.

"You're a local, Justin," Roth said, holding his cheeseburger in one hand, running a French fry through ketchup with the other. "Got family here?"

Justin chewed his burger. "Nope."

Though she never looked directly at him, Cody always found herself keenly tuned in to what Justin had to say. He had maintained a quiet, modest manner since he arrived, which mystified her. He was hard to figure out. In the barn, she had to stoke his anger to get him to talk, and from his expression, she could tell he thought she pitied him. She didn't. She identified with him, recognizing a similar toughness and vulnerability. His outburst told her a lot about his history. Adults in charge of his care had abused him. To what extent, she could only imagine. Seven months ago, she had barely escaped death at the hands of her ex-husband, who had abused her for three years. She and Justin both knew what it felt like to be terrorized.

The hands left promptly after dinner, eager to get to town. Cody and Justin ate in silence, listening to Hank and Bear talk shop. She caught her sister stealing glances at Justin when she thought Bear wasn't looking. Bear laid his arm around Sarah's shoulder and she pecked him sweetly on the cheek. "Let's get a game of poker going," Sarah suggested. "Who wants in?"

"I'm in," Hank and Bear said in unison.

"Count me in. Let me grab my cards," Justin said, wiping ketchup off his hands with a napkin. He left the table.

Cody's mouth opened in surprise. Justin normally left the table right after dinner and didn't reappear until breakfast. Sometimes she heard him strumming his guitar when she passed his room to go upstairs.

Billy's mother, Maresol, came in and cleared the table. Sarah went into the kitchen and came back carrying a tray loaded with frosted bottles of beer.

Justin waltzed back in with a deck of cards, grabbed a bottle off the tray, and sat down next to Sarah. "You in, Cody?" Surprisingly, he smiled at her, his tanned face emphasizing the neon blue of his eyes.

Her impulse was to say no, stay away from the handsome bull rider, but something in his smile melted her resistance. "Yeah, I'm in." She reseated herself next to Hank. "Prepare to lose your shirt."

"I like this shirt," Justin said with lazy amusement, shuffling the cards like a Vegas dealer. "Think I'll keep it. Better watch your own."

"Ooooh," Sarah said, her eyes lighting up. "Is this turning into strip poker?"

"You wish," Cody said, taking a swig of beer. "You'd probably lose on purpose."

"If I was wearing your shit-ugly clothes," Sarah snorted. "I'd definitely lose on purpose."

Cody shot her sister a heated look. It was returned in full measure.

Hank's voice hardened. "Sarah, watch your mouth."

Sarah flinched a little beneath his cool stare. "You always take her side, Dad."

"Don't start, Sarah."

She sat steaming. "Cody this, Cody that. Cody Miss Perfect. When do I ever get credit for shit?"

"Shut up," Cody snapped.

Sarah looked at Bear for support. The foreman said nothing. A muscle ticked in his jaw.

"Can we skip the wrangling tonight, *Ladies*?" Hank said.

An uncomfortable silence settled over the group. Cody wondered what Justin thought of their petty quarreling. Why did she care what Justin thought?

"Wanna see a little magic?" Justin broke the strained silence. He sounded relaxed, unconcerned.

All eyes turned to him. Hank looked relieved.

Justin brought out a playing card from his deck and showed everyone both sides. "The ace of spades." He rested the card on his hand, palm up. With the other hand, he pulled an imaginary string above the card. The card lifted and floated half a foot above his hand for several seconds, defying gravity.

Cody heard Sarah gasp.

Justin placed the card back in the deck, shuffled, then shot the cards back and forth from one hand to the other, so fast it was a blur. Holding the deck in his left hand, he flicked out the bottom card with his little finger. It spun like a top, floating above the deck. He held his right hand above the spinning card and gently twirled his index finger. The spinning card made a small circle in the air. Justin made a broader circle with his hand and the spinning card made a broad circle over the table and returned to his fingers. He caught it and turned it over. It was the ace of spades.

Sarah's eyes were wide with wonder. "How'd you do that? That is so cool."

"What's under that card?" Cody asked.

"Ah, we have a skeptic." He showed both sides of the card. "See, no levers, no pulleys, no invisible string." He met her eyes, held her gaze.

"What's up your sleeve?"

Justin pushed both sleeves up to the elbow, revealing nothing but skin. He grinned. "Pure magic. Plain and simple."

Despite herself, Cody smiled back. "Let's see if some of that magic rubs off on your poker game. We're playing with *my* cards."

She saw Justin and her father exchange a smile. Laugh lines fanned around her father's eyes. It was clear the two shared a special friendship. Bear on the other hand, was glaring. Cody could feel his pulsing resentment even though he sat several feet away. He downed half a beer in one gulp.

CHAPTER THIRTY-FOUR

EARLY SATURDAY MORNING, Justin drove into town. The warning symptoms of anxiety started tightening his chest as he eased his truck to a stop in the parking lot. Sitting motionless, he studied other parked vehicles and folks strolling in and out of Umpqua Bank, where he'd opened an account online. He didn't recognize anyone. He took a deep breath, walked hurriedly inside and deposited most of his paycheck. His second stop was the drugstore. Here, too, he kept an eye open while stocking up on toothpaste, razors, shampoo, and shaving cream. He looked through half a dozen greeting cards before picking one out for Avery. At his third stop, the post office, he spent a long time standing at a counter composing a letter.

The buildup of longing he felt after weeks of solitude encouraged him to get raw with his feelings. He signed his name with lots of Xs and Os, enclosed a payment toward the boots and clothes she bought him, sealed and mailed it. He hadn't realized how much he'd miss her, especially after dinner when he and Avery drank beer on the porch together and he sang cowboy love songs, and her face radiated open affection. In bed each night, memories of their lovemaking loomed in the darkness, vivid and real. He yearned to touch her body, smell her skin, hold her close. Now he understood with excruciating clarity what it meant when a woman got under your hide.

Justin snapped out of his daydream and realized he'd been hurtling down the highway thirty miles over the speed limit, fleeing back to the safety of Sterling O.

CHAPTER THIRTY-FIVE

SULLY ARRIVED at Ronnie's at seven carrying a six-pack of Bud. Living with Joe and Travis left him sorely missing female company. Having Saturday night dinners with Ronnie and Sunday night dinners with Maggie was a bonus he looked forward to all week. He pushed open the screen door and stepped inside. "Mom, I'm here."

"Back here." Ronnie came out of the kitchen wiping her hands on her apron, her eyes flashing brightly.

"What smells so good?" He pecked her on the forehead.

"Grilled chicken."

"My favorite."

"I know." She smiled.

He followed her into the kitchen and looked out at the patio. The table was set for two. Smoke was curling out of the grill. He popped open a Bud. "Beer?"

"I have wine in the fridge. Pour me a glass?" She started whipping butter and milk into a pot of mashed potatoes on the stove. "Flip the chicken for me, too."

He went outside, set down their drinks and opened the grill, releasing a cloud of fragrant smoke. He turned over the chicken, waited a few minutes, and then liberally brushed on Ronnie's homemade sauce. The tantalizing mix of citrus and herbs teased his nostrils. "Chicken's done." He forked the pieces onto a platter and sat waiting at the table, mouth watering.

"Your hat," Ronnie said, coming out with a bowl in each hand.

He placed his hat on the extra chair and ran a hand through his matted hair.

"Your hair looks nice longer," she said. "You don't look military anymore."

"Haven't cut it since I got home." Sully's Marine training was ingrained, but in the last six weeks, he had settled into ranch life like a hand in a glove. Ranching was his calling again. After piling chicken, mashed potatoes, and sautéed summer squash on his plate, he snapped his cloth napkin over his lap and bit into a juicy drumstick. "Hmmmm. You should bottle and sell this sauce, Mom. You'd corner the market." For a minute he didn't talk, just chewed, polishing off the drumstick and starting on another. In between bites he got Ronnie caught up on news at the ranch. "The first crop of hay's shooting up in the fields. I've gotten a bunch of carpentry and plumbing done. Travis is tuning up the hay baler." He took a long sip of beer. "Everything's getting spruced up."

"You're working the horses, too?" she asked, her fork halfway to her mouth.

He nodded, chewing. "Every day. They're coming up to speed. Chico's going up for sale here pretty soon. That's money in the bank."

Her brow creased into worry lines. "You're working too hard. Doing my job, too."

"No worries." He sawed off a piece of chicken, forked it into his mouth.

"I transferred money into the ranch account yesterday," she said. "It'll help pay property taxes."

He looked at her, surprised.

"Michael, you forget, I write. Doesn't pay much but I just deposit the money. What else am I going to do with it? I don't go anywhere."

He felt a stab of guilt, imagining what it must be like for his mother to be a prisoner in her own house. "Mom, why don't you come home? You don't have to live with Dad. The cottage on the creek is just sitting empty. I can get it cleaned up and painted."

Her eyes shadowed and welled with tears.

"You can be with all the animals again. Do your gardening."

She took in a deep breath. "Yes, I need to come home."

"Just say the word. I'll buy paint."

"My lease is up the middle of June. I'll start packing." Her lips curved upward, and her eyes were wide and bright. "I can't wait to see Gracie."

The grateful way his mother looked at him made his chest swell. He flushed with pleasure at the thought of having her home.

"How's your dad?" She sipped her wine, watching his expression closely.

Sully wiped his mouth with a napkin. Three weeks had passed since Joe dropped the bomb about his secret family. The initial shock had worn off but now a wall of icy reserve stood between them. "He's good. He's put on some weight and muscle. Looks halfway back to normal. He replaced the wheelchair with the ATV. He zips around the ranch like a NASCAR driver with Butch on his lap. Dog's an appendage."

Amusement touched the corner of her mouth.

He scratched the back of his head. "I have to admit, Dad's been a big help."

"What can he do with a weak arm and leg?" She brought a forkful of potatoes to her mouth.

"Everything. Feed chickens, fill water troughs, groom horses, polish tack. He and Travis planted the vegetable garden." Sully resisted telling her that Joe dragged himself to bed each night looking half dead. There was no point in Sully telling him to take it easy. He wouldn't listen.

"Does your dad ask about me?" she asked, voice cautious.

He shrugged, wanting to say yes, but in truth, Joe was too damned self-centered to think of anyone but himself. "Mom, I gotta be honest. I don't talk to Dad unless I have to." Joe and Travis on the other hand, were as tight as two sausages nestled in sauerkraut. Sully came upon them laughing sometimes and their expressions instantly sobered, like he was the bad guy. "Dad and Travis go into town together a couple nights a week."

"What do they do?"

"Drink beer. Eat pizza."

"Well, I'm sorry to hear you two don't talk. He's your father, Michael."

"Yeah, well …."

They both ate in silence listening to the music of her wind chimes.

"Do you have room for dessert?" she asked. "I made cinnamon buns."

He groaned, happily. "You're killing me, Mom. I'm stuffed. I'll have one later with coffee."

"Take the rest home. There's plenty for Travis and Joe."

"They'll be appreciated." He stacked the dirty dishes and followed her into the kitchen. "Gin rummy?"

She smiled her beautiful smile. "You bet. I haven't forgotten you owe me three dollars."

"Watch out," he said, limbering up his fingers. "I feel lucky tonight."

CHAPTER THIRTY-SIX

SULLY WALKED down to the house from the hay fields. Sunshine warmed the earth, the apple trees were covered in blooms, and Ronnie's perennials sprouted everywhere. Phlox, daffodils, tulips, hyacinths. It was good to see splashes of color after the stark months of winter. He went in to get lunch, hungrier than a bear coming out of hibernation. Travis sat at the table drinking coffee, an empty plate in front of him. Groceries were low and the men had resorted to eating sandwiches for lunch and dinner. Sully rummaged through the fridge. All the cinnamon buns were gone.

"You finish the turkey?" He opened the dairy drawer. "And the cheese?"

"We finished it last night. I just had peanut butter and jelly."

Sully pulled strawberry jam and Skippy out of the cupboard. "Time for a grocery run."

"Or we could get pizza."

Travis could live on pizza. "We're going out for groceries, Travis. We're not turning into frat boys." He put a pad and pen on the table. "Start a list." While standing at the counter making two sandwiches, he ticked off grocery items. "Milk, bacon, bread, tuna, butter."

"Slow down." Travis scratched the pad with the pen.

Sully sat at the table with his food and coffee and waited for him to catch up. "Add vegetables."

"We can buy all the groceries you want," Travis said. "Doesn't mean I'm cooking."

"I'll cook. How about salad and spaghetti tonight?"

"How about meat?"

"I'll put beef in the sauce."

Travis grunted. "I can eat spaghetti."

Halfway through his second sandwich, Sully heard the sound of gunshots coming from behind the barn. "What the hell?"

"That's Joe," Travis said calmly.

"What's he doing with a firearm?"

"Trying to shoot the damn thing."

Leaving his sandwich on his plate, Sully stumbled into his boots, hurried out to the meadow behind the barn and spotted Joe standing next to the four-wheeler reloading his Winchester rifle. Twenty-five feet across the clearing, a dozen tin cans were lined across two old lopsided picnic tables.

As Sully watched, his father tucked the butt of the rifle into his right shoulder, tried to support the stock with his weak left arm, and fired. He got off six shots, the barrel of the gun jerking each time. The shots went wild, splintering chunks of wood off the tables. "What're you doing?"

Joe glanced over his shoulder, eyes shadowed by a ball cap with a Rodeo Bum logo stitched on it. "What's it look like? Shooting a damn rifle."

"Why?"

"Why do you think? There're murdering thieves on the loose. They stole Gunner. They killed Monty. I intend to be ready when they make their first mistake."

"That's the sheriff's job."

"Not if I find them first."

His father's thinking was delusional.

Ignoring him, Joe reloaded and fired off six more rounds. The tables splintered. Clumps of earth exploded.

Sully's ears were ringing. Smoke and the smell of gunpowder lingered in the air. "A handgun would be easier."

"I'm a rifle man."

"Yeah, but with a handgun you could shoot one-handed, using your good arm."

"You know I don't have no handgun."

"You can use one of mine."

"Which gun?"

"The Glock 19. I'll show you how to use it."

Looking impatient, Joe stood the rifle against the seat of the four-wheeler. "Get the damn thing."

Sully wanted to get back to eating, then horse training. "Can we do this later? I'm busy."

"Whenever you want. In the meantime, I'll practice with my rifle."

And wear yourself out. "I'll get the Glock." Sully went back to the house, grabbed his sandwich, and took bites while walking to the office. He unlocked the gun cabinet, took out two earmuffs, several magazines, a holster, and his G19. *A safe, reliable gun.* The Glock was like a lawnmower, needing little cleaning or maintenance. It had worked one hundred percent of the time with the ammo he put in it. He went outside. Joe was leaning against the four-wheeler but stood up straight when Sully approached. He already looked exhausted.

"Lift up your right arm." Sully clipped the gun and holster to Joe's belt. "Each magazine holds fifteen 9mm hollow points." Sully inserted rounds into a magazine then took the Glock from the holster and showed him how to insert the magazine and rack the slide. Joe had been around guns his whole life. He only had to demonstrate once. He put on the earmuffs, put a pair on Joe, brought the pistol up to target with his right arm and shot off six rounds. Across the clearing, six cans jumped off the table. He crossed the clearing, stood the cans back up and returned to Joe, handed him the Glock. "Here. Try it."

"It feels light," Joe said with skepticism. "A gun this light can't control recoil."

"It's accurate, has little recoil."

Joe imitated Sully's stance, raised his right arm and fired off a shot. Missed the can. His face was set, his focus intense. Sully watched him fire off fourteen more rounds, missing every time, but his shots were coming within a half-foot of his target.

Joe pushed his earmuff back and looked at Sully, his blue eyes squinting in the sun. "Thanks, son." His voice was actually pleasant. "Tell your ma thanks for the cinnamon buns."

"Tell her yourself," Sully said coldly. "You know how to use a phone. It's the least you can do. She sits in the house alone seven days a week."

Joe winced as though slapped. His jaw worked a bit, then tightened. Sully turned his back on him and walked to the barn.

Shots rang out while Sully worked in the corral with Chico. By the time his father quit, Sully could hear a third of his shots hitting the cans.

CHAPTER THIRTY-SEVEN

THE SUN WAS straight up in the sky and it was hot and dusty in the arena. Sully was hungry but he wanted to put in more time with Chico while the horse was alert and interested. He dismounted at the water trough. While the horse drank his fill, Sully turned on the hose, removed his hat and bent over and let cold water run over his head. He combed his fingers through his wet hair and leaned back against the rail, admiring his horse. Chico would soon be on the market, going to the highest bidder. To get top dollar, the gelding had to be expertly trained. The thought of losing Chico made Sully's gut ache but life presented tough decisions, and right now he needed cash. *You better damn well do the tough stuff up front.* Joe's old sermon echoed in his ears. *Put off hard choices and you're in trouble down the road. Cut off a toe to save the foot.*

The gelding nudged Sully playfully, wanting to get back to work. Sully chuckled. That's what he loved about Chico. Attitude. He heard the clopping of hooves and saw his father hobbling up to the railing leading Whistler, saddled, ready to ride.

Joe nodded. No smile.

Sully nodded back. Joe's hat shaded his face, hiding his expression. Sully imagined it was one of criticism. Most everything Sully had learned from Joe came from criticism. The old nagging feeling he used to get in the pit of his stomach when working with Joe returned. Sully donned his hat, hoisted himself back into the saddle and resumed training, practicing the ten patterns required for reining competition. Just before competing, riders were notified which pattern they had to perform, so a horse and rider had to be highly skilled in every one. Joe had drummed into him that reining a horse was not just about guiding him, but controlling his every move. Sully put Chico through the paces. After thirty minutes he and Chico were slick with sweat and the gelding's interest was waning. Time to quit. A horse had to be a willing partner. Over-training was the best way to produce a performance that was robotic and lacking vitality. His father taught him that. Just about every thought that occurred to him while training was a retread of Joe's advice.

"You done in here?" Looking impatient, his father now stood inside the gate with Whistler, the holstered G19 snapped to his belt. This was the first time he'd brought Whistler into the arena since the morning he ran amuck. The Palomino's long silver mane and tail looked silky and his coat had been brushed to a glossy sheen. Perched on the saddle maintaining perfect balance, Butch looked about as trimmed as sagebrush, his eyes all but disappearing beneath curly hair.

"What's this? A new circus act?" Sully asked.

"Time to get back in the saddle," Joe said irritably.

"How do you plan on getting up there?"

"You're gonna help. Give me a boost."

"You're staying in the arena, aren't you?"

"Since when did you become the parent?" Joe snapped. "Mind your manners. Here, watch my dog." He handed Butch to Sully.

Sully got behind Joe, waited for him to put his foot in the stirrup, then gave a big heave. Joe settled in the saddle then took off at a lope. Sully turned away from a cloud of dust. "Thanks, Dad." Joe was steadily getting stronger. Sully had to give him credit for working as hard as he did. Some men would have given up, stayed in a wheelchair for life.

Standing on the sideline, Sully watched Joe relax his lower back and hips and sit deeper in the saddle. He could hardly see him move his body or arms but he was definitely communicating to Whistler, relying more on his legs for his turns with no visible use of the reins. The more relaxed you ride, the better a rider you'll be, Joe use to tell him. Like everything in life, the better you get at something, the less you have to do.

With Butch trotting behind, Sully led Chico deep into the barn and began removing his tack. He turned on the radio and started whistling to an old Eagles tune, "Desperado."

CHAPTER THIRTY-EIGHT

IN THE DAYS that followed, Sully and Joe fell into an easy, if barely civil, routine. Both men went about doing their morning chores, then Sully trained horses in the arena while Joe practiced his shooting skills behind the barn. Sully now heard Joe's bullets pinging tin cans eighty percent of the time, and he wore his holster every waking hour. Wyatt Earp at the OK Corral, Sully thought with grim humor. Waiting for the shootout with the bad guys who lurked in every shadow.

***

Joe's shooting practice stopped at noon and the men convened for lunch. Travis collected eggs from the hen house and made egg salad sandwiches on whole wheat.

"That's our last loaf of bread," Travis said, as they sat down to eat.

"Time for another food run," Sully said absentmindedly, unfolding the newspaper. "I'll go into town after dinner." Vaguely aware of Joe and Travis swapping conversation, he wolfed down his sandwich, read the paper, and ignored them.

Joe refilled Sully's coffee cup.

Sully looked up momentarily.

Joe held his gaze, a wistful expression on his face.

Probably hoping for a note of friendliness, or a smile. Sully wasn't feeling charitable. "Thanks," he said, no emotion, his eyes darting back to the sports section. He gulped down his coffee, then unceremoniously left the two men at the table, and went to the arena to resume horse training. Around two, he heard the ATV heading in the direction of the hay fields. His father was probably going to check on the irrigation equipment. One section of pipe had been faulty. The rest of the afternoon went by uninterrupted, Sully completely attuned to the horses. Normally he and Joe swapped places in the arena late afternoon, but today Joe didn't show. Sully groomed Chico in the barn, took him to his stall, and then cleaned the tack room. No sign of Butch or Joe.

Sully was surprised when he came in for dinner and found Travis alone in the kitchen, frying potatoes and trout for dinner. The smell of onions and garlic made Sully's stomach rumble with hunger. "Dad sleeping?" he said.

Travis looked up from the fry pan. "He's not in the house. I just checked his room. You haven't seen him outside?"

"No."

Travis scratched his chin. "I haven't seen him since lunch. I've been in the garage all afternoon working on the baler. Haven't seen Butch either." His eyes widened momentarily. "Wait, he mentioned at lunch he wanted to go hunting."

"Hunting? Today?"

"I didn't take him seriously. What in hell can he shoot with a handgun?"

Sully shrugged. "In his state of mind, who knows what he'd try to shoot. I heard the four-wheeler earlier this afternoon. Maybe he headed for the creek to try to shoot a duck or a goose. Guess I better go rustle him up."

An edge of concern crept into Travis's voice. "Take your cell. Let me know when you find him."

"Roger that."

Sully knew Joe could be anywhere along the creek, which ran for twenty miles in each direction. He went to the barn and saddled Diego and then headed up past the hayfields following the tire tracks of the ATV. The tracks ran parallel to the creek to the north end of the property and continued for some distance before suddenly veering off toward the mountains on a rarely used, overgrown horse trail. Puzzled, Sully fished his cell phone from his pocket.

Travis picked up on the first ring. "Got him?"

"No. He's headed northwest, away from the creek."

A long pause. "What fool thing did he get into his head to do?"

"Dunno. But it'll be dark here in an hour or so. It'll be hard to see his tracks. I'm gonna keep looking. I hope to hell he's headed back home."

"I'll get saddled. Don't slow your pace. I'll catch up."

"Bring flashlights.

Riding Diego at a slow trot, Sully covered a couple more miles before Travis caught up to him at a gallop, his black and white paint, Taba, damp with sweat. There was no disguising the tension on the old Paiute's face as he pulled alongside Sully.

"See anything?"

"Nada," Sully said, his sense of unease deepening. "He stopped once to let Butch have a whiz, but he didn't stray too far from the ATV. Looks like he's on a mission."

Travis pushed back his hat, eyes shining in the light of the lowering sun. "What kinda mission, out here?"

Sully blew out a breath. "Beats the hell outta me. We're gonna have to plant a tracking device on him if this is his new norm."

They both knew the trail ahead snaked through miles of thick, forested land that opened onto Misery Flats. The flats were dissected by a rugged meandering gorge with a sheer five-hundred-foot drop down columnar basalt cliffs. The Big Crow River was caged at the bottom, a tributary that ran more than a hundred miles. There was no way to cross the gorge except for an old abandoned railroad bridge thirty miles to the east.

"This isn't good elk or deer country," Sully said, worried about his father's state of mind. "If Dad's out here hunting with a handgun, he's delusional. If he's not hunting, what prompted him to come out here?"

Travis shook his head. "We'll find out soon enough. Once he's out of the woods, he'll be hemmed in by the gorge, and won't be able to go any further."

They rode through the darkening forest and entered Misery Flats as the colors of sunset melted across the mountains, drenching the desert in liquid amber. The spicy scent of sage and juniper seasoned the air.

Joe's tire tracks soon veered off the trail onto open land, skirting sagebrush, boulders, and an occasional juniper tree as the ATV forged its own path to the gorge. Sully scanned the open countryside with his binoculars but saw no movement, no telltale plume of dust stirred up by the four-wheeler.

A single, sharp crack from a handgun split the silence, coming from a distance of about two miles. The shot had a fading reverberation, which told Sully the bullet had traveled a long distance without hitting anything substantial. Two more sharp cracks followed in quick succession.

Pow-whop.

Pow-whop.

Blunt. Short distance. Followed by sounds like airborne grunts. These shots came from a high-powered rifle more to the east, and had unmistakably hit living flesh.

"Holy shit," Travis said.

A warm trickle of sweat ran down Sully's spine. Fear for his father's safety tightened his chest. "Let's go." He spurred Diego forward, following Joe's haphazard tracks until the ground hardened and became increasingly riddled with rock. They slowed the pace of the animals to a walk and repeatedly dismounted to search the earth, but the ATV's imprints became untraceable. As night thickened around them, they continued to ride in the direction of the gunshots.

***

It was pitch dark by the time they reached the rim of the gorge, which yawned across a chasm half the length of a football field, and it was difficult to distinguish where the sheer edge dropped off to the river below. Sully and Travis kept the horses at a distance. They dismounted, flashlights slicing through the night. Hit by cones of light, odd shapes that might have been an ATV became mounds of sagebrush or boulders. They walked in separate directions, trying to pick up any sign of Joe or Butch.

"Dad!" Sully repeatedly called out, moving north.

"Joe!" Travis chanted. After a while, the old Paiute's voice faded as he moved further south.

Sully's beam caught something incongruent, partially hidden behind a looming boulder. Black. Rough edges. A tire? He moved closer and his beam unveiled the ATV.

Sully heard the sudden scuffing of steps behind him. He turned, expecting to see Joe. There was a blur of movement and then something smashed down on his head. White pinpoints of light exploded in his brain and he felt himself falling, then blackness rushed in.

***

Sully woke thinking he was dreaming. Something soft and wet was flicking the side of his face. Butch ... there was a note of urgency to the poodle's whimpering and growling. Sully became aware of the hard ground beneath him and an intense throbbing in his head. His fingers traced an open gash on his scalp above his left ear, a couple inches long. Then he remembered where he was. Misery Flats. Someone clobbered him! How long had he been lying there? Where was Travis? His dad?

As he sat up his head cleared a little, but the intense pain didn't subside. Warm blood trickled down his face and dripped off his jaw.

He didn't like that Butch was alone. His father would never let him wander off, especially out here, where predators roamed at night. The poodle pawed the ground and whimpered louder.

"Easy boy," Sully said. His fingers searched the ground until they clasped his flashlight. He thumbed it on, and the beam cut slices of light through the darkness.

Butch trotted away, stopped and looked back, his body tense, waiting for Sully to follow. He yanked up his pant leg, unstrapped his .38 from its holster, and got unsteadily to his feet. Fighting nausea and a wave of dizziness, he followed Butch to the rim of the gorge. Both horses stood waiting, tails flicking nervously. A roar rose up the canyon wall from the river below. Sully pitched his beam in every direction, looking for movement.

Nothing.

He heard Butch growling. The dog stood on the edge of the rim fixed on something below, his coat blowing back in the wind. Sully's gut felt queasy as he inched closer. A strong current of cold air rose up from below. He felt a sudden wave of vertigo and imagined he was being sucked forward into the void. He stepped back quickly, waited a long moment, then lowered himself to the ground. Cold wind whipped his face and blood ran into one eye. Sully cast his beam downward and swept it over the sandy shore. A chill crawled up his spine as it illuminated a man lying face down in the sand, limbs splayed at odd angles. He heard a movement behind him and spun around, his thumb releasing the safety of his .38.

"Don't shoot!" a familiar voice rang out. Travis raised his arms against the bright light.

"Jesus, Travis! Thank God you're okay!" Sully lowered his weapon and the flashlight, heart hammering his chest.

"You're bleeding," Travis said.

"Someone knocked me out cold.

"Did you see him?"

"No. But it must have been the killer."

Travis's eyes widened. "Killer?"

Sully swallowed hard. "There's a body down in the gorge."

Muscles tensed in the old Paiute's face. He lowered himself at the rim and his beam darted left and right into the canyon. His body tensed, then he edged slowly back and heaved out a deep breath. "Let's not think the worst. Could be anyone down there."

"Why's the ATV still here? Why's Butch out here alone?"

"Dunno. But I'm not going to believe that's Joe."

Sully closed his eyes and tried to wrestle down his mounting anxiety. He, too, needed to believe his dad was alive. "Let's ride out of here and find some cell coverage. We need to call the sheriff."

"Right, but first I'm gonna take a look at your head."

Sully gritted his teeth as Travis's fingers probed the area around the wound. A fresh trickle of blood ran down his face.

"It's not bad. You'll need stitches. Hold still." Travis whipped off his bandana, dabbed the blood from around Sully's eye, and tied the bandana tightly around the crown of his head. "That'll slow the bleeding."

"Let's go," Sully said impatiently. As he took a step forward, a hammer came down like an anvil on his head. Glaring pain blocked his vision for a few seconds. He teetered, grabbed the old Paiute's arm.

Travis's voice filtered in. "You okay?"

He nodded. "Just dizzy."

"Take it slow." Travis squeezed his arm, then lifted Butch off the ground and tucked him into his sheepskin jacket. The poodle's face popped out of the collar under Travis's chin, his eyes shiny black orbs. "Let's head toward the highway."

After drinking cool water from his canteen to sooth his parched throat, Sully mounted Diego and fell in line behind Travis. A three-quarter moon peered through a break in the clouds, casting a silver patina over the terrain. Misery Flats was dead quiet all around except for horse hooves clipping the stony road. Sully's gaze probed the light and shadow of the landscape, hoping to spot his father.

They'd been on the road about five minutes when high beams abruptly bounced around a bend a hundred yards ahead, capturing them in its glare. Sully's muscles tensed as he prepared to dismount and find cover.

Blue and red strobes pulsed on the roof of the truck, fracturing the night.

The sheriff!

Then two more pairs of headlights bounced around the bend.

He brought reinforcements.

Sully and Travis dismounted and waited for the three vehicles to reach them. The trucks braked to a halt, doors opened, and Sheriff Carl Matterson and two uniformed deputies climbed out. Joe limped into view from behind one of the officers.

Sully reached Joe in a few long strides, threw his arms around him, and hugged him close. "Jesus, Dad, you had me scared to death." His voice sounded husky and his throat burned with emotion. He breathed in the familiar smell he'd known since childhood.

Joe didn't hug him back but stood limp and motionless. When Sully pulled away, he saw how pale and exhausted his father looked.

"You all right?" Sully asked.

"Yeah, I'm all right," he said in a dull tone, his eyes not meeting Sully's.

Butch whimpered and squirmed. Travis pulled him from his coat and passed him to Joe. The poodle vigorously licked the old man's face. Joe's eyes lit up briefly, then darkened again.

"What happened to your head?" Skipping a greeting, Matterson was all cop in manner and tone,.

"Got hit."

"By who?"

"Didn't see him."

"How long ago?"

"Fifteen, twenty minutes."

Matterson quickly pushed back his jacket, placed his hand near his sidearm. "So the shooter could still be out here?"

"Don't think so," Travis said. "I heard a truck peel outta here right after Sully got whacked."

"What went down out here?" Sully asked Joe.

Joe wiped his mouth with the back of his hand and Sully noticed a nervous tremor in the fingers. "Everything went haywire."

"This is an active crime scene," Matterson clipped. "Joe told us a man got shot. You see a body?"

"Yeah, in the gorge," Sully said. "A hundred yards up the road."

"Get in the truck. Show us exactly where the victim is. I need to get a recovery team out here pronto."

Sully and Joe climbed into the sheriff's Yukon, with Sully in the passenger seat, and Travis following behind with the horses. The sheriff drove slowly, tires crunching over the gravel.

"Right there," Sully said, pointing. "Across from that crop of boulders."

The three vehicles parked with their high beams facing across the wide chasm. The sheriff and deputies edged to the rim, got down on their stomachs, and directed their flashlights into the gorge, then all three men backed away and got to their feet, faces grave, brushing dirt off their uniforms.

Interspersed with static, Matterson barked GPS coordinates into his radio. "Look for our high beams facing into the gorge right above the body." He signed off and turned his attention to the group of men waiting on the road. "They're bringing in a helicopter. The coroner and forensic techs will go down on a longline with a stretcher."

Sully turned to Joe. "You know who's down there?"

Joe released a ragged breath and mumbled, "Mateo Gonzalez."

"The farrier?"

Joe nodded, misery etched on his face.

Sully felt a cold knot in his chest as he pictured the middle-aged, gray-haired Mexican. A kindhearted, jovial man. Gentle with animals. As far back as Sully could remember, Mateo had been doing top-notch hoof work for ranchers in the surrounding counties.

"Goddamn shame," the sheriff huffed. "He's got a wife and three kids."

Joe looked down at his scuffed boots and kicked a rock across the road. A damp wind blew up from the gorge carrying the smell of the river.

"Let's backtrack to the beginning, Joe, and piece this whole thing together." Matterson pulled out a notepad, angled himself near the headlights, and stood with his pen poised. "What were you and Mateo doing out here?"

In a rambling monotone, Joe relayed details, his words slurring a little. "Mateo called the house this morning. He wanted to talk to Sully, but Sully was busy with the horses. I asked him what he wanted. Mateo said he'd call back, and he almost hung up, but then he said to tell Sully he knew about Gunner. What about Gunner? I asked him. He didn't say nothing for a long time. Finally, I asked him if he knew who took Gunner. He said, yeah."

Sully felt a spurt of adrenaline shoot through his body as he pictured his champion stallion.

"Then he wouldn't say no more by phone," Joe continued. "Come out to the ranch, I said. He said he couldn't. He thought he was being watched. Just told me to tell Sully to meet him out here at seven o'clock. Then he hung up."

"Did he say anything else about Gunner?" Sully asked, clinging to a flicker of hope.

Joe shook his head. "He sounded nervous. Like someone might be listening."

"And you didn't think to tell me, Dad?" Sully's frustration leeched into his tone.

"You was busy." Joe's sorrowful eyes peered into Sully's. "I thought I could just come out here, see if there was anything to it, then go home and tell you. Save you some time and trouble."

"What happened when you got here?" The sheriff asked, his expression cheerless in the glare of the high beams.

"When I was about 400 hundred feet from the gorge, I looked through my binoculars to pinpoint Mateo's location. Saw his truck parked right here." Joe gestured to the spot where they were all standing. "Mateo got out, smoking a cigarette. He looked around, probably for Sully. All of a sudden, he whipped a gun from his waistband, aimed it southeast, and fired off a shot. Two rifle blasts fired back. Mateo clutched his chest and dropped to the ground. I saw gun smoke over there above them rocks. Butch took off like a bat outta hell. Scared of the noise."

"Then what happened?" the Sheriff asked.

"I was gonna drive the ATV over to Mateo, but then I thought it wouldn't help neither of us if I got shot up, too. So I waited. Didn't hear nothing. Didn't see nothing. So I left the ATV behind a boulder and crept over here. Mateo was gone." Joe's voice choked. He took a moment, swallowed, and continued. "I was praying he got away ... but his truck was still here."

"The killer must've pushed him over," Matterson said gently. "Go on, Joe."

"I saw Mateo's keys lying here in the dirt, so I got into his truck, and drove as fast as I could to the highway. Used a phone at a gas station, and called you." His shoulders slouched, and he tightened his grip on Butch. "That's the long and short of it."

Sully closed his eyes, an awful feeling gnawing in his gut. His father's poor judgment probably got Mateo killed. Could have gotten himself killed, too. If Sully had talked to Mateo, he would've met him at a safer place, one not tactically vulnerable to a sniper shot. Now a good man was gone, leaving behind a wife and children. With Mateo's death, they also lost their chance to learn the identities of the thieves, and the whereabouts of Gunner.

Matterson didn't waste time admonishing Joe, but stayed on course. "Cooper, Gary, you two search around that area where the shots came from. Look for casings, footprints, any sign of the shooter. Mark anything you find. Take pictures."

The two deputies strayed off, their beams scouring the ground in front of them.

Scribbling notes, Matterson quizzed Sully and Travis about their involvement for several minutes. When satisfied, he flipped his notebook closed and tucked it into his breast pocket. "As soon as the chopper and forensic team get here, I'll drive you home, Joe. Sully, one of my men will get you to the ER. Have your head checked. Travis, you can get your horses back to the ranch. We'll haul your ATV to the station, and you can pick it up tomorrow."

The loud whumping of helicopter blades came in low overhead and all faces turned skyward. Matterson pushed up the brim of his Stetson. A sheen of sweat shimmered on his face and his mouth was compressed into a tight line.

A long night lay ahead, Sully thought. With a slew of champion horses stolen, and two violent murders in as many months, the character of their county had changed for the worse.

Buy HIDDEN PART 2

A Michael Sullivan Mystery

ABOUT THE AUTHOR

Linda's love of literature and the visual arts led her to a twenty-five-year career as an award-winning copywriter and art director. Now retired, Linda writes fast-paced mysteries and thrillers. She currently lives in Oregon with her husband and toy poodle.

To learn of new releases and discounts,
add your name to Linda's mailing list:

www.lindaberry.net

Follow Linda on Twitter

https://twitter.com/LindaBerry7272